THE ART WHISPERER

ALSO BY CHARLOTTE AND AARON ELKINS

THE ART WHISPERER

AN ALIX LONDON MYSTERY

CHARLOTTE AND AARON ELKINS

THOMAS & MERCER

Published by Thomas & Mercer, Seattle

www.apub.com

Amazon, the Amazon logo, and Thomas & Mercer are trademarks of Amazon.com, Inc., or its affiliates.

ISBN-13: 9781477824559
ISBN-10: 1477824553

Cover design by 4 Eyes Design

Library of Congress Control Number: 2014934575

Printed in the United States of America

THE ART WHISPERER

The Conservation of Art: Methods and Aims. A Brief Guide

By Alix London
Price: $14.95
Paperback: 85 pages
Publisher: International Art Education Institute
Average Customer Rating: 1.2 out of 5 stars
Bestsellers Rank: #2,994,796 in Books

Reader's Forum Reviews. Newest First

★☆☆☆☆ Worse Than Useless
By Kathy Maynard
Why am I giving this book only one star, you want to know? Because there's nothing lower available. Hey, forum moderator, here's a sugges-tion. How about introducing minus-stars? There are worse things than "Poor," you know . . . and this turkey proves it!

★☆☆☆☆ Don't Waste Your Money
By Helga McGhee
Another derivative, disorganized, incomprehensible, totally unneeded little "guide" that says nothing that fifty other books haven't said . . . only this one says it worse. If Alix London really learned conservation from her crook of a father, you have to wonder how he got away with all those forgeries. Don't waste your money.

★☆☆☆☆ Clueless
By Alicia Lampert
Art restorers—Do NOT use this book as a resource unless you want to get sued for willful destruction of property. To put it plainly, the author simply doesn't know what she's talking about. As a professional restorer myself, I was flabbergasted by some of her "rules" on the use of solvents and the application of heat. Alix London really should have read a book on this subject before trying to write one.

★☆☆☆☆ Shameful and Pathetic
By Diana Anderson
So now she's a writer too. Yet another lame attempt on the part of this "expert" to cash in on the seamy notoriety of her father Geoffrey London. Shameful and pathetic.

★☆☆☆☆ Look Elsewhere
By Linda Dow
The idea that a reputable organization like the International Art Education Institute would put its name on this unedifying mishmash from the notorious Family London is enough to—

That was as much as Alix could take in one sitting, and not for the first time her fingers itched—literally, truly itched—to send in a response of her own, a fiery rejoinder that would blow these captious faultfinders out of the water, but deep down she knew it wasn't worth the bitterness of getting into a fight with them. It wasn't worth reading their "reviews" at all, but despite the self-discipline of which she was justifiably proud, she couldn't seem to stay away. It was like the hole in your gums left after a tooth extraction; it made you wince to stick your tongue in it, but you couldn't stop doing it. For two days, maybe, three on the outside, she could manage not to check, but then her curiosity would get the better of her and she'd be at it again. And, naturally, get burned again.

Talk about moths and flames.

It wasn't as if these were honest critiques from which she might learn something either. They were all part of a malicious, coordinated vendetta. Surely, anyone could see that (she hoped). After all, how could an obscure, limited-market little book like *The Conservation of Art*, with its modest objectives, be of enough interest to draw so many reviews, negative *or* positive? Who were these people (were they all really different people?) who were driven to register such passionate condemnations? Anyway, what kind of people were given to passion when it came to techniques of art conservation? No, it didn't add up.

And then, when the book, her first serious try at writing, had come out eight months ago, four reader reviews had come in over the next couple of weeks. All but one rated it four stars or more, the exception being one grumpy correspondent who gave it two stars because "it took two weeks to get here, and when it did it looked like it had been run over by an asphalt paving machine. Intolerable."

After that, no ratings at all for six months. Then, when the book was ancient history by bookselling standards, *wham!*, these personal attacks—that's what they were, weren't they, personal attacks?—started pouring in. Since then the deluge had continued, almost thirty now, one or two almost every day, and every single one of them negative—not even a three-star among them. Did that make any sense? And she had more reviews than sales; what kind of sense did that make?

Not for a minute did she believe that her book was "worse than useless" or "pathetic." And she damn well *did* know what she was talking about. *The Conservation of Art* was a good, solid little guide to the history and practice of art conservation and restoration—okay, not especially original, that wasn't its aim, but it was well organized and readable, geared not to professionals in the field, but to the lay reader who wanted to know a little more about the subject.

When she heard a low growling noise and realized she was making it, she knew a time-out was in order. Coffee. She slammed the laptop closed, sorry that she'd ever opened it, and once more promised herself that she'd never, ever, ever look at the damn review page again. She picked up the empty mug on her worktable and stomped off to the break room, muttering to herself.

. . .

Alix London, thirty years old, attractive, capable daughter of a charming and once highly reputed but famously disgraced art conservator, now reformed (she instinctively crossed her fingers or knocked on wood whenever she thought about that), was herself an art consultant and conservator with a growing reputation of her own. Unlike almost every other modern conservator, she had trained in the old-fashioned way, not at a school or institute, but by apprenticing herself for several years to the famed conservator Fabrizio Santullo at his studio in Rome. That had been when Geoffrey London's sensational conviction and imprisonment for art fraud—serial forgery—was still fresh in the public's mind, and bearing the name "London" in the American art world was like hauling around a not-so-recently dead, forty-pound albatross. Nobody wanted to get within fifty yards of her. But things were different now; she had proven her merits as a conservator in her own right.

Her current consulting job with the L. Morgan Brethwaite Museum in Palm Springs was proof of that. The museum had flown Alix down from Seattle a few days earlier for her to look at the twenty-eight pieces that they were planning to auction off, in order to determine what cleaning or restoration might be called for, and for her to present her estimate for doing the work. The Brethwaite was only a mid-sized private museum, but as private museums went it was among the crème de la crème. It was built from the personal collection of the late L. Morgan himself, and housed in the 12,000-square-foot, one-of-a-kind "Palm Springs Modern" home he had designed for himself and his family (but mostly for his art collection) in the foothills of the San Jacinto Mountains in 1969. The museum's claim to fame was its world-class collection of British and American paintings: two hundred years of the best, from Joshua Reynolds to Jackson Pollock.

By any definition, it was a plum assignment, and for Alix it was a confirmation that things were truly going her way. Finally.

And then this.

When she got back to her workroom with her own coffee, she found a young man fussily arranging coffee fixings, notebooks, and pens on the small conference table in the center of the room.

"Is there going to be a meeting, Richard?" she asked. Richard Ariano was the secretary of Lillian Brethwaite, the museum's director.

"Yes, the curators. This will probably take all morning."

"Ah."

This was the first time she'd been booted out of her workspace, but hardly a surprise. When she'd first arrived, she'd been given the regular workroom to use, but it was a windowless, cheerless place, and she'd asked if there might be something a little less depressing, and with natural light. Clark Calder, the senior curator, had suggested the conference room—roomy, airy, and blessed with a wide, wonderful view over the city and eastward across the Coachella Valley desert to the picturesque, dun-colored Little San Bernardinos—and she'd jumped at the offer, although it had come with the understanding that staff meetings would take priority.

"This *is* the conference room, you know," Richard said unnecessarily. An oily, prissy young man, he had the proprietary attitude toward his boss and her domain that is not so rarely found among personal secretaries. He had resented Alix from the start, and seemed to think that she had more access to the director and took more liberties with the museum in general than were her due.

"I know that, Richard. I didn't ask for it, you know. Clark suggested it."

"Clark," he said. Obviously not one of his favorites, either.

Well, this business with the reviews had pretty much killed any possibility of meaningful concentration for the next hour or so anyway; the truth was that she appreciated having an excuse to get away from work for a while. "It's all yours," she said, and with her coffee she went out to one of the museum's four broad terraces—one of the two open to the public, not that it made any difference at the moment, since the Brethwaite was temporarily closed while it was undergoing a major renovation of its public galleries.

She had come out onto this terrace before when she needed to unwind a little, and she could tell almost before she sat on one of the comfortable benches that it was going to do the job this time as well. It was the view that did it, northward rather than eastward, so that it took in the astonishing "wind farm" on the city's outskirts: almost seven hundred immense, chalk-white wind turbines—windmills— each an incredible forty stories high, arranged in row after parallel row, their giant blades turning slowly, slowly in the soft breeze. It was impossible to look at without thinking of Don Quixote. For Alix they were hypnotic; they would put her to sleep if she'd let them. She could feel her anger over those hateful reviews melting away and she sighed gratefully.

It didn't melt away the hurt, however, or the pain she felt on her father's behalf. Because this campaign wasn't meant to get at her, but at Geoff; that was obvious. Geoffrey London had been an accomplished and successful forger in his time—even now he claimed to be unrepentant, but that was another story—and there were a lot of people who still had good reason to wish him ill. Geoffrey had left a lot of humiliated "experts" and embittered collectors in his wake, and she was being attacked now because they knew it would hurt him. They were right, too, and it wounded her to see the guilt it caused him to be the reason for these attacks on her, hide it though he tried.

The possibility that she herself was the object of the attacks, and not Geoff, had naturally occurred to her when the whole thing started, but she soon dismissed that as unlikely.

Who'd want to hurt me?

2

It had taken a mere four months for the new senior curator of the Palm Springs L. Morgan Brethwaite Museum of Art to inspire the level of hatred from his staff that would have taken most people years to generate. They disliked him because he was newer than they were and younger than they were, because they thought his aims for the museum were crass and commercial, his personal ambitions ruthless, his speech gratuitously jargony, his manner jarringly hip and mocking, and—especially—because of the trust that Lillian Brethwaite, the museum's longtime director and the chair of its board of trustees, had come to have in his judgment and counsel, and who knew what else.

Thirty-seven-year-old Clark Calder was aware of all this and was bothered not a bit. He disliked the four staff members as heartily as they disliked him, but with one obvious and happy difference: There was only one driver's seat, and he was strapped securely into it. As such, he took pleasure in dismantling the elitist attitudes and practices that had gotten the Brethwaite into its current financial mess, and the more these fusty old dinosaurs rumbled, and quibbled, and resisted being dragged into the twenty-first century (straight from the nineteenth), the more fun it was.

"What we're talking about here," he said, leaning over the conference table, "what it has to be all about from now on, is one thing first and foremost: the maximization of monetized eyeballs."

He paused to let this sink in, waiting to see which of his subordinate curators would rise to the bait this time. As he'd hoped, it was the venerable and oh-so-dignified curator of Paintings, who was unable to repress a wince. If ever a man had a name that fit him to a T, it was the patrician and elegant Prentice Faversham Vandervere. Of all the old fogeys, Prentice was the oldest and fogeyist, trailing half a century of accolades as a famous Harvard professor and an all-knowing pundit on the nature and functions of the art museum and art itself. As such, his very presence weighed on Clark, cramped his style, even stirred feelings of insecurity, something not many other people could do to him. With Clark, the best defense against this or anything else was a robust offense. As a result, the starchy old prof was his most frequent foil.

"Uh-oh," Clark said, "looks as if I offended the delicate sensibilities of Professor Vandervere yet again, am I right, professor?"

"I said nothing, Clark." Aloof, reserved, above it all. Arrogant old fart. It was rumored that he was thinking of retiring. He'd had plenty of experience at that, already having retired from Harvard and from the Boston Museum of Fine Arts. That would be a big day, a freeing day, in Clark's life, although he'd probably miss sparring with the old coot a little. Or not.

"No," he said pleasantly, "but I spotted a telltale quiver in the right third of your left upper eyelid—a dead giveaway. Do you have a problem with the concept, professor?" He smiled. He had a great smile—a killer smile, one of his girlfriends had called it—and he knew it. Open, friendly, boyish, inviting, it was one of his best features, and he used it unmercifully.

Vandervere smiled back, politely and noncommittally, hoping now to let the moment pass. This meeting, like all of them, was Clark's show, and Vandervere had largely given up debating him to

CHARLOTTE & AARON ELKINS

no useful end. He might win the debate, but he had yet to win the war or even a single battle. Clark was too slick with words, too quick to jab, too intent on winning.

And now the senior curator continued to wait, eyebrows raised inquisitively.

Vandervere emitted an almost inaudible sigh and took up the gauntlet. "It's not a problem, really, Clark. It's only that your turns of phrase sometimes take a while for an old traditionalist like myself to accustom himself to. I think you'll agree that 'the maximization of monetized eyeballs' is not an expression that one expects from the mouth of a curator—a senior curator—at a reputable museum of art."

Vandervere's elegant and carefully crafted language, delivered as always courteously and non-combatively, and as smoothly as if it were being read aloud, was enough to give most people pause—especially people less than half his age.

Not Clark Calder. "But I'm a senior curator, and this is a reputable museum," he said innocently, "and it just came from my mouth. Ergo: there must be something wrong with your argument."

"I intended no argument. You asked me a question, and I answered."

But Clark wasn't about to let it go. "So it's my choice of terms, Prentice? Is eyeball monetization not part of the museum administration curriculum at Hah-vahd? No? But then, I suppose that monetary considerations aren't exactly high priority at Hah-vahd, are they?" He continued to smile. The climate in the room, icy to begin with, chilled further.

It was Madge Temple, the comfortably plump, forty-something curator of Costumes and Furnishings, who put an end to it. "Enough already, Clark. I think we can all agree you've made your point: *You* didn't have to go to Harvard to get where you are, blah blah blah.

10

Congratulations. So how about getting to the point of the meeting now? Or was that it?"

Madge reminded Clark of one of those Happy Buddha statuettes: plump-cheeked, with knowing, amused eyes peeking out from under half-closed lids, and a serene smile that indicated how endlessly entertaining she found the foibles of those around her. That in itself would have been only moderately hard to take, but unfortunately, like Buddha himself, she was prone to voicing her observations and dispensing her guidance for the benefit of others. If she was aware that her jokey, side-of-the-mouth comments might offend others, which they frequently did, she gave no sign of knowing. By now, Clark had come to the conclusion that she really didn't know.

"Certainly," Clark said agreeably, not as much irritated by her latest remarks as one might think. He was indeed proud of not having gone to Harvard, proud that his only college degrees were a BA in entrepreneurial studies from Black Hills State University in Spearfish, South Dakota, and an almost-MFA in art history from Montana State at Bozeman. And especially proud that he'd been born without a silver spoon in his mouth, or any spoon at all, and yet here he was with this collection of fancy-school PhDs taking orders from him. He had come from nothing—an absentee father, a motel-maid mother— had paid his own way here, and had done it on his own, with dedication, perseverance, and innate smarts. Why wouldn't he be proud of himself? The good looks and that killer smile hadn't hurt either; he had to admit that.

"Now then," he said, "you all know that Integrated Marketing Systems has been studying our operation for some time. They have now analyzed the data from the movement-sensor time recorders that were in place most of the last two months, and have turned in their report, and yesterday evening the board unanimously accepted their recommendations and directed that they be implemented. The *point* of this meeting is to inform you of them." He cleared his throat and shuffled through the few papers in front of him.

"This is not going to be good," said Madge to no one in particular. "He looks too happy about it."

On another day that definitely would have gotten under Clark's skin, but on this particular morning it slid off him like sizzling droplets from a Teflon pan. "The most substantive change thus far will occur—*has* occurred—in Photography," he said. "The IMS study makes it amply clear that the photographic wing provides our least effective client interface functionalities, in that—"

Client interface functionalities, Vandervere mouthed silently, his face a mask of pain.

"—in that our clients spend almost no time there, and most of them—*most*, you understand, not *some*—simply pass it by without a glance. So . . . as of this morning, the photographic wing is no more. The contents will be going into storage over the next few days, for future deaccession consideration."

This had the intended effect. They were stunned. One of the five curatorial divisions gone, poof, just like that? "We're closing down Photographs because it didn't get enough . . . enough *eyeballs?*" Vandervere said with a disbelief that matched the expressions on the faces of the others.

"No, not because it didn't get enough eyeballs; because it didn't get enough eyeball *time*, and lack of eyeball time is an indicator of a client-perceived shortfall in our ecosystem. If we hope to put the Brethwaite on a sounder financial footing—and by that I mean increased memberships, increased donations, increased attendance, increased admission income—such shortfalls need to be perceptually recontextualized."

"Perceptually recontextualized." The curator of Decorative Arts, aka Madge's husband Drew Temple, emitted a harsh, clipped laugh. "Forgive the expression, Clark, but that is such a total load of bullshit, even for you. With all due respect, of course."

Clark's smile broadened. He thought exactly the same thing. He enjoyed throwing in the marketing gobbledygook because it never failed to upset them, but he didn't know what the hell most of it meant either. He got most of it from a "jargon generator" on the Web: three columns of buzzwords—verbs, adjectives, and nouns— that you could combine any way you liked to produce mind-boggling business-oriented neologisms: *disintermediated cross-platform functionalities, integrated Web-enabled algorithms, orchestrated user-centric paradigms.* He'd started doing it as a joke in the early days, when they were all still friends, more or less, but to his amazement they'd never gotten it. The silly terms just rankled and confused them. So naturally, he'd kept it up.

Madge must have thought that Drew had overdone it, because she stepped in now. "I think that what Drew was trying to say, Clark—"

"What Drew was trying to say is precisely what Drew said," Drew snapped at her. "I don't see that interpretation is required."

Madge cheerfully pulled an imaginary dagger from her chest. "Pardon me for living."

What an unlikely couple they were, Clark thought. Madge was straight out of a family sitcom: fat and sassy; unable to keep her mouth shut and damn the consequences. Drew couldn't have been more different. A waspish, discontented man, other than his boringly predictable grousing over any and everything, he kept his thoughts and feelings to himself. Clark had distrusted him from the start.

"Clark, I'd like to say something here," Vandervere said in that equable, aren't-I-reasonable tone that never failed to make the senior curator grind his teeth. "I understand the need to cut back, but consider for a moment: our Photography department is a one-of-a-kind historic resource: the finest photographic record in existence of early irrigation in the Coachella Valley and the initial construction phases of the Coachella Canal."

Clark, who wore reading glasses down low on his nose during meetings, peered drolly over them. "And your point is?"

This time Vandervere declined the bait and shifted the subject. "And what will happen to Werner?"

"Yes, and where is old Wernerschnitzel, anyway?" Madge added.

"Werner won't be with us today," Clark replied. "Obviously, with no need for a Photography department, there's no need for a curator of Photography. I spoke with him earlier this morning and offered him the management of the gift shop, a new position. Oh, did I mention that the days of blue-haired lady volunteers are as of now a thing of the past? Whether Werner accepts it or not, I saw no reason for him to continue to attend the curatorial staff meetings."

This sent new shock waves around the table. *Manager of the gift shop?* Werner Mayehoff? Werner, who had been there longer than any of them, the only curator who'd been around since Day One in 1996, an old friend of L. Morgan Brethwaite's himself? If it could happen to Werner, then how safe were any of them?

"And what about the rest of the departments?"

This from the one person who hadn't been heard from until now. The curator of Prints and Drawings, Alfie Wellington, wasn't much of a contributor at staff meetings or anywhere else. Since neither museums nor the art in them excited his interest very much any longer, he was often unengaged, to put it charitably. The next oldest of the remaining curators (after Prentice), a rotund sixty-year-old with a chubby-cheeked face that was made to be merry but rarely had been in recent years, he had come to the museum as a relatively young man in 1998, in what he must have imagined to be a step toward a bigger, better future at some bigger, better museum. Yet here he was, more than fifteen years later, at the same museum, in the same position, with nowhere to go.

It wasn't entirely his fault. As with the other curators, there hadn't been much for him to do to distinguish himself. There had been no blockbuster exhibitions to set up, no major acquisitions with which to scoop competing institutions, not really much of anything, as far as Clark could see, that wouldn't have been the province of curatorial assistants or interns at any other decent museum.

The four of them were all in the same boat in that regard, and they reacted true to their own natures: Madge with her barbed and supposedly funny throwaway lines, Drew with tightly repressed resentment, Prentice with "civilized" equanimity. And Alfie? Alfie had turned to booze. He wasn't what most people would call a drunk, not the kind who goes around staggering and slurring his speech, or snoring through meetings, but he was never without enough alcohol in his system to soften life in general with a calming, distancing fuzz. Even now, at 9:15 in the morning, the smell of bourbon on his breath had the others giving him plenty of room.

And yet here he was, raising the question that no one else had dared ask.

"Ah, the rest of the departments," Clark said. "I was coming to that. Now, I want you to know there's nothing personal in this. I hope that's understood."

"Oh, that's really reassuring," Madge said dryly.

"Yes," Drew agreed, "that makes all the difference in the world."

"I have to tell you that there's going to be some necessary stream-lining in the next few weeks," Clark said. "The museum reopens in early April, and by that time . . ." He pushed the glasses up on his nose and studied the papers in front of him as if he didn't already know perfectly well what they said.

"First, Prints and Drawings." (A nod toward Alfie.) "The Prints sub-department, which failed to meet the customer-interaction criteria devised by IMS and approved by our board, will be closed down, and the number of prints sharply reduced. What remains will be combined with Paintings" (a nod to Prentice) "into a single department of Paintings and Drawings under one curator, so I'm afraid we will be eliminating one more curatorial-level position."

Alfie's head came up sharply. "You going to offer me the gift shop too, if Werner doesn't take it?"

"I didn't say that, Alfie. Whether you or the good professor will be offered the curatorship has yet to be decided. We're working on it now. Be reassured."

"Oh, right," Alfie said with a laugh that seemed genuine enough, "you're going to give it to me and tell Prentice Faversham Vandervere to take a hike. Oh, yes, that makes sense."

Clark was enjoying himself even more than he'd expected. In four months, this was the first time he'd come close to getting a rise out of boozy, laid-back Alfie. "Actually, that is highly possible," he said, with a more meaningful look at Vandervere, who returned it evenly. "As I said, it has yet to be decided. All options are on the table."

Now he turned to Madge and Drew, who were looking satisfactorily apprehensive. "A similar situation exists with your two departments. Our Furnishings gallery and two of our three Decorative Arts exhibits will be closed down for lack of interactive client activity.

Costumes, however, does very well. Therefore, the two departments will be folded into a new Costumes and Decorative Arts department under Madge's directorship. Drew, you will remain in charge of the Decorative Arts portion." He paused. "We envision an assistant curator title."

That brought a rare serious expression of emotion from Madge. "But that would mean that I would be my husband's . . . my husband's . . ." She looked to Drew for assistance.

Drew, however, said nothing, but only eyed Clark with flinty dislike.

"That Drew would report to you?" Clark said innocently. "Why yes, now that I think about it, it would certainly seem to follow, wouldn't it? That is, if it's decided that a head of Decorative Arts is necessary at all. And that"—he fixed Drew with one of his cooler smiles—"will depend largely on what we see from you in the next few weeks, Drew."

Clark gathered his papers and stood up. "That takes care of the first part of our agenda. Be back at ten thirty. Mrs. B will be here. So will Alix London. And we'll have pastries to go with the coffee."

"Wow, pastries; what a jolly affair this is turning into," Madge grumped as a frowning, abstracted Drew dragged her off. Vandervere, whose knee had been shattered in the Korean War, stood up with a wince and limped grimly away. Alfie hurried off to his desk for some Jim Beam to put in his coffee.

"See y'all at ten thirty!" Clark called happily after them. "Y'all come back now!"

3

This, Alix thought with a sinking heart, *is going to get me in trouble. Big time.*

She was standing in front of an enormous painting, seventeen feet long by eight feet wide, so large that it couldn't be hung on the museum's curving walls, but stood a few feet out, attached to a steel framework built especially for it. The picture's surface was all sweeping, brightly colored skeins and swirls, and swarms of glowing white specks and spots, thousands of them, on a field that seemed a deep, velvety black until you looked harder and saw the grays, the rusts, the umbers that ran through it. There was nothing even close to a solid form, let alone a recognizable object. It was the kind of picture that could be interpreted in a thousand ways. For some, the works of this artist conjured up the vastness of the Milky Way, for others the dark and unfathomable depths of the ocean, or the mystery of a single cell or an atom. Still others saw in it the ineffable, orchestrated chaos of the cosmos.

So it was said. But Alix was smiling to herself. She would have been willing to bet that the most common reaction was more along the lines of a bemused "My kid (my dog, my cat, a trained monkey) could do better than that."

The title didn't offer much help as to what it was supposed to be: *Untitled 1952.*

Neither did the "explanatory" legend:

Jackson Pollock (1912–1956). Pollock was an early exponent of Abstract Expressionism. He electrified the art world with his method of tacking canvases to the floor and walking up and down alongside them, flinging, dripping, pouring, and splattering paint. Many of his works, such as the one you see here, are either untitled or simply assigned numbers in order to "make people look at a picture for what it is and not what it 'represents'—pure painting." Pollock frequently attacked art critics who claimed to find hidden symbols in his work. He insisted that there was no "meaning" in the finished work, but only in the process of creating it. His advice to viewers was to "look passively and try to receive what the painting has to offer and not bring a subject matter or preconceived idea of what they are to be looking for." Any interpretation or evaluation of the finished work was a personal projection, neither wrong nor right, but perfectly valid . . . for that person.

Alix, being classically trained, did not much care for this all-in-the-eye-of-the-beholder approach to art, which she considered just this side of hokum, but that wasn't the source of her unease. What was bothering her was that she thought the painting was not a genuine Pollock. Or more accurately, it wasn't that she *thought* it wasn't genuine, it was that she *felt* it wasn't genuine. And that's what she was so depressingly certain would get her into trouble. It hadn't failed yet.

This was not one of the pieces destined for auction, but would remain at the museum, so no one had asked her to look at it, no one had requested her opinion on its authenticity, and, for sure, no one was going to be happy to hear it. But what choice did she have? She couldn't just let it pass. Well, all right, she *could*, but she knew she wouldn't.

"Jack the Dripper," somebody said behind her. "What a piece of work."

She turned. "Pollock or the painting?"

19

"Take your pick."

Jerry Swanson, in his forties, dumpy, balding, and brash as a carnival barker, was the appraiser from Endicott Fine Art Auction Galleries who was assessing the works to be sold by the gallery—twenty-eight in all. It was he who had suggested to the Brethwaite that a little competent touch-up work on some of the paintings would dramatically increase the prices they would bring; a suggestion that had resulted in Alix being there now.

"Jerry," she said, turning back to the canvas, "what do you think of this picture?"

"Hey, they don't pay me to think about them, lady, they pay me to set the expected price ranges."

Jerry's standard mode of speech was the wisecrack. With his old-fashioned, black-rimmed spectacles and his round face, he made Alix think of a smart-aleck owl. He had a snappy delivery; talking to him could be like catching a Borscht Belt comedian in mid-shtick—that, or a hang-on-to-your-wallet used-car shyster. Nevertheless, he was a friendly, engaging, outgoing guy, he laughed a lot, and he was pleasant to be around.

"Okay, go ahead and set it. What would you say the market value would be?"

"Sorry, I'm being paid to appraise exactly twenty-eight pictures, and this ain't one of 'em."

She smiled. "You only give your opinion if somebody's paying you?"

"Of course. Why would I waste a perfectly good opinion when somebody might be conned into paying me actual money for it some other time?"

"Come on, be serious for a minute. Just a general idea. I'm not going to hold you to it."

He lifted his plump chin and drew himself up. "Sorry, I have certain ethical and professional standards to which I adhere." He followed with a conspiratorial eyebrow wiggle. "So how much are you offering?"

"Well, it's pretty important. I guess I'd go as much as . . . oh . . . how about a nickel?"

"Now you're talking. Done!" He looked back at the painting. "Somewhere between ten and thirty million, I'd say."

"That much?" Her heart sank a little further.

"It's a Pollock," he said simply. "You don't know what they sell for?"

"Actually, no. A lot, I gather."

"I thought you advised people on what to buy."

"I do, but not on the basis of market value. What I try to gauge is artistic value."

"Oh, *artistic* value," he said merrily, as if it were a private joke between them. "Okay, but why all the interest in this particular one?"

"Well, actually, I'm having some doubts about it. Jerry, tell me, honestly, what's your opinion? Not its monetary value—I can't afford another nickel—but its—"

"Artistic value?" he supplied. "Well, let me see." Arms folded, he slowly scanned it from one end to the other, all seventeen feet of it. "When I look at this," he said, seriously for him, "you know what I see?"

"The vastness of the universe?"

"That, too, of course, but mostly I see the tarp under my eleven-year-old Volvo after I've finished its six-month maintenance." He grinned, hearing her groan. "Seriously, though, you're talking to the wrong guy. Artistic value just isn't my line, but I can tell you this much: People must like it because it's the museum's number-one attraction. As determined by the latest thing in eyeball mono-macro-moto-ridiculization."

21

"I don't even want to know what that means. But the thing I'm after is . . . are you satisfied it's an authentic Pollock?"

Now a look of genuine surprise. "You're not?"

She pulled in a deep breath. "I'm not, no."

"Okay, you got me. What's wrong with it?"

"I don't know," she said miserably. "Not specifically, not yet. But I do have some serious doubts—"

"Hello there, children. Should you be dawdling like this? Staff meeting resumes in ten minutes, and you know Mrs. B," a new voice interjected.

"Not my problem," Jerry said. "Nobody invited me."

"Fortunate man," said the tall, dignified newcomer with a smile.

He was the curator of Paintings, Prentice Vandervere, for whom Alix had developed genuine admiration—a sort of platonic, scholarly crush—during her three years at Harvard almost a decade before, when she had taken several classes from him. Kind, modest, and thoughtful, it was Vandervere who had instilled in Alix some of her most fundamental ethical and aesthetic values. The monthly Sunday afternoon teas (complete with crumpets and finger sandwiches) that he and his wife held at their house for students and faculty were among her happiest memories from her Harvard days. Learning that he was at the Brethwaite had been a great surprise and was probably the nicest thing that had happened to her since coming to Palm Springs. She was pleased to find him little changed from those days: his hair had thinned and receded, but his bearing was as erect as ever, notwithstanding the unbendable knee he lugged around as a souvenir of his service to his country; his straight, strong prow of a nose projected as proudly as ever; and his Clark Gable mustache was as meticulously trimmed as it had been ten years ago, if grayer.

"Prentice," she said (she was having trouble calling him anything but 'professor,' but he had gently insisted), "what's your opinion of this painting?"

"As you know, Alix, the post-war movements are not among those I claim to understand or even really appreciate, so—"

A memory of one of his musing, conversational Harvard lectures suddenly jumped up in her mind and made her laugh. "When I encounter a de Kooning, or a Twombly, or a Pollock in the company of students," he had said, "I find myself in a quandary. Should I pretend I understand what it's saying, or should I say what I honestly think? Or should I simply throw in the sponge and suggest we go and have lunch? I am ashamed to say I usually choose the last."

The first few times she'd heard him say this kind of thing, she'd reacted with the indignation that such narrow-minded observations from hidebound old professors deserve—especially from a liberal-minded young representative of the new generation. But it hadn't taken long before she was seeing things his way.

"So I am dubious about the worth of my opinion in this case," he continued now. "But aside from that, I most certainly do have a problem with it. More to the point, however, what is *your* opinion?"

"Frankly, when I look at it, I'm a little—"

"A little overwhelmed?" inquired the blond, good-looking man who had come noiselessly up behind them: Clark Calder, slimly built, boyishly handsome, with a stylishly shaggy, Ivy League haircut, a confident air, a winning smile that crinkled up the corners of his eyes, and—as far as Alix was concerned—an altogether too pleased-with-himself quality, like a snake that has just made a satisfying dinner of a mouse. Or is about to. "A little awestruck? A little—"

"A little concerned, actually."

"Oh? In what way?"

"Well, well," Prentice said, "I'd better be off to the meeting. I prefer to be on the early side."

Clark grinned at him. "Want to be sure to get your paws on those yum-yums before the rest of the gluttonous horde, eh, Prentice?"

Alix had taken a dislike to Clark the first time she'd met him, when he'd been delegated by Mrs. B to show her around the museum. He'd done so, but with that phony, bright-eyed smile plastered on his face and the air of a man who could hardly believe how sexy he was, and who had a million *really* important things he needed to be doing. And now, seeing this guy, this shallow, callow bean counter, treat her revered, eminently civil old professor this way, she bristled anew. *Creep*, she thought.

But Prentice responded only with a polite, strained smile, and left.

"You know, Jerry," Clark said, watching him go, "I don't think that man likes me." The smile broadened, the crinkles deepened. Alix expected a wink and she got one.

"Don't look at me," Jerry said. "I can neither confirm nor deny."

"Really, it surpasseth understanding," said Clark. "But Alix, what 'concerns' you about our prize possession here?"

"The museum's number-one attraction, so I hear," Jerry offered. "As determined by the latest thing in eyeball mono-macro-moto-ridiculization." Never let a good line go to waste, that was Jerry's motto.

Clark smiled. Alix didn't. She hesitated before taking it any further without something more than a feeling to go on, but inasmuch as the cat was halfway out of the bag . . . "I assume you're satisfied it's a genuine Pollock?" she said.

"And you're not?" Theatrically, he clapped his hand to his forehead. "God help us, the Art Whisperer strikes again!"

This time she did smile, but weakly. Lately she was hearing more references to herself as the Art Whisperer, and while at first it had amused and even flattered her, it was getting a little old now.

"I wondered how long it was going to take," Clark went on playfully. "I mean, I knew it was going to happen, of course—your reputation precedes you—but do you really have to do your thing with our *Pollock?* Couldn't you pick another one? *Any* other one? *Please?* There's a Childe Hassam in Gallery Two that's always gotten on my nerves. Let me show it to you and maybe you could—"

"Clark, I'm serious. There's something . . . something not right with this picture. I know it's there, I can *almost* see it, it's trying to jump out at me, but—"

"But at this point you can't say what it is. Am I right?"

She nodded dejectedly. "Yet."

"Ah, the old connoisseur's eye." He threw an amused wink at Jerry.

Connoisseur's eye, another term that was starting to bug her. Or not the term so much—it had once been used with respect—but the implied derision that often went along with it nowadays. To a lot of people in the art world—and Clark's manner indicated he was one of them—the idea that anyone could claim such a faculty was either snake oil or, more tolerantly, self-delusion. The only ways to determine the authenticity of a painting, so the prevailing wisdom went, were through painstaking scholarship and rigorous scientific analysis—*evidence*—and not some nebulous, mysterious "expert" first impression that was too woolly to put into words.

Those who took this position, and they were the majority, had a lot of history on their side. The pronouncements of so-called connoisseurs, including many of the most respected ones, had in the end been proven wrong again, and again, and again. Alix was well aware of this, but held fast to her confidence in her own instinctive judgments. Like plenty of others, she had the training, scholarship, and experience it took to offer a credible opinion on whether a painting was fake or not, but like hardly anybody else, she was also blessed (or cursed, it sometimes seemed) with the innate ability to unconsciously reduce it all into an instant, totally intuitive judgment call that she couldn't back up with words—not at first. She couldn't do it with every painting or every painter, but when the feeling was there, and when the artist concerned was an artist she "connected" with, there was no mistaking it. This was the fifth time her connoisseur's eye had spotted a fake where none had been suspected, and so far she was batting four for four. Every single one had turned out not to be what it was supposed to be.

There was one thing that was making her nervous this time around, though. Jackson Pollock was an artist with whom she *didn't* connect. She didn't especially like his paintings, and she'd never worked on one of them. So what could she possibly "see" in *Untitled*? That worried her, made her uncertain.

"Listen, Alix," Clark said more seriously, "are you planning to bring this up at the staff meeting?"

"No, I don't think so. I want to give it some more thought before I say anything to Mrs. B. I probably shouldn't have said anything to you yet either, but you sort of caught me thinking out loud."

"I'm glad to hear you say that. This painting is her pride and joy, Alix. Between you and me, I don't think it's one of his best works, but it's terribly dear to her. I know she comes off as a tough old bird, but behind those hawk-like eyes she's a pretty vulnerable old woman, and something like this would just . . . well, it'd be a hell of a blow."

"I know, but . . . well, don't you think I have an obligation—"

"I'm not sure if I see it as an obligation, but I understand where you're coming from, and you have to do what you see as the right thing. Look, how about this: You keep thinking about it, see if you can figure out what it is that's bothering you, and in the meantime I'll gather up the materials we have on the painting—provenance, evaluations, forensic testing, and so on. It's pretty weighty stuff, you'll see. Then let's meet again . . . today is Thursday, so give it a few days, and let's say, oh, Tuesday, first thing in the morning, and compare notes. After that, if you still feel that Mrs. B needs to hear, then be my guest. You have my blessing."

"That's fair enough. I'd like to have more to go on too before I say anything."

"Good. And now we'd better be off to the meeting."

"Hey, Alix," Jerry called after them as they started across the room.

He stood glowering at her from behind those big glasses, with his arms sternly crossed. "Where's my nickel?"

. . .

"Wait, hold up a second, would you, Clark?" she asked as they went by a wall of drawings.

"A second's about all we have. What is it?"

"These two drawings," Alix said, pointing. They were displayed one above the other, in simple wooden frames, each about ten inches by twelve. One was of a basket of pears, the other was of a mountain, both done in pencil, rather roughly; more than sketches but less than serious studies. They were both by the early twentieth-century American artist Marsden Hartley.

"Uh-huh, what about them?"

"I understand they'll both be in the auction."

"Yes, yes, that's right. Come on, we'd better get moving."

"Jerry told me yesterday they'd be sold as a single lot and the estimate would be fifty to seventy thousand," she said as he hustled her off. "And I was thinking: I have a friend—a collector—who might be interested in bidding on a couple of Hartleys. Would there be any problem with her coming down and looking at them here, before the official viewing at the gallery in San Francisco? She's got the time right now, but I don't know about—"

"Not a problem at all. If she likes them enough"—and the gleaming killer smile flashed—"she could make us an offer I couldn't refuse right on the spot and not have to bid against anybody later on. She could take them home with her. But it'd have to be in the next day or two, before the catalogue's mailed out."

"Seriously? She could do that? Is that legal?"

It seemed impossible, but his eyes crinkled up even more. "Surely you're not suggesting that I would propose anything extra-legal? No, seriously, yes, of course it's legal. These—"

His cell phone buzzed before he could finish. "I see," he said into it. "I understand. Certainly." He snapped it closed. "Mrs. B's gotten held up. Meeting's postponed until eleven fifteen. All in a day's work. I'll see you then. Be there." A convivial wink, and he was gone.

4

The thick, poured-concrete walls of the museum made cell-phone reception iffy, so Alix went out to one of the four twelve-foot-wide stone discs that served as entrance steps, where she knew reception was good. There wasn't a right angle or a straight line in the place; everything was curved, and the four interlocking discs at the entrance mimicked the four giant discs that made up the building itself. Alix sat down on one to make her call. She dialed a number in Seattle.

"Alix? Hi, what's up?"

The woman on the other end was her friend Christine LeMay. When they'd first met a little over a year earlier, Chris had recently resigned from her job as an IT systems/communications analyst at Sytex, an "international health care information technology advisory consultancy." Considering that those alarming muddles of multisyllabic words were beyond the comprehension of a non-techie like Alix, and that Chris knew next to nothing about art, which was Alix's specialty, they made an unlikely pair. More than that, Chris was big and raw-boned, a talkative, outspoken six-footer-plus with a startling honk for a laugh, given to flamboyant shawls and serapes and multiple rows of jangling bracelets. She was at her sparkling, noisy, funny best in crowds. Alix was the opposite. At five-nine, she was low-key and reserved, and she dressed conservatively ("classically" was the way she preferred to think about it). She kept her thoughts largely to herself, and she liked the quiet life. Well, to a point.

CHARLOTTE & AARON ELKINS

Chris had made a great deal of money when Sytex had gone public and her options had matured; she was bent on using some of it to
develop a respectable art collection, and a curator friend at the Seattle
Art Museum had suggested that Alix London was just the person to
help her build it. Whatever the reason, they had hit it off from Day
One, and Alix had wound up doing a lot more than help her with her
art collection. It had been a subtle intervention or two on Alix's part
that had gotten Chris to mend her threadbare relationship with Craig
Templeton, the man who had once been the love of her life and who
was now her husband. Chris had been enormously grateful and was
to this day determined to repay the favor. Nothing she'd come up with
had come close to panning out (they had different tastes in men), but
Alix appreciated her intentions and they were now close friends. They
worked well together, too, on Chris's budding art collection—Alix a
patient teacher, Chris an eager student—and Chris was now well on
the way to developing a fine collection of American Moderns (that
most permeable and vague art classification), including Georgia
O'Keeffe, Thomas Hart Benton, George Bellows, and Grant Wood.

But no Marsden Hartleys.

She was excited the moment she heard. "Of *course* I'm interested.
Are they really any good?"

"They're not what you'd call 'finished,' but they're nicely done.
There's a liveliness to them, and they're . . . interesting; historically, I
mean. You can see Cézanne's influence all over them."

"Fifty to seventy thousand, huh? For *both* of them? Does that
seem in the ballpark to you? Sounds kind of cheap to me. Oh, my
God, listen, to me, seventy thousand dollars is *cheap*. I've become a
terrible person." And there was the honk. "Who woulda thunk it?"

"Well, we all have our crosses to bear, you know, and yours is
being nouveau riche. My heart aches for you. Anyway, the reason it

sounds so cheap to you is that you're used to paying for oil paintings. These are pencil, and they don't bring nearly as much; people aren't that interested. And don't forget, art market prices don't have much to do with quality. They—"

"I know. You've been telling me about once an hour for the last year: Art market prices depend on art market prices. Whatever they went for at the last auction is your best predictor for how they'll be priced at the next one. Except higher."

"Very good. I didn't realize you'd been paying attention. I'll tell you this, though: They're workmanlike and attractive, and I certainly wouldn't mind having them on my own walls. They have a kind of rough energy—"

"Okay, okay, you've sold me. I want to see for myself. I'll be there tomorrow. What time would be good for you?"

"Whatever's convenient for you." Chris had a membership in an outfit called ShareJet, giving her a one-sixteenth time-share in a very snazzy Gulfstream 200, which meant she could fly just about anywhere she wanted almost any time she chose, and do it in fantastic comfort.

"Well, let's see . . ." Alix could hear her clicking away at a computer keyboard. ". . . It's about a thousand miles, so I'd have to allow about three hours, all told. How about eleven? I imagine I could drag myself to the airport in time to fly out at eight. It won't be easy, mind you."

"Wonderful! Call me before you land and I'll pick you up at the airport."

"No, not necessary. I'll just get a taxi and have it drop me at the museum. Okay, eleven o'clock, see you—no, wait, I'd better book a hotel reservation for a couple of nights. Where are you staying?"

"I just moved a couple of days ago to a lovely little place, the Villa Louisa, built in 1926, by some big silent-movie director, with a bunch of guesthouses around the swimming pool. I'm in one of the guesthouses."

"You moved? Why? Where were you before?"

"Oh, they put me up at the Colony Palms. Very nice and everything, but awfully . . . I don't know, not for me. A big, fancy place, ultra-hip and trendy, bright colors everywhere, the bars jumping at eleven in the morning. Rock music playing all day at the swimming pool, tons of Beautiful People dressed in up-to-the-minute—no, make that up-to-the-second—fashions. You know."

"Uh-huh. And at the Villa Louisa it's ugly people dressed in 1926 styles?"

"No, normal everyday people dressed like normal everyday people. It's quiet there. Restful, understated, an old wood-burning fireplace in my bedroom, another big river-rock one out on the patio. No bar. No TVs. At night they show classic movies under the stars. Last night I watched a Cary Grant from 1932. They have these lounge chairs you can lie back and snooze in if you want."

Chris was quiet for a few seconds. "You know," she said thoughtfully, "that really does sound like my kind of place."

"Good, I'll call them and make a reservation for you right now. I think the bungalow next to mine is free."

"No, not there! Good heavens! I meant the Colony Palms. Are you kidding me?"

5

Alix had been in Lillian Brethwaite's presence no more than fifteen minutes in total: once when she was offered the job, and then later, when she'd arrived to go to work, a five-minute welcoming to introduce her to the curatorial staff. Still, she knew a lot about the director, mostly gleaned during a lunch at a taqueria just south of downtown that garrulous, slightly boozy Alfie had treated her to on her first day. He'd hardly paused for mouthfuls of shrimp fajita between witty, rambling observations about the institution's short-comings, dysfunctionalities, and appalling policy changes, especially since—here he stopped to make obeisance with upraised hands—"the coming of the Boy Wonder, blessed of God, all praise him." Later there had been a couple of coffee breaks with Madge and Drew, who had been equally forthcoming. Added to that, she'd simply overheard enough griping among the staff to know that all was not well at the Brethwaite, and that the new senior curator was unloved.

Thus it was with sharp anticipation that she sat herself down in a creamy leather chair in the richly furnished boardroom, with a cup of coffee and an almond biscotto in front of her. She sat at one of the long sides of the table, between Prentice and Alfie and facing Madge and Drew, all with coffee and biscotti of their own. Some were abstractedly fingering their biscotti, but nobody was eating. Alfie was leafing through the *Desert Sun* newspaper without really reading it.

The others were silent and frowning, sunk in their own thoughts. Neither Clark nor Mrs. B had shown up yet.

When several minutes had passed without anyone saying anything, Alix, having grown uncomfortable, said: "People? Is anything wrong? Has something happened?"

"Don't ask," Alfie said, without looking up from his paper.

"Yes, 'something' has happened," Drew said with an arid laugh.

"There are a few organizational changes being considered," Prentice said.

"Ha." Drew again.

Another thirty seconds of silence, and then Madge, whom Alix already knew to be an eager gossiper, couldn't hold it in any longer. "Oh, there's no reason to keep the poor woman in suspense. It's not exactly a secret."

"And if it were, you wouldn't exactly be the one to keep it, would you?" Drew said meanly.

Over the past few days, Alix had chatted often with the curators and had learned a lot about them. From her standpoint, Drew Temple was the least likable of the bunch, a dour, unhelpful, vaguely reptilian man with a long nose that drooped at the tip, like a cartoon witch's, and a thin-lipped, extraordinarily wide gash of a mouth that made her think of a Muppet, but without the sunny disposition. He said little, but what he did say was unfailingly critical or negative, and delivered with a condescension she found immensely irritating. Behind the tiresome, rote carping, she sensed someone who was keeping a tight lid on a long, meticulously maintained list of bottled-up grievances.

His comment had no effect on his wife, who explained the morning's bombshell clearly and succinctly: The Photography department had already been scrubbed and its curator dumped—that was now history. But beyond that, Prints and Drawings (Alfie's department)

34

was to be combined with Paintings (Prentice's department) into a single department of Paintings and Drawings; and Decorative Arts (Drew's department) and Costumes and Furnishings (Madge's department) would become a single department of Costumes and Decorative Arts.

Alix nodded. "I see." No wonder they all seemed so worried. "So then, what used to be four departments will become two."

"Clever woman," Drew observed. "Not much gets by her."

Alix ignored him. "Are there only going to be two curator-level positions then?"

Not even Madge seemed eager to answer that question, and it was Prentice who finally did. "Yes, only two. According to Clark, Madge will be the Costumes and Decorative Arts curator, and Drew will become assistant curator responsible for the decorative arts segment. As for Paintings and Drawings, it has yet to be decided as to whether Alfie or I will assume the mantle."

Alix stared at him. Was he serious? *Has yet to be decided?* Prentice Vandervere or *Alfie?* She liked Alfie, she had nothing at all against Alfie, but compared to Prentice . . . !

Alfred Carpenter Wellington, she had learned (from Alfie himself), had been born to wealth and status, the scion of an old Virginia family. He had done well in school, but everything had come too easily and he had grown lazy and bored. He was sent to Yale, where he partied and enjoyed himself, working all the way up to a PhD in art history without expending much time or effort. After that he'd taught at an exclusive Connecticut prep school for a while but didn't enjoy it, and quit. He'd married an aspiring singer who later joined a rock band that came up with a huge hit. From then on she had been a celebrity and Alfie had shrunk into a sort of hanger-on. It wasn't long before he'd started drinking. One too many of his scenes in public soon led to a divorce. From there things continued to go downhill. He lost most of his money in the stock market crash of 1987, and had taken on a succession of jobs he couldn't hold on to. In 1998, the Brethwaite came through with a surprise job offer and he'd been there ever since: still in the same job after sixteen years. Still the same person too: still bright, still lazy, still unambitious (this is all Alfie talking), and still a boozer, though a more moderate one than he'd been before.

Still an amiable person, too, and pleasant to be around, but miles shy of Prentice in experience, ability, presence, and everything else. What kind of game was Clark playing at?

Alfie had obviously been asking himself the same question. "Does anybody here seriously think Clark would put me over you, Prentice?" He shook his head. "Get real."

"It's hardly as ridiculous as you make it sound, Alfie," said Prentice. "You have a good many—"

"Of course it's ridiculous! It's his nasty little joke, Prentice. He's just saying it to demean you, that's all."

"And what makes you think he won't *do* it to demean him?" Drew asked.

Alfie took a swig from his suspect mug. "If he did, I'd never accept the position," he said with dignity. "Prentice is a legend. The museum is lucky to have him."

"I don't agree with you, Alfie," Prentice said, "and I sincerely urge you not to do that. But I want you to know how much I appreciate your words."

"Oh, I'll do it, all right," Alfie said and went back to his newspaper. "It would be a travesty."

Well done, Dr. Wellington, Alix thought with a swell of affection, *good for you*. But, she wondered, what about the other change that was in the works: the one that would make Madge her husband's

36

superior and, presumably, boss? Drew didn't strike her as the kind of man who'd be able to handle that. It wasn't altogether a matter of chauvinism, either. In some ways he could make a pretty good case that, on paper anyway, the curatorship was going to the wrong person. He, too, was a Yale PhD in art history, and had been an adjunct professor at Brown when he applied for the position at the Brethwaite. Madge, by comparison, had no "Dr." in front of her name and wasn't really an art historian at all. She had an MS in costume design and technology from the University of Cincinnati and had worked in theater and taught continuing education courses at a community college in Providence when Drew had been at nearby Brown. When Lillian Brethwaite had hired Drew, Madge—then his fiancée—had come along as part of the package, to install and head the new, relatively small Costumes and Furnishings department, which had since grown considerably. Alix had no doubt that Madge herself thought she was fully competent to curate the entire new Costumes and Decorative Arts collection and was the right choice for the job. That Drew saw it that way was doubtful in the extreme.

Alfie was now reading the newspaper with more attention, and Alix glanced at the front-page story that seemed to have caught him up: "Phantom Strikes Again: This Time the Ocotillo Lodge."

"The Phantom," Alix said, making conversation. "What is *that* about?"

"Actually, it's interesting, there's this thief, the Phantom Burglar, they call him, he never leaves a clue, the police don't—uh-oh." He set down his cup and straightened up. "Gird thy loins," he whispered, "man the bulwarks, hoist the . . ."

There had been a perceptible stiffening in the room as those in it sensed the director's imminent entrance, which she made with long, quick, confident strides and more than a hint of swagger.

The Iron Lady, they called her, and she looked the part, a keen-eyed, wiry old woman with a face full of crosshatched wrinkles, weather-beaten and parched by nearly six decades of desert sun. She wore the same expression Alix had seen during their single face-to-face interaction, one eyebrow slightly arched in a lemme-see-you-try-and-put-one-over-on-me-pal look. She wore her straight, gray-streaked hair long and bound in a none-too-neat, old-fashioned bun with a nasty-looking dagger of a tortoiseshell comb stuck through it. When Alix had seen her before, she'd been wearing a mannish, well-tailored pantsuit. This time she was in a beat-up denim jacket and jeans worn over an old, much-laundered, open-throated white shirt. She looked as if she'd just arrived from breaking in a stubborn horse or two that had been too much for the hands down at the ranch. As a matter of fact, she did own a ranch a few miles south of town, so who knew, maybe she had.

Twenty years earlier, in her mid-forties, she had married a manu-facturer of plastic barrels for ballpoint pens, a man with the unlikely and uniquely unsuitable name of Lillienburger, but, to no one's sur-prise, marriage didn't suit her. Soon divorced, she had quickly and understandably discarded the "Lillian Lillienburger" name and gone back to "Brethwaite." At the museum, she preferred to be addressed as Mrs. B ("not Miz, if you don't mind"), and so it was.

Her approach to running the museum fit the "Iron Lady" sobri-quet too. She was the founding director, having been handed the reins directly by her father when it opened in 1996. The museum consisted almost entirely of his own collection, and she had indeed ruled it with an iron fist and a protective, frostily possessive attitude. She was demanding and domineering with the staff and no less dictatorial with museum visitors. There were strictly enforced, prominently displayed standards of dress and deportment for those members of the public who ventured onto the premises.

These premises had been her childhood home, after all. She had grown up with most of the works of art that were on the walls now, so as far as she was concerned, visitors were little more than vulgar interlopers and rubberneckers to be tolerated only because her father had so willed it, and only so long as they behaved themselves. She was famous for having once called the police to demand that some poor guy be arrested and hauled off for "willfully despoiling private property." He had been eating a donut and drinking a carton of milk—while leaning against his car, out in the parking area.

As to the board of trustees, they were local businessmen and -women whom she herself, as its chair, had appointed, and at whose pleasure they served. A dozen years ago, two of them had stood up for themselves and voted against her on some now-forgotten issue. By the next day they had been dismissed, and since then no further insurgencies had arisen. People didn't mess with Lillian Brethwaite.

But according to what Alix had been hearing, things had changed four months ago, which was when Mrs. B had met Clark Calder at a meeting of the Association of Private Museums. She had been impressed (or charmed, or smitten, or conned, depending on whom you talked to) by the glib, patently ambitious Clark to the extent of creating a new position for him as senior curator. He had taken up the job within the week, and it quickly became clear to the others that he could do little wrong in Lillian's eyes. Almost everything he proposed had either been implemented or was scheduled for implementation: relaxing the dress code to the extent that nothing short of showing up topless or with bare feet would deny you entrance; extracting a $15 "suggested donation" from visitors (admission had previously been free); creating Patron-level and Fellow-level museum memberships at $250 and $500 respectively, whereas there had previously existed only the $50 General level (shortly to become $75); and various other changes to remedy the museum's dire financial situation.

And of course it had been on Clark's recommendation that IMS be brought in to do the two-month study of "client interface experience" that had resulted in the monumental shakeup now under way: the deaccession by auction of many "surplus" works of art (the first deaccessioning in the museum's history), the banishment to storage of many others that failed to meet monetized eyeball criteria, and the resultant shrinking of curatorial departments. It was also Clark who had engaged Endicott to handle the auction, and who was now negotiating terms and arrangements with them.

Through all of this, so Alix had heard, Mrs. B had sat back as her Golden Boy implemented his twenty-first-century business marketing strategies. And to his credit (this was said grudgingly, with qualifications), the desperate financial circumstances that the Brethwaite, along with so many other non-profits, had found itself in with the recession had markedly improved since his arrival, and it appeared that the museum might actually be in the black again in the not-too-distant future.

Nonetheless, it wasn't Mrs. B's nature to fade decorously into the background. Every now and then, Alix had been told, Clark would step out of line or get a little too pushy for her, and she would cut her senior curator to pieces as brutally as she would anybody else. This was a source of rare pleasure for the staff, and apparently, this was to be one of those mornings. She began without preamble.

"Clark, before we get to the agenda—I've decided not to present to the board your proposal to include a graphic novel show to next year's exhibition schedule."

"Oh, I think that might be a mistake, Mrs. B. The last time the Institute of Graphic Novels put a similar show on the road, six museums in California and Arizona took part, and the income it generated for each of them in a single month-long exhibition was equal to—"

"There is more to museums than income generation, Clark, as important as that may regrettably be."

From the corner of Alix's eye she saw Prentice's chin dip in a barely perceptible nod of approval, and it brought to mind another remark of his—actually in one of his published essays—that had stuck with her through the years. "Income—profit—must never be the goal of an art museum, but only the means to higher ends. Otherwise, what exactly is the point? Self-perpetuation? There is a great difference between running a museum in a businesslike manner, which is a good and necessary thing, and running it as a business, which is neither."

"The heart of the matter," Mrs. B went on, "is simply this: I am not having comic books on display alongside my father's Audubons and Whistlers. It won't do."

Clark threw back his shaggy blond mane for an airy laugh. "Graphic novels are a long way from your father's old Superman and Captain America comics full of *Bam!*s and *Pow!*s, Mrs. B. They're taught in literature seminars now, and reviewed in serious journals as the postmodern supra-literary constructions that they are. Nowadays, they're rightfully seen as unique, sequentially generated narratives, which make possible levels of subtext that ordinary—"

But Mrs. B refused to put up with the jargon. "I know what graphic novels are, Clark. They are strips of cartoonish, generally morbid drawings of people and talking animals with dialogue balloons over their heads. Otherwise known as comic books. And we are not having them at the Brethwaite."

She spoke with severity, snapping off the words, and Alix saw surreptitious satisfaction shine on the faces of Drew, Madge, and Alfie. Even Prentice looked discreetly pleased.

"Mrs. B, they'd be in the temporary exhibition area, completely separate from the permanent collection. You wouldn't even be able to see—"

"Have I been unclear, Clark? I don't believe I have been unclear. Does anyone else think I have been unclear? Pay attention now, Clark. We . . . are not having . . . that crap . . . in the Brethwaite. Would you like me to say it one more time—more slowly yet, so that you can grasp it in its entirety?"

Wow, Alix thought, if Clark was supposed to be her favorite, he had it wrong; this really *was* one tough old bird.

Clark's cheeks flushed, but he managed to laugh it off with twinkling good grace. That smile of his really was a winner. "Not necessary, Mrs. B. I think you've pretty well seared it into my brain."

Mrs. B relaxed into a near smile herself, having made her point: When push came to shove, she still held the whip hand. "Good. Let's move on. Alix, the board has unanimously accepted your bid to clean three of the paintings going to auction—the Sargent, the Eakins, and the Mary Cassatt still life—as long as you can guarantee to have the work completed by the time of the auction."

"Thank you, Mrs. B. I should have them done in ten days; two weeks on the outside."

"However . . ." Mrs. B's long, knobby fingers drummed delicately, perhaps nervously, on the glossy tabletop. ". . . However, there is one issue—"

"The Stubbs," Alix said. "*Chestnut Stallion with Two Spaniels.*"

"Yes, the Stubbs. Can you explain?"

"Explain what?" asked Madge Temple. "What about the Stubbs?" The word *issue* had grabbed her attention. If there was an issue in the making, she wanted in on it.

"Alix declined to clean it," said Clark, who had apparently been briefed earlier.

"You *declined*?" Madge said. "Why? It's our oldest painting and it looks like hell. The varnish has turned so yellow the damn stallion looks like Lassie. And then there are all those fly specks, and what about the paint blisters that are starting—"

"I didn't 'decline' to clean it, Madge, I said it can't *be* cleaned."

"Which means *you* can't clean it," Drew said. "Maybe we need to find another—"

"No, I meant that you couldn't find any knowledgeable, reputable conservator who would even try."

"Then we know what has to be done. Our course is clear," Alfie contributed with a swig of his bourbon-laced coffee. "Only where do we find a disreputable one?"

Mrs. B ignored him and spoke to Alix. "Explain, please."

"Of course—"

"Are you aware," Clark interrupted, "that the Stubbs is the cornerstone of our auction, the unit that is projected to bring the greatest return?"

"No, I wasn't aware of that," Alix said. "And frankly, that surprises me. It really isn't one of his better works."

"That's so," Prentice said. "It's little more than an oil sketch."

Clark's friendly, boyish, snaky smile gleamed. "I agree with you both—I mean, who am I to disagree with you two?—but the pertinent fact here is that Stubbs's *Gimcrack on Newmarket Heath* sold at Christie's London not very long ago for more than thirty million dollars, the third highest Old Master price in auction history. So as you can imagine, that brings everything by Stubbs, including doodles on napkins, into the best-of-breed class when it comes to sales. *Quality* is not the issue we should be concerned with here."

"Quality is not the issue we should be concerned with?" Prentice echoed. "What are we aspiring to be, a used-car company, a—"

"All very interesting," said Mrs. B, "and pertinent, I'm sure, but can we get back to my question? Alix: Why can't it be cleaned?"

"It's because of the materials he used in some of his paintings from this period, and unfortunately this is one of them."

George Stubbs had been a late eighteenth-century English painter known for his pictures of animals, and especially for his portraits of famous horses, the champion *Gimcrack* being the prime example. But apparently in an attempt to make his paintings on wood panels as smooth as enamel, he had experimented with various arcane waxy materials— some of them so obscure that they had never been identified—to thin and smooth his pigments. The problem, as Alix now told them, was that no one had yet come up with a solvent that could safely dissolve the darkened varnish without also dissolving the wax-impregnated paint underneath. Unfortunately, as Alix had determined, *Chestnut Stallion* was one of these paintings.

"Well, all right, perhaps not a thorough cleaning," Mrs. B said, "but surely a light application of mineral spirits would help at least a little without doing any harm."

"Not even mineral spirits. Not even water," Alix said. "And as for pressing out the blisters, Madge, you need heat to do that, and whatever Stubbs was using has a melting point of about 140 degrees. It simply starts flowing at anything over that. Obviously, it's been tried before with *Chestnut Stallion*, probably in the nineteenth century, probably more than once, which is why it looks the way it does now."

"Muzzy," opined Alfie, who was half off in his own world.

"Muzzy is the word," agreed Alix.

"Couldn't you at least see if you can get rid of those damn fly specks?" Madge asked. "They're really disgusting."

"I'm sorry, my opinion is that anything we do would make things worse."

"Prentice," Clark said, "why have you never thought to mention this?"

"I didn't know it until now."

"You didn't know it? You're our curator of Paintings." He was still smarting from his put-down by Mrs. B, Alix thought, and Prentice was taking the brunt of it. "You're supposed to be—"

"Yes, but I'm no conservator. I believe I *have* mentioned the need for a conservation specialist here at the museum."

For once Clark decided not to engage with him. "According to Jerry," he said, appealing to Mrs. B, "if it were spruced up, even a little, it could go for millions. In its present condition . . . a few thousand at best. Probably no more than five figures."

"Then that's the way it is," said Mrs. B. "Clark, you will please have it removed from the auction. It was one of my father's favorites and I really was not happy with seeing it leave us."

"But—"

"Please do as I ask. The matter is closed." She burrowed into him with those raptor eyes of hers, daring him to challenge her. Alix began to think that the reports she'd been hearing about Mrs. B's infatuation with Clark were seriously overblown.

"Of course, if that's what you want," he said now, but he wasn't able to manage a smile this time.

"Very good. Alix, you may leave now. Oh, one more thing. The narrative budget you turned in for the cleaning work was adequate for its purpose, but I would appreciate it if you would put together an itemized line-item budget for the restoration work and leave it on my desk before you go for the day."

"It'll be there. Thank you."

"And now, before we move on to the agenda," Mrs. B said, addressing the others as Alix got up, "I wish you all to understand that the organizational and personnel changes Clark discussed with you earlier today have my approval and are not open to discussion or reconsideration. Furthermore . . ."

Alix got a brief, wan nod from Clark as she got up. Poor guy, he wasn't having much of a day and Mrs. B wasn't making it any easier for him. Alix almost felt sorry for him.

6

Clark wasn't the only one having a lousy day. Alix's wasn't going too well either. She'd known for a while now that she'd been developing a reputation for being trouble. At first it was because of her father's notoriety; lately, she'd been earning it on her own, and this morning was a good example of why. In the space of a single hour, she had declared her suspicion that the most popular exhibit in the museum—the Pollock—was a fake, and that the item they were counting on to bring them the most money at auction—the Stubbs—wasn't fit to go on the block and nothing could be done about it. Quite a morning's work. They would soon start to wonder if they didn't have a Manchurian Candidate on their hands, sent to ensure the destruction of the Brethwaite.

She sighed and shook her head. Well, what was true was true, and she wasn't going to pretend that everything was all right when it wasn't. If people didn't like it, or didn't like her on account of it, that was their problem, not hers. Her independent-minded mother had drummed that into her head when she was still in pigtails, and even if Alix had learned that it was hardly a universal truth, she did try to live by it.

But for now she had other things on her mind. Mrs. B's request for an itemized line-item budget on her desk by morning had come as a surprise. She'd thought the general estimate that she'd already submitted—admittedly, rather vague; so much for materials, so much for time required, so much for travel—had been all that was required. It had taken exactly sixteen lines, and it was as much as she'd ever had to do for any previous job. This itemized budget thing, this was something else.

There went her afternoon, she thought glumly; it would have been the first substantial chunk of free time she'd had, and she'd been hoping to take the aerial tramway up into the San Jacintos for a few refreshing hours in the snow. Well, she'd be around for a while, the San Jacintos weren't going anywhere, and, this being February, the snow wasn't going to melt any time soon. She got herself a cup of coffee from the break room (you'd think a fine-art museum's break room coffee would be something special, but it was run-of-the-mill at best, as in every other break room she'd ever been in), sat down at her worktable, and mulled things over, planning the best way to approach the task. After a couple of minutes she nodded decisively. She knew exactly where to begin.

She picked up the telephone and dialed.

"Chris," she said, "what the heck is an itemized line-item budget, exactly?"

. . .

A lot of work, as it turned out, half-and-half mind-numbing drudgery and finger-in-the-air guesswork. It not only took her the rest of the afternoon, but carried well into the evening so that she had to renege on her acceptance of the dinner invitation she'd accepted from Prentice and his wife. It was almost nine when she wearily closed her laptop, got the four densely printed sheets out of the printer, put them in Mrs. B's mailbox, and drove to her hotel, where she tossed the laptop on the bed, popped a couple of aspirin for her itemized-line-item-budget-inspired headache, and headed out to a late dinner at Lulu California Bistro, a highly recommended Art Deco restaurant on Palm Canyon Drive, Palm Springs' main street.

It was a rotten choice for a solitary diner. "At Palm Springs new-est and hippest restaurant" was the way it described itself on the menu, and the diners were working hard to make it so. Everybody in the place seemed to be having such a hip, noisy good time Alix thought it might make her grumpy, so she asked for a table on the sidewalk terrace instead, where the darkness and the relative quiet suited her mood better.

Not a good idea. Although there were a couple of other lone din-ers, they were mostly couples enjoying a quiet, romantic dinner in the velvety evening air: laughing, clinking glasses, gazing at each other with those adoring sheep's eyes that look so wonderful when you're on the receiving end, and so utterly sappy when you're on the outside looking in. It brought home all too strongly the dearth of romance in her own life. Careerwise, she was doing fine. Relationshipwise, it was another story. To put it in a nutshell, her love life was nonexis-tent. In the last year, Chris had several times convinced her to go out with one of her high-tech friends. "Alix, you're petrifying right before my eyes, and you're too damn young, and too pretty, to be a fossil," Chris would say, or some variation of it. And Alix would go out with some perfectly nice guy, but find halfway through the evening that her smile was calcifying and she wished she were home with a good book. It wasn't that any of them were creepy or strange—Chris never once picked a real loser—but there just wasn't anything there. Zero sparks, zero desire to ever see the guy again. Was it today's men? The strange, evolving times? Her?

No, not her. She was capable of feeling sparks, all right. It was only a year ago that Ted Ellesworth had made that clear, and the pang that came with thinking about him now was almost a physical ache. How could she have thrown that budding relationship away with a few stupid, thoughtless comments? Why hadn't she taken them back on the spot? And if she hadn't been able to do that, why in God's name hadn't she apologized and explained afterward? What kind of idiot was she?

No, stop right there. She wasn't going to go there. Much, much too late now.

A bowl of shrimp gazpacho, a glass of Chardonnay, and back to her hotel.

. . .

Palm Springs has no shortage of distinguished old resort hotels dating back to the town's heyday as a refuge for Hollywood stars in the '30s, '40s, and '50s. Some have remained quite grand and chic, even through the town's doldrums in the '70s and '80s; some have turned into dowagers—still respectable, even stately, but threadbare and down at the heels; while others, once opulent or in vogue, are now downright seedy. A very few others, small ones, had started off as modest, unpretentious places, more like B&Bs than hotels, and had managed to last, thanks to a dedicated clientele through the decades. The Villa Louisa, where Alix was staying, was one of those. It consisted of a main house with a dozen or so rooms, and a set of eight cottages around a swimming pool. Everything was clean and well tended, but it had been a long time since any real money had been put into it. Faucets leaked, pipes clanked, carpets were frayed. In Alix's view, this made the place homier, and as she'd told Chris, she liked it. Her cottage, the Greta Garbo Bungalow, named for the actress who had supposedly stayed in it for a week in 1928 when the cottages were still houses for guests of the owner, suited Alix just fine. Nothing fancy, but a big two-room place with a lovely wood-burning fireplace, which she'd lit on two of the frostier nights she'd been there.

She'd walked the five blocks to and from the restaurant, had gotten chilled on the way back, and was looking forward to having a fire tonight too. And maybe another glass of wine in front of it, along with something good on her Kindle. If luck was with her the fire had already been laid, as it had on other days, and all she would have to do would be to press the button for the gas flame that set it alight. She'd do it the minute she walked in. But when she opened the door and flicked on the entryway light switch, nothing happened; the room stayed black.

Damn. Well, she was familiar enough with the layout to know where the switch for the living room lamps were, and she fumbled her way along the wall toward it. She could see a little; her eyes had adapted to the dark during her walk—once one gets even a block away from the busy downtown routes, the old streets of central Palm Springs are not oversupplied with streetlights—and the soft lighting around the hotel's pool had only slightly diminished her ability to see in the darkness.

After a couple of steps she blinked and stared. Across the living room, the French doors that led out onto a back patio were open, and not just open, but wide-open. She stopped. Dead bulb, doors open when she was positive she hadn't left them that way . . . no, no, this wasn't good. She spun back around to make for the front door but was shocked into freezing when she found something—*someone*—directly in her path, barring her way. A person, a man, crouched and crablike. But instead of a face, he had a . . . what was it . . . a sack of some kind? . . . covering his head, with a horrible, rudimentary face painted on it: sinister little holes for the eyes, two dark, big circles for nostrils, and a mouth like a carp's but crammed with pointy teeth, the whole thing misaligned and off-center, like one of those crude, frightening masks from some jungle midnight ritual in New Guinea or Africa, made of burlap, and meant to scare the bejesus out of adolescent initiates.

Well, it sure did the job with her. "*Hey . . . !*" she yelled, more an involuntary shriek than a word.

He switched on a tiny Maglite and threw its brilliant, blue-white beam straight into her eyes. It hit her like a blow, seeming to light up the inside of her skull, and she swatted at his hand, caught it in a lucky shot, and sent the flashlight flying across the room to hit the brickwork surrounding the fireplace and then blink out. But the brief flash had left her worse than blind, in a pulsating ocean of swirls and sparks and sizzles. *Like being submerged inside that Pollock*, she thought inanely.

Her entire body was thrumming with the sudden rush of adrenaline, but her mind remained clear and steady, or at least it felt that way. This was no simple burglar caught in the act. If he'd been that, he would have run as soon as he'd heard her key in the lock, but he'd stayed to meet her head-on, and he was assuredly not there to explain himself or wish her well. He blocked her way back to the entry door, but across the room were those open French doors. What with that flash, she couldn't see them now, but she remembered well enough where they were and ran for them. She couldn't see the heavy wooden pedestal table and chairs that were in her way either, but unfortunately she *hadn't* remembered those. Two running steps and she barreled into them hard, the table gouging her hip and drawing another yelp. Two of the chairs went clattering over the wood floor and Alix sprawled across the table, which tilted from her weight and dumped her facedown onto the floor as well.

He was on her the instant she hit, scrambling and groping at her with ice-cold hands, and for a second her heart seemed to stop. *Oh my God . . . was he trying to rape her?* But just for a second. The next second, spurred more by anger and by sheer affront—*the hell you are!*—than by fear, she was kicking and flailing her way out of his grasp. Her fist smashed into his face and she felt something give way . . . his nose? She hoped so. And when he gasped with the pain or shock of it, she felt like a boxer who'd just seen his opponent stagger. She went at him with everything she had—both hands, both knees, her elbows, even her head. Grunting, panting, they struggled on the floor. She sensed a faltering, an indecision, in him, as if this wasn't what he expected and his heart was no longer in it, and now he *would* run if given the chance.

Oh, no, I'm not through with you yet, was her immediate thought, but she was sensible enough to know that was not a wise attitude to take, and she rolled away to give him room. With her returning eyesight, in the dim light coming through the doors she saw at once that neither flight nor rape was what he was thinking about. They were still sprawled on the floor, a foot apart; his arm was raised over her, and in his hand the heavy, rectangular onyx ashtray that had been on the table. Was he out of his mind? He'd crack her skull open if he caught her a good blow with that thing. She kicked out ferociously, catching him in the wrist and drawing another satisfying gasp, so that the ashtray popped out of his hand and bounced noisily off the floor. She—

"Hey, in there! What the hell is going on?" The voice came from the next cottage, just a few feet away, and it immobilized both of them. "It's after ten o'clock, for Christ's sake. We're trying to get a sick kid to go to sleep. How about showing a little consideration?"

The intruder stared at her for a moment, or rather she thought he did. What with those dead black eye holes, it was impossible to tell. Then he jumped up and bolted for the French doors, leaping across the patio, on the way grabbing a duffel bag he must have stashed there. He took a stumble over the foot-high brick wall that

CHARLOTTE & AARON ELKINS

served as a border, quickly recovered, and was onto the path that led to the main building and out of sight in no more than two seconds.

Alix sank to the floor again, her anger and adrenaline-induced strength melting away and pouring out of her like water down a swimming pool drain.

"Sorry," she called weakly to her irate neighbor. "It won't happen again."

"I certainly hope not." And a window slammed down.

"I'll drink to that," she mumbled and dragged herself to the telephone to dial 9 1 1.

7

A good game, a nail-biter, the Yankees leading 3 to 1 in the eighth, but the Angels with the bases loaded, only one out, and Mike Trout coming up. Joaquin Maximilian Cruz was so engrossed that he didn't hear the phone ring, didn't hear his wife come into the den with the cell.

"Jakie, is for you." And with a sympathetic shrug: "Is Lieutenant Mitchell." She held out the phone.

Cruz turned from the game with exactly the why-me look you would expect from a police detective who had put in a long and productive day's work in the service of the citizens of Palm Springs, had come home to a hearty, home-cooked meal of Tex-Mex fried chicken, red rice, beans, and tortillas, and had only twenty minutes ago sat down to digest same in front of the TV with his belt buckle comfortably undone and his second Coors Light yet to be opened beside him . . . and who had now been told that his lieutenant was on the phone demanding to talk to him.

"Thanks, Marita," he said glumly and took the phone from her. She gave him another sweet, sympathetic shrug.

"Spike?" he said into the phone.

"Yeah, Jake, sorry to bother you at home, but I thought you'd want to know. Looks like your boy is at it again."

That focused his attention. He signaled to Marita to turn off the television set and straightened up. "The Phantom?"

"Well, we don't know that, but it has all the markings. This would be what, the third one this month already?"

"Only the second, assuming it's the same guy. But four last month and three the month before. So where was this latest one? And when?"

"Villa Louisa, you know it? One of those little old-time places below East Baristo, near—"

"I know the place."

"Call came in twenty minutes ago. I've sent the property detectives and the crime scene techs over there for prints or possible DNA, or whatever, and to canvass the neighbors for witnesses. The detectives will be back in the morning, when it's light, to follow up. It's Denny Campbell's beat; he should be over there by now, taking the victim's statement, so the bases are pretty well covered." He cleared his throat. "Pregnant pause at this point."

Cruz filled it in for him. "But," he said.

"But I thought as lead detective on this character's cases you'd want to know and maybe—"

"Maybe get my ass over there too?"

"Amazing, you read my mind. I've already let the sarge know about it, and don't worry, we'll put you down for overtime. Listen, there's a difference this time around. The woman whose room it is— she came in and caught him in the act. They wrestled around before he took off. So for once there might be some forensic evidence— blood, skin, DNA, who knows?"

"He actually physically tussled with her? Hey, that's great."

"I'm not sure she'd agree with you on that."

"Oh, hell, you know what I mean, Spike."

"I know what you mean, Jake," Lieutenant Mitchell said, laughing. "You mean that, technically, we're not just dealing with just another two-eleven. This time he's upped the ante to strong-arm robbery and he's in major trouble. I like that too."

"He's in major trouble if we ever catch him," Jake amended. "The girl, the woman—she's okay?"

"Woman. Alix London, some kind of consultant. She's here doing something for the Brethwaite. And as far as I know, yeah, she's okay. Couple of bruises, I guess. She's refused to go to emergency, says it's not necessary."

"Okay, that's good, and I assume we've got a few units prowling the streets for anything that catches their eye?"

"Yeah, sure, two of them, but unless he's running or starts yelling 'Arrest me, I give up, I did it!' I don't know what they're going to see."

"They don't know what he looks like? If she wrestled with him, she must have seen him."

"No, it was dark and he was wearing some kind of sack or bag on his head, or so she says."

"Well, hey, that'll make it easier. All they have to do is look for a suspicious-looking guy with a bag on his head. Listen, could she at least say whether he—"

"Jake, what are you asking me for? I already told you everything I know. Go ask her."

"Right, lieutenant. I'm on my way."

He set the TV on Record so he could watch the rest of the game when he got back (although he knew himself well enough to realize he wouldn't have the patience; he'd just fast-forward to the end), popped the beer back in the refrigerator, and kissed Marita.

"I'll be back when I get back, honey," he said. "Don't wait up."

"I wait up," she said.

"Babe, it's not necessary. It's just an interview."

She kissed one of his cheeks and patted the other. "I wait up. Don't shoot nobody."

. . .

Palm Springs patrol officer Dennis Campbell was the youngest, sweetest-looking cop Alix had ever seen. Slender, intense, smooth-cheeked, he looked as if he were wearing his big brother's uniform.

"Ma'am," he said, having introduced himself and the officers with him, "we've arranged with the manager to use a nearby bungalow where I can take your statement, so we can get out of the way while these officers here process the crime scene, if that's all right with you."

Is that what her homey little bungalow was now, a "crime scene"? Suddenly, it wasn't so homey any more. "Fine," she said, "let's go."

She followed him down the row of cottages to the Joan Crawford Bungalow, according to the wooden plaque on the door. She was glad when they sat down at the round dining room table. With the adrenaline rush having dissipated, her legs felt as if they didn't have any bones in them. She'd been surprised by how unsteady she'd been on the brief walk from the Greta Garbo cottage.

Campbell took the seat opposite, pulled out a notebook, and set a small recorder on the table between them. As he did, a hank of straight brown hair flapped down over his forehead, turning him even more into a fifteen-year-old. He smiled, quite appealingly. "Ready?" She nodded.

Campbell turned on the recorder. His expression composed itself into something more formal. "This is Officer Dennis Campbell. I am speaking with Ms. Alix London. This interview is being conducted on February 7, 2014, at the Villa Louisa in Palm Springs . . ."

And on it droned. Alix was having a hard time focusing. *I could really, really, use a cup of coffee,* she was thinking. There was a twenty-four-hour urn in the lobby, its contents stale and bitter by now, but the stronger the better at this point. "Officer Campbell," she said, "I'm sorry to interrupt, but I am in real need of—"

At which moment the door swung open and an older man in civilian clothes came in. "Sorry to interrupt. Hello, Dennis. Ms. London, I'm Detective Cruz. I'll be sitting in on the rest of this, if it's all right with you."

If Campbell looked like a kid playing a cop in a high school play, the shambling, bearlike Cruz more than made up for it by looking exactly like the detective everybody knows from having seen him a dozen times in movies or TV crime series; not the dashing lead, but the second banana: the decent, slightly tired, older family man who's been talking about his retirement party next week, but who you just know in your heart is going to walk into that decrepit, supposedly empty apartment and get himself killed.

He sank into a chair with a washed-out sigh. He was wearing a rumpled gray suit, a tired white dress shirt open at the neck, its collar points limp and wilted from a few dozen launderings too many, a loosened tie, and a world-class five-o'clock shadow. He made a go-ahead motion to Campbell. "Please continue."

The young officer looked surprised. "Me, sir? Not you?"

"No, young Dennis, you go right ahead and do it the way they taught you. I'll just sit right here and apprise you of your mistakes so you can learn from them."

"Thanks a bundle, sir. I appreciate this opportunity to partake of your wisdom."

It seemed to Alix a pretty cavalier way to begin, especially with her sitting right there, but then maybe they were just more laid-back in Palm Springs and this kind of badinage was routine. In any case, the young police officer, not observably rattled by Cruz's oversight, couldn't have been more professional and efficient with the interview. He was considerate, too, charmingly so. When he asked if the intruder had "tried to take advantage of you in a sexual manner," he'd apologized for the question and might even have blushed. Cruz offered no direction or questions of his own, merely listening amiably and non-judgmentally, and jotting an occasional note in a pad of his own; he could have been watching a TV show that he'd seen before but that still held some points of interest. Despite the world-weary, seen-everything look, he couldn't have been more unthreatening.

Somehow, the moment when it had seemed appropriate to ask about coffee had passed, but at about the twenty-minute mark, the worried resident manager showed up with a cart loaded with a thermal coffee carafe, cups, and a dozen or so cookies on a plate. Alix went for the coffee the way a drowning man goes for a life ring. Cruz poured himself some as well, but not Campbell. No takers on the cookies.

"Does this matter have to be in the paper?" the manager wanted to know. "Are we going to have TV reporters all over the place?" A hesitation and then an eager whisper: "Was it the Phantom?"

He was sent on his way with sincere thanks for the coffee and not-so-sincere prevarications on the questions, and Campbell resumed the interview, which took fifteen more minutes. Cruz had yet to ask a question or make a comment of his own, but once Campbell had finished, he took command with easy assurance.

"Dennis, go and see if anything's turned up over at the other bungalow, and then give the techs a hand searching around the outside, will you? Crime Scene will be back out in the morning when it's light, but it wouldn't hurt to have a look now, while everything's fresh. Pay special attention to the area around the patio, especially to the ground on the other side of the brick border, where the lady says he stumbled over it. Might have dropped something when his foot caught, or something might have popped out of his pocket."

"Will do." Campbell unholstered his flashlight and pulled on a pair of plastic gloves as he left.

"Oh—" Alix suddenly said. "*He* was wearing plastic gloves too. I forgot. Or maybe rubber." After another second she said, "So there won't be any fingerprints, will there?"

"Not if he was wearing gloves, no. But then there never are, with this guy."

"'This guy?' You think he's this Phantom Burglar I've been hearing about?"

"That," he said, "is the working hypothesis. Subject to change at any moment, of course." He was sitting back in his chair with his hands folded over his stomach, looking wise and canny. "So. You said your laptop's missing—probably in that duffel bag you saw. I don't suppose it has built-in tracking, or did we get lucky for once?"

"Uh . . . I don't know."

"Is it an Apple?"

"No, something else. HP, I think. No, Acer . . . oh, wait . . ."

"And you never subscribed to a service that . . . no, I can see that you didn't. I hope you had all your data backed up in the cloud somewhere," he said, obviously doubting it.

"Actually, I do." Chris had insisted on teaching her how to set that up on SkyDrive and once done, it took care of itself. Now all she would have to do was get a lesson on how to retrieve it.

"That's good. Okay, your answers to Officer Campbell's questions were very clear. I just have a couple more. You've said he was a male."

"Yes."

"But you couldn't see his face, and he wasn't especially big or strong, and he never said anything, so you never heard his voice. So how do you know it wasn't a woman?"

"It wasn't," she said with certainty. "Women and men have different ways of moving, of gesturing. You can't always tell, but when you can, you can, even if you can't explain exactly how. And this was a man." The good old connoisseur's eye, in other words.

Cruz seemed to accept this. "More coffee?" At her nod, he topped off both their cups. "So, listen, how do you think he got inside? No signs of a forced entry. Did you possibly leave those doors unlocked?"

"It's possible, but I really don't think so. But remember, during the day, there'd be staff coming in and out. Someone might have accidentally left them unlocked."

"Where do you keep your room key when you're out?"

"In my bag. It's back in the other bungalow right now."

"But in general, does it stay with you all day?"

"You think someone got the key out of my bag to get in?"

"The thought crossed my mind, yes. So, does it stay with you all day?"

"Pretty much. I mean, I keep it in my desk at the Brethwaite. If I'm just going to be gone a few minutes, I do leave it there."

"Ah."

"Oh, wait a minute, detective, it's the only place I ever leave it. And the museum isn't open to the public right now. The only people who get in are the people who are supposed to be there. Surely you're not suggesting that one of the Brethwaite staff—"

"Well, I'm not discounting it. That's my best guess yet as to how this guy's been getting into these hotel rooms. He gets hold of a guest's key card somehow, runs to their hotel, unlocks the door, and uses something—a match, a paper clip—to leave it propped open a crack. Then he runs back—if it's in Palm Springs, it can't be more than a few minutes away, can it?—and puts the card back wherever he found it, and returns to the hotel later, at his leisure, but while the guest's out."

Doubtfully, she shook her head. "I don't know, I think you're on the wrong track there. I just don't see one of the staff sneaking into my desk to steal my key so they can sneak into my room that night and steal my laptop. I just don't see it."

"Well . . ."

"Besides, if it's the Phantom Burglar we're talking about, he's obviously been able to get in pretty much anywhere he wants. Why assume it has to be someone who works at the museum? Anyway, maybe he gets into the rooms some other way. Maybe they're—I don't know, inside jobs or something."

"Well, and so they may be," he said agreeably. "As I said, it's only a hypothesis. The entire notion of a Phantom Burglar—a single person behind all these thefts—is no more than a hypothesis. Could well be wrong. Hello, Dennis, lad, what have you got there?"

Officer Campbell had returned, beaming and bearing aloft what Alix at first took for a plastic shower cap in a see-through plastic bag.

"Oho, what do we have here?" Cruz asked again. Everything seemed to be a game to him. "Bring it here, Denny."

"It's a, what do you call it, a shoe cover, isn't it?" Alix said as Campbell placed the bag on the table. "The kind of thing they wear in operating rooms to keep them germ-free."

"In this case," Cruz said, "I think the more apt comparison would be with our crime scene investigators, who are almost certainly wearing them this very moment a few yards from here, to keep from messing up the scene with their own DNA or anything else. Where exactly did you find it, Dennis?"

"Exactly where you told me to look, Jake. I'm impressed."

"Well, I am a detective, Dennis," Cruz said nonchalantly. "It's expected of me. Now, if you're done out there, would you do me the favor of going to the main building and getting to that manager? Find out if they maintain any surveillance videos that we might look at."

"Sure thing, but I doubt it."

"I doubt it too, but do it anyway. And then move on to any garbage cans and dumpsters on the grounds. I want you to go look in every single one of them and see what you can find."

"And I am specifically looking for . . . ?"

"Plastic gloves, another shoe cover, and some kind of sack or bag made into a mask. He wouldn't want to be caught on the street with any of those. He'd get rid of them right away. And, if he's panicked, there might be a laptop too. And anything else that catches your eye. Use your noodle."

Campbell turned to go, but Cruz stopped him and cocked a cautionary eyebrow. "And when I say 'look' in the dumpsters, that includes climbing in and rooting around with your hands if need be, which it probably will. Understood?"

"Yes, sir, thank you, sir. And here I thought, being the new guy, that I wouldn't get any plum assignments for months and months."

"Kiddo, I've been in more dumpsters than you've got years. The development of skilled dumpster investigation techniques and strategies is your pathway to becoming a big, important detective man."

"You mean like you, sir?"

"Well, no. I wouldn't shoot as high as all that. No point in setting yourself up to be disappointed."

"I'll keep that in mind, sir. Thank you for your valuable advice— your ceaseless, constant, all-pervasive, never-ending . . ." He was still coming up with adjectives as he exited. These two had quite a shtick going, Alix thought. Perhaps it was intended to relax people. If so, it was working with her. She was smiling.

"Pay no attention to that boy," Cruz said. "He's still finding his way. Now: the more I see here, the more I believe it is our elusive Phantom Burglar—whoever he might be. Your running into him may not have been the most pleasant experience you've ever had—"

Not the worst, either. It had been anything but pleasant at the time; it had been shocking and frightening and deeply upsetting, but in retrospect, other than losing the laptop and bruising her hip, it had been . . . well, kind of enjoyable. Exciting, anyway. She'd gotten in a few good licks, and they'd felt marvelous. At the very least he was going to have a few sore spots when he woke up tomorrow morning.

"—but it was a break for us. We now have this shoe cover, for one thing, and I'm hoping he put it on before he put on the gloves so we might be able to turn up some prints. And I'd be really surprised if he didn't leave some DNA in your room. It's hard to wrestle around with somebody on the floor without leaving some of yourself behind, so to speak. We'll want to check your hands and fingernails and so on too, as soon as we're finished here, if you don't mind, and we'll want to collect the clothes you were wearing—well, I guess that would be the clothes you're wearing now. I don't suppose you were considerate enough to bite him?"

She shrugged. "Sorry."

"Oh, that's all right. And at least now we have some confirmation on how it was he could pull off all those burglaries without leaving any kind of evidence. Covers his head, covers his hands, covers his feet. We figured as much, but we didn't *know* it before. Now let me ask you another question. Apparently, you never screamed or yelled for help. Why not?"

"I didn't? No, I guess I didn't, did I? I suppose I just didn't think of it. I was too busy fighting with him, and it was all over in what, not even a minute."

"Huh," was his non-committal response, and then: "Well, next time, scream like hell, that's my advice."

"I will certainly take it into consideration, detective," Alix said coolly. She didn't like being told what she *should* have done any more than anybody else does, especially when you know the person who's telling you that is right. "I will also make sure to bite him first. Or do you recommend it the other way around?"

"No, seriously, screaming your head off is your best bet for bringing help, but more than that, most bad guys will turn tail if you do it loud enough. And if he doesn't run, then at least you know what kind of person you're dealing with: You're in big trouble and you better be ready to go all out and fight for your life." He eased up a little and smiled. "Which I admit, you did just fine. End of lecture."

He looked up, surprised, to see young Campbell, who had left only a minute ago, back at the door. "Well, that was fast."

"I didn't get to the main building yet, Jake. I stopped at the first dumpster I came to. No gloves, but . . ." From behind him, as if he'd been hiding a present, he produced another plastic bag, this one with a rubber mask in it. Alix instantly saw that she'd been wrong about the cutout sack. This was what he'd been wearing over his head, a rubber mask, a crude one.

Cruz stared at it, scowling, then looked at Campbell. "Butthead!"

Campbell quailed, not play-acting this time. "Sir . . . ?"

"No, I'm not calling you names, Denny, I'm telling you who this mask is supposed to be. Didn't you ever see *Beavis and Butthead*?"

"Well, yeah, sure, I . . . hey, you're right, Jake. It *is* Butthead. Sonofagun."

"Is this what your man was wearing, Ms. London?" Cruz asked.

"It is, yes. I'm not sure why I thought it was a canvas sack or something—because it's so crudely done, I guess." She was glaring at it as if the intruder's head was still inside it.

"Yeah, well, Butthead was a pretty crude kid," Campbell said. "I always liked him, though."

"I only saw a few clips of it," Alix said. "I thought it was pretty bad, to tell you the truth." No, the truth would have been that one clip had been enough and she'd thought it was beyond inane, and repulsive as well, but she didn't want to hurt the young officer's feelings.

Cruz was smiling. "I guess we should consider you lucky that it wasn't Beavis you ran in to. He was the really nasty one."

"I don't agree, Jake," Campbell said with a smile of his own. "I think Ms. London would have beat the crap out of him too."

8

After the interview, Cruz took Alix back to her cottage for a walk through with him at her side, and then to provide the crime scene people with the clothes she'd been wearing, and with various biological specimens that might prove helpful in analyzing and identifying any trace evidence they came up with: fingernail scrapings, blood sample, hair sample, and so on. It wasn't until one a.m. that the police began to wrap up, and the manager, who'd been anxiously hovering outside, immediately offered to move her to another room where she might feel safer. Alix said no. She thought it extremely unlikely that the guy would strike again, and in any case she didn't want to give Mr. Phantom the psychological victory of running her out of her room. So she preferred to stay right where she was, if the manager didn't mind. But it was Detective Cruz who minded, saying that in his experience she'd get a better night's sleep if she spent the rest of the night elsewhere. So she accepted the manager's offer of the Joan Crawford Bungalow, which was bigger and *very* much nicer, he emphasized, practically wringing his hands, and which ordinarily went for a much higher rate, but would be given to her at no additional charge for the remainder of her stay.

It *was* bigger, she realized when she went back, a full-scale apartment, really, with a kitchen and two bedrooms instead of one, which meant she'd have a home office to spread out in if she needed it. And yes, nicer too. Unlike the Ginger Rogers Bungalow, its pipes didn't clank. And it looked as if the rugs had been replaced sometime since 1926. Luxury.

She'd hoped to get a few hours' sleep, but she was far too wired, mind and body. It was impossible for her to stay still for more than twenty seconds at a time, let alone sleep.

Lying on her back, staring at a ceiling that was too dark to see, she fidgeted and sighed, replaying the events of the night in her mind and then doing it again, an unending loop of increasingly agitated what-ifs. What if she'd failed to kick the ashtray out of his hand? What if her neighbor hadn't called out? What if—

At two thirty she gave up, climbed out of bed, and used the biggest mug in the kitchen to make herself some hot tea. She spent the rest of the night over her iPad (which had remained safe in her purse), successfully resisting the pathological urge to check her reviews, and instead digging into the techniques and materials of John Singer Sargent, Mary Cassatt, and Thomas Eakins, the three artists whose paintings she would be taking on. Toward morning, she used the Internet to order next-day delivery on the bare essentials she needed to get started on the work: cotton swabs, brushes, disposable chloroprene gloves, a few types of cleaners, a few different adhesives, a variety of varnish softeners and removers. Given a day or so, she'd be able to determine what else would be needed. Fortunately, the museum already had a good table-mounted binocular magnifier stowed away under a dust-coated plastic cover in a corner of the storeroom. No one seemed to know what it was doing there, but she'd make good use of it.

She stuck with these chores until six a.m.—nine o'clock on the East Coast—and then put in a call to FBI headquarters in Washington, DC, in response to an e-mail that had shown up on her late lamented laptop the day before. For over a year, Alix had been on the list of approved consultants to the FBI's Art Crime Team (the "art squad," as everybody called it, including the team members), and she had been on three assignments for them. The first one had almost been her last. She'd been playing a supposedly undangerous, semi-undercover role on the *Artemis*, a fabulous mega-yacht in the Mediterranean, more of a luxury vacation than a work assignment (so she was told), but a few little flies in the ointment had turned up, starting with her getting knocked senseless on the first night, very shortly continuing with the murder of a crew member, and winding up with an outstanding grand finale, an all-too-close encounter with a wild, gun-waving Albanian mafioso. But she'd come out of it only slightly bruised, and, from the FBI's point of view, she'd done a fine job.

From her point of view, it had been a disaster.

She'd been under the long-distance supervision of Ted Ellesworth, the FBI agent whom she'd first met a few months earlier, while helping Chris look into a questionable Georgia O'Keeffe landscape being offered by a gallery in Santa Fe. After a rocky start in New Mexico, she and Ted had hit it off, Ted had been impressed with her abilities, and it was he who had recommended her to his boss as a consultant to the Bureau and gotten her the assignment on the *Artemis*. Halfway into the cruise it turned out that Ted was needed on the yacht as well, and he'd come unexpectedly down from the sky in a noisy racket of rotor blades. They had been able to spend a little time together over the next few days, and there had been a renewal of the lovely spark of mutual attraction that had flitted between them in New Mexico. There, on the juniper-scented, sun-soaked Aegean, it had been on the verge of really turning into something. With both of them being on the undemonstrative side, however—Ted even more so than she was—they hadn't yet gotten around to doing anything about it. They hadn't even done anything that could reasonably be called flirting, not in the twenty-first century. Probably not the twentieth, either. The nineteenth, maybe.

But it was in the air, it was in the air.

Until, on what should have been a romantic post-cruise lunch at the fountained Garden Court of the National Gallery in Washington, she'd totally, thoroughly, irrevocably, unconditionally, and single-handedly screwed it all up. All with a few ill-chosen words. To his great surprise and obvious disappointment, instead of excitedly accepting the new plum assignment he had gotten for her, she had responded with a vitriolic . . .

No, she wasn't going to go there, not again. It never got her anywhere, and it didn't matter anymore anyway. Since then, he'd kept his distance. In all these months she'd never seen or heard from him again, and she'd known better—or had more pride—than to try and get in touch. The two consulting jobs she'd been offered since then had been arranged and managed by one of his assistants, a bright, vibrant woman named Jamie Wozniak, whose job Alix had never gotten straight—she wasn't at the special-agent level—but she pretty much seemed to pull all the strings, much in the way that the resourceful executive secretary of a CEO might pretty much pull the strings in the company. The e-mail Alix had received yesterday had been from Jamie, and had been seven words long: "Lookin' for work? Give me a call."

As usual with Jamie, the phone seemed to be picked up almost before it rang.

"Ever been to Fairbanks, Alix?"

The abruptness, the lack of a greeting, didn't bother her. Over the year they'd been in occasional contact, they'd become friends, and Alix had learned that with Jamie, when it was business, it was all business. And business meant they wanted her for another assignment.

"Fairbanks, Alaska? No."

"Wanna go?"

Hell, no, she didn't want to go. She'd damn near been killed a few hours ago, she hadn't slept all night, and she was still finding new scrapes and bruises. The last thing she needed was to put herself at risk on another "safe" FBI venture. Maybe in a few months she'd be ready to give it a try, but she'd need time to think about it.

She was still trying to figure out how to get all this across to Jamie without having to unpack for her all that had happened—she just wasn't up to it—when Jamie said, "Alix? You there?"

"Yes, I'm here. Sorry."

"We're not talking about right now, this minute," Jamie said. "Couple more weeks."

"It'll still be February. Isn't it dark for, like, twenty hours a day? And freezing cold?"

"I believe I may have heard such rumors."

"Then pardon my asking," Alix said, "but why would I want to go to Fairbanks?" And a moment later: "Why would anyone?"

"Anyone, I don't know, but for you, we've got a pretty good inducement: Anthony van Dyck. There's supposed to be a lost—or should I say 'newly found'—late Van Dyck up there, that turned up in a junk shop—excuse me, an antiques gallery—a big-as-life, knock-your-eye-out *Charles I on Horseback*. It's a little beat-up, but if it's authentic, it's the find of the decade. But our respected coterie of Flemish Baroque experts are split down the middle. Half say fake, half say it's the real thing. They've practically come to blows. As for forensic tests—and I *know* this will shock you—they've been inconclusive: maybe real, maybe not."

She was surprised to find herself beginning to waver. She greatly admired Van Dyck's work, she knew it well, and she had a good feel for it. It would be wonderful to work on one of them, even a purported one. Maybe, now that she thought about it, an interesting new case and few days in an exotic new environment might be just the ticket.

"So as you can imagine," Jamie was saying, "Ted would very much like to have your opinion."

Any thought of Anthony van Dyck flew out of her mind. ". . . Ted?" *Oh, Lord, tell me my voice didn't really crack when I said that.* But she knew it had and she knew it wouldn't get by Jamie.

Not that Jamie would let on, of course. "Well, yes, Ted's the lead agent on this, but I should tell you—"

—he probably won't be up in Fairbanks at that particular time.

"—he's got another assignment going and he won't be able to be there then."

Good, no possibility of an awkward meeting. That was a relief. Yeah, right—if she was so relieved, then why the unsettled, fluttery feeling in her stomach? Was she disappointed that he *wasn't* going to be there? Could you be relieved and disappointed about something at the same time? Apparently, you could.

What was going on here? Was she really that hung up on this guy? She knew she'd made a bad mistake with him, but she'd truly believed she'd put it behind her. Well, maybe not "truly," because every now and then, on some solitary evening, she'd rehearse in her mind just how she'd frame her apology and smooth things over if their paths ever did cross again. And now that the possibility of running into him had so suddenly popped up and just as suddenly been snatched away, it had left her not knowing *what* she felt. Or what she wanted.

All right, you're not over it, you might never get over it. Big deal. Live with it, put it behind you, get on with your life. Enough already. "Okay, I'm interested," she told Jamie. "Tell me more."

Arrangements were quickly made. Alix would fly up at the end of the month, would be oriented and escorted by Special Agent Jacobs from the FBI's satellite office in Fairbanks, and would be put up for two nights at the Westmark. Compensation and expense reimbursement would be as provided by her contract.

"Listen, Alix . . ." The softening of tone announced that they were about to shift to something more personal. ". . . I know this is a touchy subject, but I was wondering about, you know, these nasty reviews you've been getting, and now that really awful new blog that's out there, and I was thinking, well, we're the FBI here, we've got a lot of resources on hand, maybe we can do something about it, maybe I should talk to Ted about the possibility of looking into—"

Alix headed her off. "No-no-no-no-no," she said. "No, no, no. Absolutely not." Jamie's interest in her reviews was a personal thing, the concern of a friend. She had assured Alix that she'd never once spoken to Ted about them, and although Alix had taken her at her word, the possibility of it happening still worried her. "I do not want Ted involved. I do not want the FBI involved. Forget it," she finished.

Jamie sighed. "Honestly, Alix, I wish you'd just come out and tell me what you really think."

Alix wasn't ready to joke about it. "I do not want Ted involved. Please, Jamie, promise me you won't talk to him about it."

"Well, I think you're making a mistake, but all right, if that's what you want, I promise."

"Say it like you mean it."

"I *promise*. Sheesh, Alix."

"All right, then. Ah, look, Jamie, it's not that I don't appreciate the thought, it's just that . . . well . . . you know."

"Excuse me?" Jamie said after a couple of soundless beats went by. "We seem to have a bad connection. I didn't quite get that. It's just that *what?*"

"I'll tell you when I figure it out," Alix said, laughing now. "In the meantime, I expect you to keep your word."

"I will. And I'll be in touch on Fairbanks within the week."

It was only when Alix had shut the telephone that one of Jamie's remarks hit home.

She glowered at the phone, chewing on her lip. *What* really awful new blog?

.   .   .

Jamie was in a rare bad mood when, without putting down the telephone, she pressed Ted's number. At heart, behind the wisecracks and banter, and despite a mere thirty-five years of age, she was a motherly old soul, and it just plain annoyed her these two people of whom she was extremely fond couldn't get their act together. If any two people were ever made for each other—*needed* each other—then Alix London and Ted Ellesworth were the ones. It was perfectly clear to her. Why couldn't they see it? Well, heck, they did see it, she knew that; they just wouldn't admit it. You didn't have to be as good as she was at reading people to know—

He was on the line. "Hiya, Jamie, what's up?"

"I wanted to let you know that Alix accepted the Van Dyck assignment. She'll fly up at the end of the month. I just finished talking to her."

"Oh, good." And then, after a short break. "So how're things going out in Seattle?"

Typical Ted, Jamie thought, tossing it out as if he couldn't be less interested. And managing to ask about her without even using her name.

"Alix is doing fine, but she's not in Seattle, she's in Palm Springs."

"She's moved?"

"No, she's down there for a couple of weeks, doing some conservation work for a museum."

"In Palm Springs? An art museum?" She could practically hear his frown. "Not by any chance the Brethwaite?"

"Yes, the L. Morgan Brethwaite Museum of Art, why?"

"Am I mistaken, or hasn't their name shown up somewhere in the Lord & Keen investigation?" The rustling she heard suggested he was thumbing rapidly through the Lord & Keen case file.

Lord & Keen was an upscale, long-established art dealership in Lower Manhattan that was now under federal investigation. At issue was its suspected involvement in the sales of several forgeries of works by major early and middle twentieth-century European and American artists, including Seurat, Matisse, Rothko, Pollock, and de Kooning. As far as Ted was concerned, there was no "suspected" about it; they were in it up to their eyeballs. So—and this was more common than not—the difficult part of the job was not so much to determine guilt as it was to come up with proof that would a) first be accepted into evidence by the judge, and then b) convince the jury. So far, he hadn't been doing too well.

The rustling continued, but Jamie only had to think about it for a couple of seconds before she came up with what he was looking for before he did. "You know what, you're right. I knew the name rang a bell. The Brethwaite, they're one of the outfits that did some business with Lord & Keen, aren't they? But they're not subjects of the investigation, or are they?"

"Subjects, no. They didn't sell anything through Lord & Keen, they bought something *from* them, so if anything, they're victims." The rustling stopped. "Yeah, here they are, right on their list. We just haven't gotten around to them. It's a long list."

"Hunh," Jamie said.

"Hunh, what?"

"Hunh, pretty coincidental that Alix is down there working for them right now."

"Sure is," Ted said. "Look, I better get back to work. Anything else you wanted to talk about?"

Yes, plenty, but Alix made me promise I wouldn't. "No, nothing important," she said.

And then, to herself, as she put the phone down, a resolute and self-assured look on her face: "But she didn't make me promise that *I* wouldn't look into it."

.   .   .

The look on Ted's face when his phone clacked into its cradle was anything but self-assured. He leaned uneasily back in his chair with a rare sigh. Alix London. Had he ever botched anything as badly as his relationship with Alix? He'd thought he was doing her a favor by dropping a glamour job in her lap for her first assignment, with promise of more to come, but it hadn't worked out that way. It damn near hadn't worked out at all.

Some glamour assignment. Yes, there was a lovely cruise among the Greek islands on the sumptuous *Artemis*, and a supposedly undemanding task that perfectly fitted her abilities and tastes. But it had wound up a nightmare.

And it was his fault, it really was. From the first he'd done everything wrong: It was her first assignment for the Bureau and he'd put her out there, innocent, untrained, and unarmed, all alone with no backup, no partner, and only minimally informed about what she was getting herself into. As far as the job was concerned, she'd done good work, but it was sheer luck he hadn't gotten her killed. Even thinking about it now made his temples throb. He was the head of the Art Crime Team, for Christ's sake, he had almost a decade's experience at it, he'd been on over a dozen undercover assignments himself, more than any other member—how could he not have known better?

He'd been toying absently with the Lord & Keen case file, and now he threw it disgustedly down on the desk. Deep down he knew exactly why he'd been so rash, and it wasn't because he didn't know better. Over the few days that he'd been in her company in New Mexico, Alix London had gotten to him in a way that no woman had, not since the days of his sappy teenage crushes. And he'd done precisely what you'd expect from a sappy, love-struck teenager: He'd tried to impress the hell out of her. *Hey, look at me, how cool I am, what a high mucky-muck I am in the FBI. I can get you these fantastic, exciting experiences; I can put you in a world of opulence and luxury that to most mortals is as remote as the rings of Saturn. And all it takes is my say-so.*

Stupid. Juvenile.

And the kicker was that he hadn't impressed her at all. She'd grown up with wealth—not in the *Artemis* class, but plenty rich enough. Then, when her father had gotten himself into that forgery mess ten years ago, every cent of the family money had gone to lawyers' fees and civil suits. From what she'd told him, the whole affair had devastated her, and estranged her from her father, but there were no signs of that now. After a few rocky years, her relationship with Geoffrey London (who was still a bit dodgy if you asked him) had repaired itself, and they had become close again. And as for missing her old world of wealth and privilege, he couldn't see any sign of that either. As much as anyone he'd ever known, she had put the past behind her with all its regrets and missteps. She was intelligent, amusing, and capable, and she was focused on the present and the future, no longer on the past. She was charming, upbeat, sexy, and just plain nice to be around.

She was, in other words, as close to the perfect woman as he was likely ever to run into. So, for once in his life, he'd waded right in . . . and promptly screwed it up. Their last meeting had been a lunch at the National Gallery in Washington a few days after the cruise. He had come to it with an attractive new undercover assignment to offer her, this time with adequate preparation at the Quantico training center, and with an experienced partner (he himself) on the job itself. There was almost no chance of things turning nasty, and in the unlikely event that they did, he would get her out of there in a hurry. Along with all this was the unspoken likelihood that there would be more undercover work with him to come, that they would almost be . . . well, long-term partners. He'd thought that was an absolutely terrific notion.

And yet he'd been nervous about presenting it. He had yet to absorb how harrowing her experience on the cruise must have been for her, but he did sense a certain aloofness, a coolness toward him that hadn't been there the last time they'd been together a few days before, dining on salmon and champagne on a romantic, moonlit night among the millennia-old ruins of the Minoan palace of Knossos. The feeling made him hesitate with the offer of the job—what if she refused?—but he sucked it up and plowed ahead anyway.

And she refused. She came up with a bunch of wordy reasons, none of which made a lot of sense, but the underlying message was clear. He had blotted his copybook and she was uninterested in risking her life again in his company or under his so-called tutelage. That her aversion was to him was personal and not directed at the Bureau as a whole was clear enough; since that time she had accepted two more assignments with the art squad—but none of them undercover (Ted was the lead on all undercover operations), and none of them on cases in which he had any personal involvement. He had gotten the message, and had kept out of her way.

"What the hell, it's over and done," he muttered. He picked up the Lord & Keen file again. *Let's just hope whatever she's doing for the Brethwaite people will also be over and done if it turns out the case requires me to go down to Palm Springs to talk to them.*

79

9

On the other side of the continent, two-and-a-half thousand miles distant, in Palm Springs, California, the scene in Ted's office was being almost exactly duplicated, this time by a young woman who sat in a swivel chair, staring at a telephone without seeing it, the furrow between her eyebrows marking the intensity of her thoughts. Even the subject of those thoughts was the same as the one on Ted's mind: that misbegotten lunch at the National Gallery. Her perspective, however, couldn't have been more different. Like Ted—like anyone—Alix's memory was selective, whimsically so. Sometimes it chose to retain only the positive things, the things that brought pleasure, that made her feel good about herself. Sometimes not. This was definitely a "not."

This is the way she remembered it: Over a meal of roast beef, chicken potpie, and root vegetables (the luncheon theme that month was American), Ted had offered her a new undercover job. She could tell from his animated manner that he was excited about it and he was sure she'd see it as the terrific assignment he thought it was.

Instead, he'd gotten a lecture. Did he remember a book he'd recommended to her by the founder of the art squad, Robert Wittman? Did he remember how Wittman had described the essence of undercover work? *First you befriend, and then you betray.* Did he recall that Wittman had expressed the feeling that either you were cut out for undercover work or you weren't? (She wasn't actually shaking a finger at him by this point, but she might as well have been.) Well, she hectored him: She wasn't cut out for betrayal, for schmoozing first and gaining your new "friends'" trust and amity, and then dropping a ton of trouble on them, and, frankly, she was surprised that he could stand it. (That had been then. Now, a year later, she'd come to the conclusion that there were quite a few sleazeballs she'd betray in a heartbeat.)

The longer she talked, the more sober and restrained he became, and no wonder. She'd done it in a self-righteous, better-than-thou way that no self-respecting man with an ego (and Ted had plenty of that) could have taken in any way other than as a put-down, personal and professional. She should have apologized on the spot and she knew it, she'd known it even then, but . . . she hadn't. The words were out there and when she tried to take them back, they had stuck in her throat. And afterward, the more time that passed, the more impossible it became.

There hadn't been any "scene." In fact, they had parted with smiles and best wishes. But the deed had been done. Ted still valued her expertise—thus the continuing consulting offers—but he himself had dropped out of her life.

When she was startled by a sudden jerk of her head, she realized that she'd dozed off. The need for sleep had finally caught up with her. Quickly, before it passed, she lay down fully dressed and was asleep instantly. She didn't awaken until almost nine, much refreshed.

After soaking under a long shower and wolfing down every crumb of an enormous waffle-and-bacon breakfast at a bakery restaurant on the way to the museum, she told the security man who let her in that she was expecting a visitor in an hour or so, and if he would buzz her, she'd come to the entrance to meet her guest.

In the meantime, her intention was to sit down with a mug of tea in front of the easel that held the Cassatt and begin thinking about where she wanted to start, but that "really awful new blog" that Jamie had mentioned had been rattling away inside her head, so instead she logged in to the desk computer to find it. It didn't take long. When she searched for her own name in Google's blog search engine, the second blog title that came up was *The "Art Whisperer."*

Steel yourself, she thought. The term *art whisperer* could go either way, but if you put quotation marks around it, the clear implication was that the person so described was a faker, or a poseur, or both. Or maybe worse. From Jamie's tone when she'd mentioned it, that's what Alix was expecting: worse.

She clicked through to the blog itself. The Art World Insider, the well-designed logo read, and then, underneath:

The Continuing Saga of the "Art Whisperer"

By Peter Bakeworthy

PETER BAKEWORTHY IS AN ASSOCIATE PROFESSOR OF ART HISTORY AS WELL AS AN ART CONSERVATOR AND RESTORER IN PRIVATE PRACTICE.

One of the conundrums of today's ingrown world of art conservation is the continued, persistent presence of self-described "art whisperer" Alix London on the scene. Discredited and scandalized again and again, she simply refuses to go away. Most recently, London (also fondly known as the Harbinger of Disaster) has been contracted for some sort of unspecified restoration project by Palm Springs's L. Morgan Brethwaite Museum of Art, a heretofore well-thought-of institution. Apparently, the Brethwaite people don't read the art news. If they did, they would know that the celebrated Ms. London has been nothing if not consistent. Everything she touches winds up being a police matter one way or another and leaving behind a trail of human wreckage: prison sentences, ruined reputations, lost fortunes—to say nothing of the horrendous damage she's inflicted on the works entrusted to her.

Let's look at a few pertinent facts—

Shocked and incensed, she stopped reading to search for a few facts—a few answers—of her own: What else did this Art World Insider discuss other than Alix London's villainy and incompetence? What kind of history did the blog have? Answers: None and none. There was only one entry and this was it.

For answers to other questions—When had this been published? Who was Peter Bakeworthy?—she left the blog itself and went back to the search engines. The blog, it turned out, had been published February 6—*yesterday!* As for "Peter Bakeworthy," in all the world there was no such entity, unless both Google and Bing had missed him; an impossibility for someone who was both an art history professor and a professional conservator. The man didn't exist.

Surely he (or she) also had to be the person behind those malevolent book reviews. How could more than one person hate her this much? It had seemed to her before that some of the names of the "reviewers" were contrived as well. Helga McGhee? Please. She'd be amazed if they weren't all fakes.

She tabbed back to the blog itself and found that there was no contact address for Mr. "Bakeworthy" or any way to get in touch with him. She returned to her reading.

Let's look at a couple of pertinent facts:

Fact: London has a cloudy but well-documented association with the infamous Albanian mafia.

Fact: In the last year alone she has managed to be "a person of interest" to the FBI in three (yes, three) major forgery cases.

Now, a charitable person might point out—

There was a brisk double-rap on the open door behind her. "Alix, do you have a minute?"

It was Mrs. B; the first time she'd gone out of her way to find Alix. "Of course, come in, Mrs. B."

The director was dressed cowhand-style again: faded denims, threadbare at the elbows and knees; old white shirt with a ragged collar edge; and scuffed lizard-skin cowboy boots. In her hand she was brandishing a typewritten sheet of paper. "You need to see this," she said and plopped it down on the desk.

Alix reluctantly took it. What now? *You need to see this* was not generally a precursor to anything good.

Mrs. B stood, rigid and straight-backed, her bony, sun-browned hands on the back of a chair, her thin lips pursed. Definitely *not good*, Alix thought. And it wasn't. It was, in fact, a printout of The "Art Whisperer", the very blog page to which her computer was open.

"It was in my e-mail in-box this morning," Mrs. B said. "I don't know who sent it, and I don't want to know."

"I was just reading this myself," Alix said, turning the computer so the older woman could see. "And I have no idea what this is about. I hope you know that everything I've read so far is . . . is . . ." She flicked the sheet with the back of her fingers. "'A well-documented association with the infamous Albanian mafia'? Well, sure, if by *association* he means being used as a shield and choked practically to death by an Albanian thug trying to get away from the Albanian police. And, and calling me a person of interest when I was actually—"

"Alix, I don't want to hear your explanations."

Alix felt the back of her neck grow warm. "But surely you can't believe—"

"You misunderstand." There was a slight easing up, a barely perceptible warming of tone. "I detest cowardly, anonymous mischief-making like this. Even if I didn't know you, I would never believe a single word of it. Believe me, my opinion of you is the same as it was before I saw this, and that is very high, indeed. I'm bringing this to your attention only because I think you should know that someone is actively trying to do you harm."

"Thank you for that, Mrs. B," Alix said humbly.

"What do you intend to do about it?"

"I don't know."

"If it were I," said Mrs. B, leaning over the back of the chair and speaking confidentially, "I would find out who the bastard is and tell my lawyers to get on his case and stay on his back the way shit sticks to a blanket, pardon my French."

Alix couldn't help laughing. "I'll certainly keep that in mind. Thank you again."

What in the world did the staff have against Mrs. B, she wondered afterward. As far as Alix was concerned, the Iron Lady was a sweetie.

She returned to the blog.

Now, a charitable person might point out that she has never been arrested or convicted, that all of this is strictly coincidental, an unlucky tendency to turn up in the wrong place at the wrong time. But where there's smoke there's fire, says the old maxim, and Alix London's professional life has been one smoke signal after another. Who else do you know who . . .

She shut the site down and sat there, her heart pumping angrily away. This was far worse than the reviews; not just opinions and value judgments, but outright lies and contorted half-truths. And not about the book, but about *her.* There wasn't a single sentence in that blog, not one, that was true. Not one of those "facts" was even close to being factual. Surely, nobody could believe—

She jumped at the sound of the telephone buzzer, took a deep breath, and let it out through her mouth. It seemed to settle her, and she picked up the phone.

"Ms. London? It's Jock downstairs. I got these people here for you."

"People? Plural?"

"Well, there's this lady, Christine, uh—"

"LeMay. Yes, but she's the only one I was expecting."

"Well, there's two guys with her. One of 'em's your father. I know because that was the first thing that came out of his mouth. He couldn't wait to tell me." He switched to a wildly off-base simulation of Geoff's plummy English accent. "'Alix London, why, yes, she's my daughter, don't you know.' And the other one, I didn't get his name, but I tell you, I don't know about that one. He looks like the Incredible Hulk—"

"You mean he's green?" She had recovered enough to make a small joke, and she had every intention of putting that miserable blog out of her mind, for now at least.

"No, not green, but he's gotta be three hundred pounds and he's built like a, like a stand-alone freezer."

"I know who he is, Jock. Don't worry, he's harmless. I promise, he won't break anything. Be right down."

So Geoff had flown down with Chris, she thought as she jogged around the three spiraling levels to the entrance. Well, that was a surprise, and a pleasant one at that. They'd come a long way, she and Geoff, since their estrangement after his stupid, reckless (but brilliant) string of forgeries. For almost a decade, she wouldn't even let herself think about forgiving him, but eventually, maturity and time had done the trick . . . along with Geoff's warmth, his damnably irresistible lovability, and his genuine goodness. But it had taken her a long, long while to come to grips with the notion that being a genuinely good man—even an ethical one—and being a crook weren't necessarily mutually exclusive.

Even as short a time recently as a couple of years ago, after he'd served his eight years at Lompoc Federal Penitentiary in California and had moved to Seattle, he'd never have dropped in on her without an invitation, and if he had, he'd have been unwelcome. Now, here he was popping up without warning in Palm Springs.

And she couldn't have been more pleased.

As for the Incredible Hulk, she had no trouble guessing who that might be, and he was equally welcome, the man she loved most in the world after Geoff, a three-hundred-pound ex-con gorilla named Beniamino Guglielmi Abbattista, but now predictably known by one and all as Tiny (except by Alix when she would occasionally revert to childhood and call him *"Zio Beniamino"*—Uncle Benjamin). He wasn't actually related to her, though; he was an old, old friend and "business associate" of Geoff's who now worked for Geoff's business, the Venezia Trading Company, "purveyor of authentic, high-quality reproductions of fine objets d'art, in quantity and at reasonable prices." (Most of his clients, as might be expected, were second-rate motel chains interested in arty-looking furnishings that didn't cost an arm and a leg to replace when light-fingered, absentminded guests happened to leave with them. Geoff's biggest seller, by a country mile, was their hard-plastic "Aztec-style synthetic onyx soap dish," which he got by the pallet—and sold by the gross—from a family manufactory in Bangladesh.)

The three of them, Geoff, Tiny, and Chris, had stepped back from the building and were waiting outside, on the lowest of the four stone discs that formed the stairway leading up to the entrance. They were pointing at different parts of the structure and jabbering away at each other.

Tiny was the first to spot her, and his face lit up. "'Ey, *mia cuccio-lina!*" My little puppy. He'd been born over a barbershop in the Bronx's Little Italy, but he frequently reverted to the epithets and ejaculations of his Sicilian mother and father, and he always had some Italian term of affection at the ready for her. And they always warmed her heart.

There were hugs all around, and Chris explained that, since she had the whole Gulfstream to herself and didn't enjoy traveling alone, she thought that Geoff and Tiny might like to fly down with her, and on the spur of the moment she'd invited them along.

"And on the spur of the moment, we accepted," Geoff said brightly, "and here, as you see, we stand before you . . . and before this, ahem, unusual structure."

"That is one weird place," Tiny agreed, tilting his head up at it.

He had a point. The Brethwaite, built on an uneven, markedly sloping site, did have the look of four gigantic stone wheels that had dropped down out of the sky and haphazardly landed in an intersecting circle, each one slightly overlapping the one to its left and being overlapped by the one on its right. The low roofs were all slightly canted too, none of them exactly at the same angle or in the same direction, and no two of them were exactly the same size. In the center sat a surprising, pleasant little open-air atrium with a neatly cropped lawn and a few picnic tables for visitors to have coffee or snacks that could be bought at the small café.

"Is that thing really an art museum," Chris asked, "or are we looking at a pileup at the Flying Saucer Airport?" That made everyone laugh, it was so apt.

"Well, why don't we all go in?" Alix suggested. "We'd better head up to those Marsden Hartley drawings first, Chris. I saw Clark in his office when I came in just a few minutes ago, so we can probably catch him if you still want to make an offer after you see them. And then I can show everyone around the place, although there isn't a lot on the walls right now."

Chris, Tiny, and Geoff were issued clip-on visitor passes at the security desk, and then Alix led them up two levels (each level being a few inches higher than the one to its left, so that you had to mount a single, wide, curving six-inch step to get to it) to the small bay that had held the Drawings gallery. Many of the items that had been on the walls were no longer there, having been demoted to racks in the storage room, probably never to emerge. What was left was a largely undistinguished smattering of mountains, deserts, horses, Native Americans, and one lonely, unsmiling Mongolian herder in a fur hat and a long, padded tunic. In their company the Hartleys, rough as they were, stood out as the work of a genuine artist.

The four of them quietly studied the two small drawings, their attitudes restrained and circumspect—except for Chris, for whom restraint and circumspection were behaviors that went against nature.

"I *love* them!" she declared. "I want them! I *need* them!"

Tiny was less impressed, bordering on disdainful. "Hey, if what you want is Cézanne imitations, I can knock off a couple of them for you, in, like, one afternoon, that are better than those. And that includes a coffee break."

Alix saw his point. Both of them might have been homages to Cézanne, especially the one with the mountain, which was very obviously Mt. St. Victoire, near Aix-en-Provence, the subject of never-ending fascination to the great French artist, who had painted it more than seventy times. These two pictures showed the enormous influence Cézanne had had on the young Hartley.

"Now, Tiny," Geoff said with a smile, "you really shouldn't go around saying such things. Not everyone might understand that those days are long behind you."

As with Geoff, Tiny's disputes with the law—every one of which he'd lost—had been the result of his brilliantly executed forgeries and the not-so-brilliant frauds stemming from them. And as she did with Geoff, Alix still had the occasional nervous-making misgiving about just how "rehabilitated" he was.

But Tiny responded to Geoff with umbrage. "Hey, come on, I wasn't gonna *charge* her. I was gonna do it for free. There's nothing wrong with that."

Geoff immediately apologized. "Indeed, there is not. Forgive the implication."

The big guy wasn't altogether mollified. "And I *could* do better Cézannes than those," he grumbled, "and you know it."

"I never said you couldn't. But these aren't Cézanne copies, Tiny, or imitations either. Look at them more closely. Hartley has used Cézanne as a starting point, yes, but he's added something of his own, a touch of the vibrancy of America, of the American West, that one does not find in the very Gallic, very European Cézanne."

Tiny didn't hesitate with what he thought about that. "Sheesh," he opined, but Alix supported her father. "That's so," she said. "Hartley was nowhere near the artist that Cézanne was, but he came at things a different way. A Cézanne still life is, well, *still* . . . settled . . . but when you look at Hartley's bowl of pears here, they only seem to be resting for a minute. You get the impression that if you turned around for a second and then looked back at it, they would have re-arranged themselves." This was the kind of airy-fairy art talk that Alix generally deplored and she was a bit embarrassed to hear herself doing it. "Sort of," she added by way of amends.

"Enough already," Chris said. "The majority vote says go for it." She clapped her hands together, a single snapping *clack*. "Let's go talk to this Clark person, Alix."

"Wait, before we do, there's a painting I'd like everybody to have a look at. It'll just take a minute. It's on the way."

It was the Pollock that she took them to, of course, and from twenty-five feet away, Geoff said, "Oh, I didn't know the Brethwaite had a Pollock. From the drip period, obviously, perhaps 1948 or '49?" The question was addressed to Tiny.

"Ehhhhh . . . I don't think so." Tiny was looking at it, his head to one side. "A little later, I think, just before he got, you know, darker. I'd say 1951 or '52."

"Very good, Tiny," Alix said. "According to the plaque, it's 1951."

Tiny beamed. "Nothin' to it. It's a knack I picked up. In my former life."

After they'd gotten closer and had a chance to view it from a few different angles, Geoff asked: "Is there a particular reason for our looking at this, Alix?"

"I wanted your opinions. There's something about it . . ."

"You think it might not be genuine?" Chris asked.

Alix nodded. "But I can't point to anything very substantive; nothing that would convince anybody. It's not much more than a kind of mental tickling, a gut feeling."

"And we all know about your gut feelings, my dear," Geoff said, stepping back for a broader view. "One would be wise to take them seriously." After half a minute of intense study, he spoke again. "As you know, Abstract Expressionism is hardly my métier. When I was at the Met, I did do a little work on a Pollock of theirs, but it was a sort of Indian sand painting, but done in gouache and colored pencil in 1941. Nothing at all like this, so I don't know what my opinion is worth, but I would have to say that nothing leaps out at me that would make me suspect it. It may not be one of his most striking works, but it looks fine to me."

"What about you, Tiny?" Alix asked. "Did you ever do anything with Pollock?"

"Uhh . . ."

She smiled. "In your former life, I mean."

"Well, actually, if you want to know, I almost gave it a shot once." Like Geoff, Tiny didn't have to be coaxed very hard to talk about his old career, as long as it was in the right company. "This lady wanted one about like this one here. So I studied Pollock's techniques and his materials and stuff—everything. But I finally turned the job down."

"Too big?" Chris asked. "Too much work?"

"That's exactly right! Way too much work for the money, when I could do a Picasso knockoff—or a Cézanne, for that matter—in one afternoon and get paid just as much. And it costs too much to do, too. Look at all the paint that's on there, even if it's just plain house paint."

"He used *house paint*?" Chris said.

"For the drip paintings? Sure. In gallon cans. Straight from the nearest hardware store. Then he went stomping around with the can in one hand and spritzing it all over the place with the other."

"Tell me, though, Tiny," Alix said impatiently. "Does it seem to you something might be wrong with this one?"

He looked uncomfortable. "I can see you'd like me to say yeah, honey, but the truth is, I don't. It looks okay to me too. Sorry."

"Alix," Geoff said, "a moment ago you said you couldn't point to anything very substantive. Does that mean there's something *un*substantive you can point to?"

She hesitated. "Well, yes, a couple of things, but they're so nebulous I don't like—"

"Spit it out," Chris said. "You're among friends."

"All right. First point: To my eye, it's too neat, too pretty for a Pollock."

They waited for her to enlarge on this subject, but that's all she had. On to point number two.

"At the same time, it has no center, nothing that focuses the eye. It just wanders off toward the edges and kind of flows away and disappears over the sides. That's not typical of Pollock."

"I don't know, Alix," her father said. "'Not typical' and 'fake' are two different things."

"I know that, but taken together—"

"What else you got?" Tiny asked.

She had kept the strongest, such as it was, for last. "The straight lines. They're *too* straight."

"But lots of Pollocks have straight lines," Geoff said, and Tiny nodded.

"Not his drip paintings, not this many, not that I've ever seen. Sure, you can get an occasional random straight line from dripping or flipping paint onto the canvas, but not easily. This has them all over the place, some of them fairly long. Someone must have laid them down with a brush or some kind of tool, I think."

"Anything else?" Tiny said, unimpressed.

"That's it. Now you know why I don't feel ready to talk to the director about it yet. It really does all come down to the feeling I get." She shook her head. "Only what am I doing getting a feeling about a *Pollock*?"

"It *is* a bit nebulous," Geoff agreed gently.

"Hey," Tiny said, "isn't there this foundation that specializes in Pollock authentications? I forget the name, but I remember they have a good reputation. Maybe they could help?"

"The Pollock-Krasner Foundation," Geoff supplied. "But they stopped doing it years ago, probably for fear of being sued. Just announced that all genuine works by Jackson Pollock had been accounted for and anything new that turned up therefore had to be a fake, and disbanded. Speaking for myself, I wouldn't be so sure." He hesitated. "You know, child, I still know some people who might very well be helpful in establishing certainty one way or the other. Would you like me to look into it for you?"

"Thanks, Geoff, but I don't think so, not yet, anyway. Let me sit on it a little longer. Maybe I'm just imagining things."

"If so, it'll be the first time," Geoff said stoutly. "You've always been right in the past. Four out of four, if I'm recalling correctly."

"Yes, right about a Manet, an O'Keeffe, a Renoir, a Titian. But Pollock? That's another kettle of fish. No, I just want to let it percolate in the back of my mind for right now. I'll be talking to Clark about it next Tuesday, and we're going to go through all the paperwork on the thing. Maybe things will be clearer after that." A beat, and then: "Or maybe I'll just drop it. I'm out of my element here."

"And speaking of Clark," Chris said, "let's go find the guy and you can watch me negotiate the socks off him."

10

Geoff and Tiny were left to explore the museum on their own for half an hour, at the end of which time Alix would find them and then take everybody out to lunch. In the meantime, the two women headed to the level where all the senior staff cubicles were, including Clark's. (Ironically, Alix was the only person other than Mrs. B whose workspace had solid, honest-to-goodness walls that reached to the ceiling, and a real door that closed and opened.)

They could hear Clark's voice as they approached his cubicle. He was turned three-quarters away from them in his swivel chair and speaking into the telephone. Although his voice was dialed down, his whisper carried, and there was no mistaking the anger in it.

"Absolutely not, a deal is a deal, let's just stick to it. . . . No, I do *not* want to take into consideration . . . We made an agreement, and I intend to . . . (Sigh) Okay, I grant you that. All right, maybe we can. What did you have in mind? . . . No, I'm sorry, seven is out of the question. I can't . . . Six? . . . Six is possible, yes. All right, we'll say six."

At this point, he spotted Chris and Alix out of the corner of his eye. Without turning, he raised one arm and lifted a forefinger: *Give me just a second.* They stopped where they were, about fifteen feet from him.

"Don't push your luck," he said into the telephone, his voice lower but still audible. "I said okay, didn't I? . . . I have to go . . . I know . . . All *right*, Melvin. See you there. Jesus." Clark slammed the phone down in its cradle. "God damn it," he said to the ceiling. "Some people."

"You know," Alix whispered to Chris, "this might not be the best time to negotiate the socks off him."

"You just watch me," Chris said and urged Alix forward. "Come on, into the lion's den."

Alix rapped on the edge of one of the cubicle's entrance partitions to make sure that they really were welcome.

"Yeah, come on in," Clark said, swiveling slowly toward them. "I swear, some of the things you have to deal with . . ." He shook his head.

But as he took them in, the annoyance that had been on his face vanished, and the Smile took its place. Alix realized for the first time that his smile for women was different from his smile for men: wider, more inviting, with more eye involvement. More genuine, Alix might have thought if she hadn't known him. Actually, she wasn't altogether sure that he liked women that much. And as cinematically good-looking as he was, she wondered if women liked *him* that much. Speaking for herself, he was starting to make her skin crawl.

"Ah," he said, eyeing Chris, "this must be the lady who's going to make us a lovely, generous offer on our Marsden Hartleys and save herself the risk and effort of having to bid for them against a rapacious crowd of Hartley lovers. Please, sit." His gesture took in both of them.

One of the great perks of the museum curator's life is the opportunity to outfit one's office with works of art not currently on public exhibit. Most of the curatorial staff at the Brethwaite had taken full advantage: paintings, drawings, desk sculptures, various objets d'art adorned their cubicles. Drew, as curator of Furnishings, for example, worked at a spectacular, silver-filigreed, nineteenth-century slant-top writing desk. But Clark's surroundings were relentlessly, uncompromisingly utilitarian, more like a chief clerk's office than a senior curator's office: steel and Formica desk, laptop, steel filing cabinets, chairs of green vinyl and gray steel, a few books, a few folders, a printer. No art, none at all. It was a subject of debate among the staff as to whether he was making a point, had no taste, or just didn't give a damn. Alix had yet to form an opinion, but she was pretty sure it wasn't the second. He dressed too well for that.

Alix had wondered how Chris would react to Clark. Her friend, while very happily and faithfully married, had an unfortunate tendency to melt when in the presence of a good-looking male face, but maybe Clark was a bit too pretty, or oily, even for her, because she looked about as meltable as a glacier on Mt. McKinley. "No, I'm the lady who's going to make a conservative but reasonable offer on your Marsden Hartleys that will save you both the expense of insuring and packing them, and the risk of having them go for an even lower price at auction or, worse, fail to be sold altogether."

"Whoa," said Clark, eyes widening. He grinned at Alix. "She's *good.* I've known her all of two seconds and I'm already impressed."

And well he might be. Chris at her forceful, confident best cut a formidable figure. Even sitting, she towered half a foot over the two of them, and the capacious blue-and-black-checked tartan shawl (cape? mantle? cloak?) that swathed her shoulders this morning made her loom even larger.

"So," Clark said, "what's your offer?"

"What's your reserve price?" Chris shot back.

"The estimate, provided by the Endicott Gallery, not by us, is that the lot will go for fifty to seventy thousand dollars."

Bracelets jangled as Chris dismissed this with a wave of her arm. "No, not the estimate—the reserve."

Unlike the estimate, which is made public and typically appears in the auction catalogue, the reserve price is the real minimum price the seller will accept to let go of the item, and it is kept confidential until that price is actually reached in the bidding. If it isn't reached, the item is withdrawn.

"Ah, well, you know," Clark said playfully, "that's a secret."

But Chris wasn't interested in game playing. "I'm going to assume it's the usual: eighty percent of the low estimate. That means it's forty-four thousand dollars."

"Well, you're not going to get it for that price," Clark said. "I can tell you that. Damn summer colds, I hate them. Worse than what you get in the winter, why is that anyway?" He'd been sniffling and dabbing at his nose with a series of tissues since they'd come in.

"And I wouldn't expect to," Chris replied. "Here's what I'm willing to pay: fifty-five thousand. That's reserve price, plus twenty-five percent."

Alix was impressed too. A year ago Chris had known as much about auctions as Alix did, which wasn't much. Now she sounded like an old hand. And she had come prepared, as the figures that were popping so easily out of her mouth now proved

"It's also just five thousand over the low-end estimate," Clark said. "No, I'm sorry, I think we can do better than that at auction."

"It's fifty-five thousand dollars you can have right now, this minute. Bird in the hand . . . " She gave him her first smile.

Thoughtfully, he dabbed at his nose. "Well, look at it this way. If you were to bid at the auction and manage to get it at that price, which I seriously doubt, you'd also have to pay the auction house their fifteen percent buyer's premium, which would bring it to sixty-five thou or so—"

"More like sixty-three, actually. And let us not forget about the seller's commission on the hammer price that *you'd* have to pay the auction house if you sell it through them. I'm guessing we'd be talking somewhere in the ten percent—"

He held up his hand. "All right, tell you what." The Smile was back, collegial now, and accommodating. "You up your offer to the sixty-three you were just talking about and we have a deal that I think we can all live with."

Chris didn't hesitate. "Okay, then, I guess we have a deal." She stood up and extended her hand.

He shook his head and warded her off. "No offense, but I wouldn't advise shaking hands with me. I'm contagious."

Chris pulled out her checkbook and wrote out the check. Clark said he would have the paperwork ready for her before the day was done and the drawings safely packed for carrying on the plane, and negotiations were closed.

"Pleasure doing business with you," Chris said.

"Call again any time," said Clark, waving the check beside his face as if it were written in old-fashioned wet ink. "I'll call the printer's right now and ask them to take it out of the catalogue."

Chris frowned. "Could that be a problem?"

"No, there won't be any problem," he said while he dialed, "because they haven't printed it up into hard copies yet, and with every lot on a full page of its own, all they have to do is to digitally delete this one page and then renumber . . . oh, hi, Sal, this is Clark Calder"—with his fingers he waggled a goodbye to them, and went on talking—"and I have a small change for the catalogue—"

"I'm glad you got the drawings," Alix said when they were safely out of earshot, "but I'm not sure I know who came out better. He did a pretty smooth job getting you up to sixty-three thousand, I thought."

"Are you serious? Listen, I walked in there fully prepared to pay seventy, maybe even seventy-five. I got away easy. The man's a pussy-cat." She smiled. "He is *hot*, though, I'll say that for him. Whew." She fanned her face with her hand.

"You really think so? There's something about that guy that really repels me, something I don't trust."

"Who's talking about trust? What's 'trust' got to do with 'hot'?"

Alix laughed. "Anyway, you could have fooled me," she said. "Knowing you, I figured you might swoon when you met the guy, but there was never a sign."

"I'll withhold comment on that 'knowing you' crack, but I'll tell you that where money is involved, I do not swoon." She tugged exuberantly at Alix's sleeve. "Hey, come on, I wanna look at my beautiful new possessions one more time. Oh, I *love* being rich."

· · ·

A few minutes later, Alix left Chris mooning over her new acquisitions and went to look for Geoff and Tiny to show them what she knew they were most interested in, namely, the three paintings she would be restoring. Both men made suggestions—not always in agreement—for solvents and methods for the different pictures, which Alix appreciatively and dutifully wrote down. They both supported her decision not to touch the Stubbs, which she also appreciated. Despite the sureness she hoped she'd projected, she had felt all alone and just a little bit out on a limb when telling Mrs. B and the staff about that.

"Thank you both, that was really helpful, especially on the Cassatt," she said. "I feel more sure of myself now. And now let's go see if we can tear Chris away from her new treasures for a while."

· · ·

They found Chris prowling around the second level, peeking into alcoves and corners and looking cross. "Don't they believe in coffee in this place?" she grumbled. "I just gave them sixty-three thousand dollars and nobody's offered me a cup."

Alix took them to the break room, where they got mugs off the wall hooks, filled them, and took them out to one of the shaded picnic tables in the atrium.

Chris's first sip brought back her usual happy humor. "I like this museum," she said. "Different. And this outdoor area, this is pleasant."

That started Tiny and Geoff off on a string of reminiscences about their favorite outdoor areas at Lompoc, accompanied by much laughter.

"I guess I better tell you about this," Alix said as their stories wound down. "I had myself a pretty interesting experience last night. When I walked into my room."

She tried to tell it matter-of-factly, playing down the physical part, and Chris remained calm, as Alix knew she would, but Tiny and Geoff were up in arms, pressing for details and bombarding her with questions. Why hadn't she told them right away? Why hadn't she called her father *last night*? What were the police doing about it? Was she sure she was all right? Why hadn't she gotten herself checked over at a hospital? Had she heard back from the police this morning?

Warmed by their concern, Alix answered patiently, but when it seemed they were never going to run out of questions, she held up both hands. "Truce. Can we please get off this subject for a while? Through lunch at least?"

"Yeah, lunch," Tiny said, brightening. "Boy, I'm ready."

"Good, let's go. You're going to love this place, just wait."

11

Geoff had his nose in the air, nostrils twitching, like an English hunting dog zeroing in on the fox. Tiny looked much the same, practically straining at the leash.

"Ah, those aromas," Geoff said. "Heavenly."

"Wow, it smells great in here!" exclaimed Tiny, his eyes closed. "I could be in the Carnegie right now. Somebody, quick, bring me a corned beef on rye!"

"Well, since the two of you never stop griping about the New York delis you can't find in Seattle," Alix said, "I thought you'd enjoy this place."

"This place" was Sherman's Delicatessen & Bakery, which Madge had recommended as the best Jewish delicatessen in the city. It advertised itself as a "New York–style deli" and was obviously modeled on the old-time delicatessens that New Yorkers of a certain age remembered with such fondness.

The Brethwaite people seemed to like it too. There, a few tables away, sat the curatorial staff, minus Clark—Prentice, Madge, Alfie, and Drew. And Mrs. B's secretary, Richard. Alix had waved to them coming in, but they'd had their heads together and hadn't seen her.

"It sounds like a New York deli too," Chris said, pointing out that the man standing at the central cash register was yelling to his old customers and ribbing them, and the staff was loud, jokey, and kibitzing with the patrons to the point of rudeness.

"I detect a subtle difference, though," Geoff said. "Here, I have the sense that we're witnessing a sort of genial playacting, not serious, with everybody merely *pretending* to be raucous and rude."

"Whereas in New York you get the genuine article?" Chris offered slyly.

"Precisely."

Alix had dropped out of the conversation. Like the others, she had her eyes on the menu, but she was thinking about that venomous blog again, and only now realizing that there'd been no mention of her father, despite the opportunities to sling more mud at him. Did she have it wrong, then? Was *she* the object of the blog and the reviews—and not Geoff? But who could possibly be so spitefully determined to stigmatize her, to shred her reputation, her livelihood . . . her life? And why? And what would have prompted the creation—*yesterday*—of a brand-new blog totally devoted to her wickedness and ineptitude?

She realized Geoff was speaking to her and tuned back in.

". . . just that you seem a bit, ah . . ." he was saying with some delicacy.

"Just that something's bugging you," Chris said bluntly. "You're a million miles away. What's up? Still chewing over what happened last night, huh?"

"Actually, no, something else. I came across this new blog, this website, The "Art Whisperer", which . . ."

Three smart phones were immediately whipped out of their hiding places and flicked on. Alix knew better than to compete with smart phones, so she just shut up and sipped water while they read, each of them muttering comments as they went along.

Geoff: "My word . . . Oh, my . . ."

Chris: "I don't believe this . . . You gotta be kidding me . . . How could they? . . . Jeez . . ."

Tiny (in a rumbling, ominous mutter): "*Cavolo . . . Cazzo . . .*"

They were interrupted by their waitress, a short-haired, middle-aged dyed blonde in white shirt and trousers and a black apron. "Get the matzo ball soup," was her greeting. "Stay away from the stuffed kishke, that's my advice for today." She tilted her head toward the man at the cash register. "Don't tell Airhead I said so." Her nameplate read *Donna*.

"Your secret is safe with us," said Geoff. "I believe I'll have a pastrami sandwich, please."

"On rye?"

"Of course."

"Good choice," Donna said, writing. "Anything to drink?"

"You wouldn't actually carry Dr. Brown's celery soda, would you?"

"We got it. I'd stay away from that too, though."

"Nevertheless," said Geoff politely.

Donna shrugged. "It's your stomach."

Tiny ordered a pickled herring appetizer, a bowl of mushroom-barley soup, and the knockwurst and corned beef dinner plate. Chris, who was almost as hearty an eater as he was, got an entrée-sized Cobb salad and a Reuben sandwich, and Alix ordered the hot corned beef sandwich.

"This blog," Geoff said as Donna left with their orders. "Don't you have any idea of who's behind it? Anybody with a reason to bear a grudge?"

Alix didn't, and neither did the others. "But even if I did, what would I do about it, sue him?"

"Damn right!" Tiny said with some heat.

"Honestly, Tiny, I do not want to upend my life, and spend thousands of dollars, going through a suit."

"Actually," Chris said, "I think you do have grounds for a suit here. I'm no lawyer, but—"

"Neither am I," said Geoff, "but I do happen to have some familiarity with the issue. Not *everything* they said about me at the trial was true, after all, and I looked into the possibility of a suit myself. From what I learned, Chris is right. This is libel, pure and simple: an effort to injure your professional reputation with defamatory, untrue accusations."

"So did you wind up suing anybody?" Chris asked him.

"Ah, no. In the end, I didn't feel I had a convincing case. I was a disgraced conservator and a convicted felon serving a long jail sentence for fraud. Exactly what 'reputation' was I protecting? Alix, however, is not in that situation." He knocked twice on the tabletop.

But Alix had a friend who had filed a suit a few years ago under similar circumstances. The suit, rancorous and time consuming, had yet to be resolved, and the friend now bitterly regretted ever having gotten into it. "It's eating up my life," he'd said.

"Sorry, folks, but no thanks," said Alix. "Anyway, since we have no idea who's behind it, it's pointless to even talk about it, so let's just forget it."

Geoff shook his head at her. "My dear, this is important—to you, I mean, to your reputation in this small and highly competitive field. I believe it's worth every effort to try and find this person, and when you do—when we do—then you must take some kind of action to counteract it. If suing is the most appropriate route, then sue it should be. You know you can count on us for all the support we can give."

"Absolutely," Chris said.

"Nah, Alix is right, screw this *sue* stuff," Tiny said. "Listen, we find out the name of this bum, this *cafone*, I give my Uncle Guido a call, he whacks the guy the same day. Problem solved." Tiny had a pretty thick Bronx accent to begin with, but here he'd broadened it to his over-the-top version of Mobspeak. *We fin' ou' da name a dis bum, dis cafone . . .* "Bada bing, bada boom," he finished, making the appropriate thumb-and-forefinger trigger pull.

"I like it," Alix said, laughing. "Case closed. And here comes our lunch. Let's eat."

"'Ey, *mangiamo!*" cried Tiny, urging Donna on with an expansive wave.

· · ·

During the flight from Seattle, Chris had learned that Tiny was a huge Frank Sinatra fan, and to accommodate him she had called from the plane to book a tour of Twin Palms, Sinatra's famous Palm Springs residence and a major tourist attraction, but had no success.

"Sorry, Tiny," she said, turning off her phone, "no openings for the rest of the week."

Tiny's face fell. "Nuts. He's my absolute favorite singer. Maybe I can come back another time. Thanks for trying, Chris."

"They did say we might be able to get into Elvis's house, though. Interested?"

He lit up. "That'd be *great.* He's my absolute *second* favorite singer."

And so she'd made reservations for the four of them on the two o'clock tour of the "Elvis Honeymoon Hideaway," where Elvis and Priscilla Presley had spent the first nights of their marriage. As soon as lunch was over, Alix put the address into the GPS and drove off with them to the ritzy Las Palmas District. They got lost on the district's winding streets near the end, and Tiny, who was also a dedicated movie buff (Alix was learning some surprising things about him today), was in heaven. At the airport he'd bought a guidebook to the

106

old movie stars' homes, and he ticked them excitedly off as they passed. "Wow, right there, that was Kirk Douglas's house . . . That was Dinah Shore's . . . Whoa, that was Edward G. Robinson's . . . That one right here on the corner? That's where Donald O'Connor lived . . ."

After all that, the Honeymoon Hideaway was a bit anticlimactic and more than a little strange. With a dozen or other visitors, they were greeted at the door by their guide, a fully costumed impersonator—not your everyday, ho-hum Elvis impersonator either, but a Priscilla impersonator (the only one in the world, she announced) who was indeed a near look-alike to Ms. Presley. Standing in the entrance foyer, "Priscilla" offered a spirited introduction to the story of Elvis's time at the house, going so far as to provide different voices for the King, Priscilla herself, Frank Sinatra, and even Elvis's father.

The tour proper then began. Straight walls must have been considered gauche by Palm Springs's mid-century, because, like the Brethwaite, the house was built of intersecting circles, with no straight walls. They began in the kitchen, with its huge, hooded (circular) charcoal grill, and then were taken into the living room, where they were encouraged to sit on the original curved, built-in banquette for snapshots—"If you look right above you, you can see photos of Elvis and Priscilla sitting right where you are now, on these very same cushions"—and to strum a guitar purported to be one of Elvis's own. Then through the sliding glass doors onto the back patio where they looked at the swimming pool, heard more stories, and went across the lawn to see the roof of Marilyn Monroe's house just below, and to stand on the very spot on the lawn where Sinatra had parked to help the Presleys flee to Las Vegas for their wedding to escape the gimlet-eyed gossip columnist who lived next door.

Alix and Chris decided to sit out that part of the tour and instead they waited for the others in a couple of lawn chairs beside the pool.

"I've been thinking," Alix said. "Maybe you all have a point about that blog. Maybe just ignoring it isn't the right thing to do. But is it even possible to find out who's doing it? Can you trace the what-do-you-call-it, the URL?"

"The URL doesn't tell you anything. It's the IP address you need—the address of the individual computer that it was created on—but even if you get it, it's still a hassle identifying the guy himself. First, it's next to impossible, and it takes months, if not years. You see, even if you get the IP address, it's not necessarily the IP address of Mr. Creepo's own computer. How do we know he's not sending it from a library computer, or a computer rental place? And even if he's been using his own computer, the ISP, the Internet service provider, isn't going to give you his name without a court order, and in order to get a court order you'd have to prove that a crime had been committed, which in your case is the catch, because in order to do that you'd have to first—"

Alix lifted her hand. "Forget it, I'm sorry I asked. I'm already bored with the whole thing and we haven't even started. Really, I just don't think it's worth it."

When the rest of the tour group returned, Alix and Chris rejoined them to see the bedroom ("Feel free to sit on the bed where Lisa Marie was conceived"), the bathroom ("Climb into the Jacuzzi if you want to"), and the toilet area ("Have a seat on the 'throne,' if you want. You can even use it when we take a break").

Tiny, who had happily sat on the banquette and strummed the guitar, was reluctant when it came to sitting on the bed or in the Jacuzzi, and incensed about the offer to use the toilet.

"That's disrespectful," he growled, and being the size that he was and looking the way that he did, no one took Priscilla up on the offer.

For the rest of the tour he remained out of sorts, and at the end, when Priscilla said, "If you enjoyed our tour, please go to our website, where you'll find a link to TripAdvisor, and give us a good review," he muttered, "And if we don't like it?"

It had been meant for Alix, Chris, and Geoff, but Priscilla heard it and cornered him to plead. "Just don't one-star us, please. Just tell me what we did wrong and if there's something we can do to improve it."

"Yeah, don't let anybody sit on the can," Tiny grumped.

.   .   .

By the time the tour ended it was three thirty. Geoff and Tiny were scheduled for a five o'clock commercial flight back to Seattle, so Alix drove them to the airport, first swinging by the museum to let Chris off—she was staying in Palm Springs another day—to do a little more exploring on her own. Tiny, with his guidebook tightly gripped in his huge fist, resumed his edifying lectures on the way there. ("Look, there's Leo Durocher's house. Wow, you know who lived there? Carmen Miranda! Look . . .")

In the airport parking lot, Geoff leaned back into the driver's side window for a final word to Alix. "I want you to put me on speed dial, my love."

"You're already on speed dial, Geoff."

"I'm glad to hear it. But you know what I'm getting at. I want your promise that you will let me know at once should you have any more problems with phantom burglars."

"Or vice versa," Tiny contributed, hefting both their bags.

"I promise, Dad."

Calling him "Dad" always brought a sentimental softening to his features, although it was Geoff himself who had first instructed her to use his given name, against the wishes of her mother. That had been when Alix was twelve, and only recently had she begun to try an occasional "Dad." It still felt awkward, but she knew it pleased him so she kept working at it.

"Good. And if I can be of any use at all, you know that I'll be there at once."

"I know. Thank you, Geoff. Dad."

A kiss on the cheek from Geoff, a "*Stai bene, principessa mia*" from Tiny, and they were gone.

When she arrived back at the museum, she found Chris in the break room, a mug of coffee in her hand, fidgeting in front of the window that looked down on the atrium.

"It's about time!" she declared. "Come with me, I have to show you something!"

. . .

What she had to show Alix was the object destined to be Lot 22 in the auction. Having been buried in storage for years, it had been pulled out of the basement and was on a temporary easel with a few of its fellow travelers, awaiting shipment to the Endicott Auction Galleries in San Francisco. Unassembled picture crates, each one custom-made for its particular contents, stood along one wall, giving off the pleasant scent of freshly cut raw wood. No glue smell, though, as most museums were on the fussy side about getting glue anywhere near their art pieces. No hammers allowed either; the crates would be sealed with screws that would be inserted into predrilled holes.

Lot 22 was a dark blue felt–covered panel about two feet by three, on which were mounted twelve small oval portraits in three rows of four each—six women, four men, and two children, all in mid- or late-eighteenth-century dress. The largest of them was less than three inches in height, the smallest about an inch and a quarter. Alix had passed by them once or twice before, but they hadn't caught her interest and she hadn't looked closely at them.

"Aren't they lovely?" Chris asked. "Look at those tiny little faces. They're so appealing, so . . . so damn *lovable*! Especially the two kids at the bottom, on the right, they break my heart."

"Sure they're lovable, they're supposed to be lovable. They're portrait miniatures."

"Are they made to be pendants? There are those little metal loops on most of them."

"Right, for a cord or chain to wear around the neck. Or if you were a man, it'd have a cover on it like a watch cover and you'd keep it in a vest pocket. These things weren't like regular full-size portraits, Chris. They weren't painted to hang on a wall for anybody to see, but strictly as personal, private keepsakes—lovers, parents, children. They're mostly watercolors on ivory, and that, I'm afraid, pretty much exhausts my store of knowledge on portrait miniatures." She leaned closer to the rows of gentle, minuscule faces that looked back at her so very innocently and openly across two-and-a-half centuries. "And yes, they are affecting, aren't they?"

Not one was smiling or laughing, but not one had on a "public face" either. They reminded her of the kind of semicandid snapshots that might be taken at a family gathering today: "Hey, Uncle Ed, look over here for a minute!" All of them had convex glass covers— "crystals"—and were framed in gold, most of them simply, some more ornately. The majority appeared to have been done by eighteenth-century "limners," self-taught painters who were closer to artisans than artists, and who went from town to town peddling their services. These were pleasant to look at, with a naïve folk-art quality. But a few of them, including the two that had drawn Chris's attention, exhibited the subtleties and nuances of accomplished artists, all the more impressive for having been rendered on a three-square-inch surface.

"Lovely," Alix murmured.

"The boy and girl are a set," Chris said. "The cases match, do you see?"

Alix nodded. "Probably brother and sister."

"Do they cost a lot?" Chris asked.

"I don't think so, no. On a guess, I'd say you could get the whole panel for a lot less than what you paid for the Hartleys." She straightened up and threw a sidewise look at Chris. "Wait a minute, don't tell me you're thinking about buying these, too."

"Hm, do I note a certain disapproval in your tone?"

"You can buy whatever you want, Chris, but they'd be anachronisms. Where would they go in your collection? They're completely different from anything else you have."

"I like them, they appeal to me, isn't that reason enough? I'd like to have them on my wall to look at. Is something wrong with that?"

"No, of course there isn't, but . . . well, in a way, there is, yes. You're a collector, right? And you've worked hard. You've got a wonderful collection going that's getting better all the time—"

"But . . . ?" Chris was standing erectly, feet wide apart, arms folded across her chest. One eyebrow was lifted.

"Quit looming, Chris. You're plenty intimidating as it is."

Chris laughed and relaxed. "I can't help it. It's what I do when somebody makes me mad."

"Well, I certainly wouldn't want to do that, but look, here's my 'but.'" She paused to get her thoughts together. "All right. An art 'collection' isn't just any old bunch of paintings or drawings, you know that. To be a collection it has to have a theme, a focus. It has to be *about* something. And yours is American Modernism, first half of the twentieth century. The Marsden Hartleys are a great addition to that. But these"—she gestured at the panel—"sure, they're attractive, but they're from a different time and from a wildly different culture. If O'Keeffe and the rest had been influenced by artists like these, you'd have a point, but they came at their work with a totally—*totally*—different set of aims, and values, and techniques. There's no connection. If you—"

"Say, do I get to say anything here? Of course, I realize that it's only *my* collection, and *my* money I'd be spending, so maybe I don't have the right—"

Alix smiled. "Okay, your turn."

"It's just this: I *like* these miniatures, Alix. It makes me feel good to look at them. Somebody's going to wind up with them, and I don't see why it shouldn't be me."

"Let me put it differently," Alix said. "Where are you heading with this? Where would you rather be in five years, surrounded by a comprehensive, orderly *collection*, or just by a hodgepodge of things that make you feel good to look at?"

Chris looked blankly at her, eyes opened wide, and Alix stared right back, and both of them broke out laughing.

"Do I really need to answer that question?" Chris choked out.

Alix shook her head until she was able to speak. "Point made," she said. "And you know"—she leaned closer to the panel again—"those two children are really beautiful, really well done. They're almost like Peales, or even—"

"John Singleton Copleys," said Jerry Swanson, who had materialized behind them. "Am I right?"

Alix turned. "You are right. That's exactly what I was thinking."

"If only," Jerry said, prayerfully turning his eyes to the ceiling, "Nope, they're by a guy named Joseph Dunkerley. You know him?"

Alix shook her head. "Not a familiar name."

"Well, neither does anybody else who doesn't specialize in minia-tures. American, last half of the eighteenth century. Born in England, I think, but mostly worked in Boston. As far as I know, miniatures were all he did, and as you can see, he's pretty good—better than most. I've valuated his stuff before, and the Copley question usually comes up somewhere along the way, because he does paint a lot like Copley—in this teeny-tiny version, anyway—but it always gets shot down. These particular ones, they've got an ironclad provenance that goes all the way back to the day when Dunkerley sold them . . . back to the original commission, in fact, if I'm not mistaken."

"No such thing as an ironclad provenance," Alix said. "You ought to know that."

"Yeah, but you haven't seen this one. Oh, it's the real thing, all right. Trust me, we'd *love* to be able to at least say 'attributed to Cop-ley.' That alone would quadruple the price. Thought about 'school of Copley,' and I suppose we could have gotten away with that, but, I don't know, it seemed like it was reaching a little. Copley didn't really have a 'school,' did he?"

"No, he wasn't a unique or original painter in that sense. He just painted in the classical English style—only better than ninety-nine percent of the Brits did."

"What I thought. According to the records, these two right here were commissioned by Mr. Jeremiah Hobbie, Esquire, of Oldham, Mass, 1770. The kids' names are . . . oh, hell, I forget—Alfred and something—but it'll be in the catalogue. Anyway, if you look at them closely, like with a magnifying glass, you can see they're not anywhere near as delicate as Copley's miniatures." He laughed. "That's what they tell me; what do I know?"

"Well, who's looking at them with a magnifying glass?" Chris asked. "I think they're beautiful. I think they're all beautiful. What's the estimate range on this lot?"

"Twenty to forty thou, and most of that is based on those two kids. Good Dunkerleys go for about ten thousand each, and these are good. The others aren't worth much, between you and me."

"I think they're wonderful," Chris insisted.

"You should put in a bid at the auction, then. Well, I'd love to stay and chat, ladies, but duty calls."

The moment he left, Chris rubbed her hands together. "I *want* them," she said in a low growl. "Let's go see the Man."

"How much are you expecting to get them for this time?" Alix asked. "It's more interesting to watch if I know where you're going."

"I don't know, but if I can't get them for thirty, I'll be very surprised."

"He'll probably nail you for that fifteen-percent premium again."

"And I'll pay it if I have to, which I probably will. I really love these little guys."

12

They found Clark hunched over a putter, stroking balls into a spring-loaded contraption that popped them back to him. "One second," he said, and hit one more that rolled off to the left and missed. "Darn, that's what happens when I have a gallery." He leaned the putter against the wall. "So. Something more I can do for you?"

Again, Alix felt uncomfortable around him. She thought briefly about excusing herself, but decided her interest in watching the negotiations outweighed her repulsion and she took the same seat she'd had earlier.

He and Chris had the hang of each other's styles now, so things went more smoothly than they had the first time. In five amiable minutes they'd settled on exactly what Chris had predicted: The miniatures were hers for $30,000 plus fifteen percent, for a total of $34,500. Chris was obviously delighted, and Clark seemed pleased too.

"Our printer's going to love me when I do this to him," he said merrily, dabbing at his nose. This was a monster cold, all right. His nose was even redder than it had been in the morning, and his eyes were heavily bagged. She almost (but not quite) sympathized with him.

"They chewed me out about the Hartleys, but"—big boyish grin—"if I'm not good at sweet-talking, then what am I good for? Piece of cake. Let me do it right now."

He wasn't on the phone thirty seconds before his fragmentary comments made it clear that things weren't going well.

"You're joking . . . But you had no trouble with the Hartley page, why would there be . . . ? You did? Already? As fast as that? . . . Well, can't you get them back before they're actually sent out? We'll pay for the additional costs . . . Okay, all right . . .Yes, I understand. Goodbye, Sal."

He put the phone down, his electric smile nowhere in sight. "Can't be done. I'm sorry. The catalogues have already been mailed, two hundred and seventy-five of them. They went out an hour ago."

"You mean they printed them up, bound them, and mailed them off between eleven o'clock this morning and one o'clock this afternoon?" Chris asked. "That's kind of hard to believe."

"Yeah, that's what I said. But according to them, the printing and collating only took an hour, and they're not bound, they're just center-stapled. All they had to do after that was to slip them into pre-addressed envelopes and drop them off at the post office. Just two hundred and seventy-five of them, all told. I'm really sorry, Chris."

"Clark," Alix said, "why is this a problem? Couldn't you follow up with an announcement—a correction—saying that this particular lot is no longer available?"

"Not possible, Alix. The implication would be either that we've withdrawn it because of some problem with it—authentication, condition, who knows—which would cast doubt on all the rest, or that we had presold it to a customer with special access—"

"Which would be the case," Alix said.

"And which—*while perfectly legal*—would create the impression of having given certain people special treatment. Nobody else but Chris got a chance to buy anything ahead of time. That would—"

"You had no qualms about that with the Hartleys," Alix pointed out.

"Of course not, the catalogues hadn't gone out yet."

"In other words," Alix said, "the problem isn't that the miniatures were being sold ahead of time, the problem is that people would know about it."

A big smile, a conspiratorial wink, somewhat complicated by weeping, swelling eyes. "By George, I think she's got it!"

. . .

"Well, I'm disappointed, sure," Chris said a few minutes later, "but it's no big deal. I can just bid along with everybody else and hope for the best. If I can't get to Frisco, I'm sure I can do it on the phone."

They were in two of the lawn chairs scattered about the central atrium, with coffee they'd brought down from the staff break room. With her mug cradled in both hands on her lap, Chris turned her face up to the sky. "Oo, that desert sun feels good. Guess what it was doing in Seattle when we left."

"Mm, that's a hard one. Let me think . . . This is a wild guess, but was it raining, maybe?"

"Raining, definitely." She shifted a little, stretching out her long, jeans-clad legs. "Can I take back what I said about Clark earlier? About his being hot? Well, no, he *is* hot—even all clogged up with that terrible cold—but there's something awfully . . . slick about the man. Fishy. Not to be trusted. Do you get any sense of that?"

"I do," Alix said, seizing on the comment to raise something that had been on her mind but was almost too silly to say out loud. "In fact—now, I know you'll say I'm crazy, but I've been wondering—"

"I would never say that about you, Alix. If anyone in this world has both feet on the ground, it's you."

"I'm glad you feel that way, because what I was wondering was whether Clark could be the man who attacked me last night."

Chris jerked upright in her chair. "Are you crazy? The senior curator of the Brethwaite Museum is the Phantom Burglar?"

"No, I'm not saying that. I never thought that. What I'm saying—what I'm wondering—is if he's the man who attacked me last night."

"You're losing me. I thought the guy who attacked you *was* the Phantom Burglar."

"No, that's just what the police think."

"Well, if they think it was the Phantom—"

"Chris, for God's sake, forget the Phantom Burglar for one minute, will you? Pretend you never heard of him. Just think about Clark."

"Yes, but—"

"Hear me out. Yesterday his nose was just fine. No sign of red, no sign of a cold. Last night I socked somebody in the nose, hard, right through his stupid mask. Today, suddenly, Clark's nose looks like a pink potato."

"Alix, the man has a world-class cold. Didn't you see all that sniffling? And his eyes were getting red and puffy, the way they do when you have a bad cold. Didn't you notice?"

"Yes, but do you really develop a cold like that overnight? He was fine yesterday. And today it wasn't only that his eyes were red, there was a kind of bruising around them too," Alix said, "sort of purplish, like a couple of black eyes starting to develop. Didn't *you* notice that?"

"Frankly, no," Chris said more loudly. She was starting to look a little alarmed. "Look, think for a moment, Alix. Why in heaven's name would Clark want to steal your laptop?"

"Maybe to make it seem to the police that he *was* the Phantom Burglar. Maybe what he was really there for was to . . . I don't know, to kill me, maybe?"

"*Kill* you?" Chris shook her head. "Alix, you're starting to worry me."

"I'm telling you, the more I think about it, the more it hits me that that's exactly what he was trying to do. That ashtray he had in his

CHARLOTTE & AARON ELKINS

hand—that wasn't one of Geoff's Bangladesh knockoffs, it was *heavy*. Solid stone. There was a dent in the floor where it hit. There would have been a dent in my head, too, believe me."

"All right, think about that. If he was there to kill you, wouldn't he have brought something more appropriate with him, not just looked for whatever he happened to find in the room? Explain that to me."

"Same explanation," Alix said. "To make the police think later that he was just there to burgle, and it was an accident that he got caught in the act."

"Okay, he wanted to mislead the police, that I can buy. But why would he want to mislead *you*?"

"How did he mislead me?"

"He wore a mask. Why would he do that if he intended to leave you dead?"

"In case he didn't succeed. He didn't want me to be able to identify him. Which, may I point out, is exactly the way it turned out."

Chris shook her head. "You have answers for everything, I'll say that for you." Soberly, she placed her hand on Alix's wrist. "Alix. Now listen to me. For your own good, don't go around saying these things to anybody else. Even to me it sounds, well . . ."

"Paranoid. I know," Alix said with a sigh. "But wait, there's something else—I forgot. The detective that came out said he thinks whoever did it probably got my hotel key out of my bag, and the only times that bag was out of my sight—the only possible times he could have done that—were during the day when I was away from my desk for one reason or another—*in* the museum. That would mean it almost certainly had to be somebody from the museum, wouldn't it? And if—"

"Stop right there, Alix. I just heard one 'probably,' one 'thinks,' and one 'almost certainly' in less than three complete sentences. And there was an 'if' in there not very long ago too. You're reaching, kid."

"But if you put all the 'ifs' and 'mights' together—"

Chris put a hand to her lips. "Sh. Company."

It was Prentice, who had come from the building and was approaching. "Hello, again, Chris," he said, having apparently run into her earlier in the day. "Alix, I wanted to ask you: The gentleman I saw you with earlier today—not the large one, but the other, the older one—wasn't that your father?"

"Yes, it was."

"Ah, I thought so. He's changed a bit, of course, but then a couple of decades does that to a man."

To say nothing of ten years in prison, Alix thought, not that Prentice would be ill mannered enough to mention it.

"I did have several opportunities to chat with him years ago—a delightful and accomplished man, and I would dearly love to do it again. On the off chance that the four of you are free later this afternoon, Margery and I would like very much to have you all to cocktails. We'd make that a dinner invitation, but we have later obligations ourselves."

"Oh, I'm sorry, Prentice, Tiny and my father have already left. I know they would have loved to come. They'll be sorry to have missed it."

Chris's glance indicated that she knew Alix was lying through her teeth. They would never have accepted. Geoff had been chastised and snubbed too many times by the art world elite to chance getting burned again (not that Prentice would ever have done it), and Tiny was unhappy around aristocrats like the Vanderveres on general principle.

"Oh, dear, that's really too bad," Prentice said. He looked glum for a moment, then brightened. "But how about the two of you? Are you available? Would you like to come?"

"We'd love to!" Chris practically yelled, speaking for both of them.

"Excellent. You have our address, Alix. This will be entirely informal, just the four of us. What you're wearing is fine. Shall we say five thirty?"

Chris was smiling as he left. "What a nice man. A gentleman of the old school."

"You'll never meet anybody nicer—or more worth listening to when it comes to art."

"Back to what we were talking about," Chris said, her smile fading. "Let me ask you just one more question. *Why* would Clark Calder want to kill you? I seem to have missed that part."

Alix nodded. "That's the question, all right, and I don't have a clue. I've never harmed him. I hardly know him. But there's something about the guy. The more I think about it, the stronger the feeling gets. Not only that so-called 'cold,' but his whole manner, the way he looks at me when he thinks I'm not watching him—"

"Halt! Stop right there. Consider. You're constructing one hell of a case against someone on the basis of what? A red nose. All the rest is conjecture, and pretty wild conjecture at that, if you don't mind my saying so."

Alix took a sip of her coffee, the first in a while, but it was stale and cold, and she grimaced. "You're probably right. You know, last night shook me up pretty good. Maybe it made me a little strange."

"You're not going to go to the police with this, are you? They'd probably put you away."

"No, I won't go to the police. Come on, I'll drive you to the Palms. You can check to see that they've really brought your bags up to your room and then we can just kick back and talk for a while around the pool before we head for Prentice's."

"Sounds good to me. I need you to tell me more about portrait miniatures."

"You mean in order to better plan your orderly, comprehensive hodgepodge?"

"Bingo."

. . .

When Alix had told Chris that she'd pretty much exhausted her fund of knowledge on miniatures, she'd been telling the truth, so she didn't have much more to say on that subject, but she promised to look into it and, at the very least, to provide Chris with some good reference material. That, plus getting Chris settled in her room, took them almost to five o'clock. Alix asked if that would allow time for her to show Chris a little of Palm Springs on their way to the Vanderveres'. "The heart of downtown, anyway," was the way she'd put it.

"That won't take us long," Alix said as she started up her rented Dodge compact. The heart of downtown Palm Springs, she explained, and then demonstrated, lived up to its vibrant, glittery reputation: lots of foot and vehicular traffic, plenty of good restaurants—mostly jammed—and a surfeit of trendy, busy shops. But the whole thing was only four blocks long: the half-mile of Palm Canyon Drive that ran north and south from Tahquitz Canyon Way. And the heart was all there was. No limbs, no ribs, no head. Go two blocks above Tahquitz to Amado Road, or two blocks south to Baristo, or leave Palm Canyon Drive in any direction, and you run out of downtown in a hurry.

Except for the occasional restaurant, or hotel, or shopping center, Alix had learned during the last few days, the rest of this city of nearly fifty thousand consisted of thirty-two precisely and officially defined residential neighborhoods, a few of which were supremely elegant and luxurious (Vistas Las Palmas, where they'd been a few hours earlier, was an example), but most of which were not supremely elegant and luxurious. As with any city.

"And which one do the Vanderveres live in?" Chris asked.

"I don't know. I've never been there. I'm trusting the GPS to get us there. It doesn't look too far, but we'd better head over now. I've saved the epicenter, the very *heart* of the heart of downtown, to show you on the way back."

13

As expected, the Vanderveres lived in a very nice neighborhood, on a quiet cul-de-sac. When Alix pulled into the driveway alongside an aging but beautifully maintained Lexus, she was struck by what a long way this house was—geographically, culturally, and historically—from where the Vanderveres had lived just off the Harvard campus in the old days. There, their house dated from the 1760s and looked it: a small, clunky, wood-shingled saltbox right around the corner from the Longfellow House. The poet's home, now a National Parks historic site, had served as General Washington's headquarters during the siege of Boston, and one of Washington's colonels had been billeted for several weeks in what would become the Vanderveres' home a couple of centuries later.

Here, their house, low-slung and sleek, with white stucco walls and a pebbled roof, had probably been built in the 1950s, when Western ranch style had been the rage. Alix couldn't say it was one of her favorite architectural fashions, but she had to admit that the stark design aesthetic went well with the desert ambience. Still, it was strange to think of Prentice and Margery, so elegant and cultivated and old-fashioned—so *Eastern*—living here.

Alix and Chris were met at the door by a slim, middle-aged Hispanic woman in a white uniform dress. "Professor and Mrs. Vandervere are waiting for you on the patio, if you will follow me."

They were taken through a living room and dining room sparely furnished with Scandinavian-designed chairs and tables, clean-lined and modern, and mostly made of sand-colored teak. The Vandeveres must have left their heavy, dark, old furniture behind when they'd come out here to all this sun and open sky, Alix thought, and all things considered, it had probably been the right decision.

"You know, that's what I need," Chris whispered as they trailed the woman. "A maid. And maybe a butler too."

"What, no footman?" Alix whispered back. "No groundskeeper?"

Prentice and Margery Vandervere were sitting in the shade of the awninged patio with tall highball glasses on the table in front of them, and a smiling Prentice stood up to greet their guests when they were ushered outside. But Margery didn't get up. Time had been harder on her than on Prentice. She was in a wheelchair now, drawn and pinched, and with a lightweight summer blanket over her legs. She had dyed her hair a jet black that Alix thought unfortunate. And whereas Prentice had kept the pink-cheeked, smooth complexion that so many of the rich and wellborn seemed to retain into their later years, Margery's face was age-mottled and wrinkled. To see her this way came as a sad surprise. Back in the Harvard days, Mrs. Vandervere, unashamedly gray-haired then, had been a fixture at the afternoon teas; active, lively, and funny.

But that had been ten years ago, after all, and she had probably been seventy then. *Tempus fugit.* Even at thirty, Alix had learned that the older you get, the faster it *fugit*s.

"Hello, Mrs. Vandervere," Alix said, extending her hand. "It's wonderful to see you again."

Her manner must have given away what she was thinking, because Margery barked a short laugh. "Alix, please, despite appearances, I am not in extremis or even permanently wheelchair-bound.

The reason you see me thus"—a graceful flutter of both hands took in the wheelchair—"is that my knees began refusing to follow orders despite my many threats and admonitions, and so I finally turned them in for a new pair. The operation was only last week, you see, and I haven't yet gotten used to them. Nor they to me."

"I hope we aren't putting you to any trouble," Chris said.

"No, no, none at all. I don't really do anything even when all body parts are more or less operational. Prentice only keeps me around for ornamental purposes."

So the old Margery was still in there, Alix was glad to see. And if she'd had both knees replaced a few days ago, then she had every right to look a bit drawn.

"Lena, God preserve her from harm, takes care of everything," Margery said. She made a brief finger wave in the direction of the house and two seconds later Lena came hustling out.

"Now, what would you like to drink?" Margery asked them. "Prentice is having a Manhattan and I'm drinking a Tom Collins. Lena does them both very well."

Alix couldn't help smiling. They might have left their 1950s furniture back on the East Coast, but not their drink habits.

"Just a glass of red wine for me," Chris said to Lena.

Alix asked for a Tom Collins, partly because she'd never had one, but primarily because it looked so good, thirst-quenching and crystal-clear in the ice-frosted glass at Margery's elbow.

When the drinks came they chitchatted for a while, mostly about Alix's career and Chris's collecting. Prentice in particular was interested in Chris's predilections within the American Modern ranks and showed obvious approval for her disinterest in the Abstract Expressionists among them. Chris spoke excitedly about the collection she was building with Alix's help, and Prentice offered his own ideas on what made a sensible private art collection. Chris chose not to mention the miniatures she had tried to buy just that afternoon—a wise choice, in Alix's opinion.

The Vanderveres were the same good hosts they'd been a decade ago, showing more interest in their guests than in talking about themselves, but eventually the conversation broadened and Alix found an opening for a question she'd been waiting to ask. "Prentice, you seemed really disappointed not to have had the chance to talk to my father. I can't help wondering why."

"Why would I not want to? A fascinating man, a man of principle. I have a great deal of admiration for him. Always have."

Now there was a stunner. Of all the people in the world to be the first one in ten years—certainly the first establishment type—to express admiration for Geoffrey London, Prentice Vandervere would have been her last pick. Prentice himself was her model of probity and integrity, but as for Geoff, while there was much to admire (and love) about him, he was, to put it charitably, a little flexible when it came to matters of ethics.

"You look surprised," Prentice said, laughing, "but what I said is true. I followed his trial with great interest, you see. It was extraordinary . . . unique, really. That a respected authority on conservation, a Metropolitan Museum conservator, should be accused defrauding his private clients out of millions was unbelievable."

"But true," Alix pointed out. "He did make exacting copies of those paintings, sixteen of them, and he did give the owners back the copies rather than the originals, and then he did sell the originals to other buyers for millions of dollars." None of which was left after court costs and suit settlements, she might have added. "And he went to jail for eight years, and even he very readily admits it was justified. Legally."

"Yes, legally. Exactly. That was the aspect of his many reported comments that intrigued me: that legally he might be guilty of violations of the criminal code, but ethically, morally, his actions were actually commendable. It's a topic I'd have liked to explore with him."

It was also a topic that Alix had often explored—that is, argued about—with her father, and over time Geoff had brought her a lot nearer to his point of view. It was his contention—and the facts supported him in this—that the sixteen original owners he defrauded had all come to him to restore their beautiful seventeenth-, eighteenth-, and nineteenth-century paintings in preparation for selling them in order to be able to buy late twentieth-century works (*monstrosities* was Geoff's word for them) that in the current bizarre market were worth more in money and prestige than the works of the Old Masters themselves. It was Geoff's position that he had "rescued" these paintings from Philistines who didn't know the difference between art and junk, and put them into the loving hands of culturally literate people who understood and appreciated their artistic value. And the fact that his switcheroo had also happened to put those millions of dollars in his pocket? Irrelevant. Beside the point.

Maybe so, but it was what had sent him to jail; that, too, was a mere technicality. In his view he stood unconvicted of any ethical misdeeds. What he had done was illegal, yes, but he had done nothing *wrong*. It was what he'd maintained at his trial and it was what he maintained today.

"You see," Prentice said, "I feel much the same sense of moral outrage when I see a museum like the Brethwaite demean itself by selling off—'deacessioning,' if you prefer the gentler euphemism—its most glorious possessions so that it can buy the works of momentarily fashionable artists in their place. It's pathetic, really. Artistic merit—beauty—doesn't enter into the decision at all."

"I don't understand," Alix said. "I thought that the paintings that were being auctioned off were for general museum upkeep, not to buy anything new for the collection."

"That's so, but the reason they are being auctioned off, or banished to the basement, is that they don't bring in 'eyeballs.' They're not popular, you see, or entertaining. They don't 'grab' the average person, don't interest the youth. But when did it become the purpose of the museum of art to entertain the 'average' person, whoever that might be? When did it—"

"Prentice, dear, you're getting a little exercised," Margery said. "Try the bacon-wrapped shrimp. She cooked them with rosemary this time and it's made all the difference in the world. They're wonderful."

This was in reference to the varied plates of hot hors d'oeuvres that Lena had brought out on a rolling cart a few minutes earlier. Chris and Margery had eaten a few and made appreciative noises as they did, but Alix and Prentice had been too engaged in conversation to try them.

In response to Margery, Prentice dialed down his fervor a little, but kept on talking. "In any case, the auction isn't really what I was referring too, it's just the latest indication of the museum's direction, one more straw. It's the Pollock that I was thinking of."

"The Pollock?" Alix's interest spiked. She remembered him expressing "concern" about the painting when they'd been standing in front of it talking to Jerry and Clark the other morning. "Do you think there's something wrong with it too?"

"Wrong with it?" Prentice repeated, frowning. "You mean other than its being a Pollock?"

Alix smiled. She was thinking that the fact that she didn't care for abstract art and contemporary art in general—more than once she'd been called a snob about it—was hardly surprising, given that her most influential mentors had been Prentice and Geoff.

"I wouldn't know if there was anything 'wrong' with it or not," Prentice went on. "No, I was referring to the deaccessioning that we went through in order to purchase it."

"I didn't know you did."

"Oh, yes. It cost the museum *sixteen million dollars*, can you imagine?" He winced at the thought. "The most expensive object we ever purchased. We had to sell—"

"Deaccession," Margery said with a twinkle in her eye. "Let us not be commonplace, Prentice."

That made Alix think of something she'd heard Geoff say: "Have you ever noticed that the art museum is the only business in which one 'buys' things, but never 'sells' them? It merely 'deaccessions' them. So much more civilized."

"—*sell*," Prentice continued, "nine of our finest paintings, arguably our very finest, to afford it. Nine paintings that had come from Morgan Brethwaite's personal collection." His face grew longer as he remembered. "There was a wonderful, luminous Bierstadt of a clearing storm in the Rockies; a Degas horse race, not his best, but charming all the same; a magnificent storm at sea by Turner, no more than twelve by fourteen inches, but filled with stupendous power; a Vuillard; a somewhat slapdash but affecting Gainsborough family group; a Constable; a—"

"Dear, I would say you've made your point," Margery said sweetly.

"Wow," said Alix. "Mrs. B must have wanted the Pollock an awful lot to give those up."

"Well, you know Clark by now." He shook his head. "He can be immensely persuasive when he wants to be, at least"—and the corners of his mouth turned down—"to those susceptible to his famous charms."

As far as she remembered, it was the first time she'd heard him speak disparagingly, let alone sarcastically, of anyone (with the sole exception of the Abstract Expressionists and their anarchic, anything-goes descendants). Obviously, Clark had gotten to him in a way that few others ever had.

"But you do have to admit, my dear," Margery said to Prentice, "that his judgment has proven sound in the end. Since the installation of the Pollock, attendance has increased something like thirty percent, has it not?"

"I do have to admit that attendance numbers have increased, yes, but I don't admit that Clark's judgment was sound. We sacrificed quality for quantity. We surrendered enrichment and refinement for entertainment and celebrity. Are we to think of ourselves as being in competition with sports events and rock concerts, then? If so, to what end?"

At this point Chris got into it. "But isn't an increase in museum attendance a good thing, Prentice? Don't you want more people to come in and see the museum, the rest of the art? And to see the Pollock, for that matter, and make their own judgments about it?"

"I'm not so sure, Chris. From a financial perspective I suppose so, but is high attendance a worthwhile goal in itself? Can you really have a meaningful engagement with a work of art when you're standing in a gallery filled with garrulous people elbowing their way in front of you to get a better look—a thirty-second look—at whatever it is that you're trying to *see*?"

"Well, then what about this? You know, to a lot of people an art museum is a mysterious, off-putting place they have no interest in going to. Don't popular works bring them in and help demystify the experience?"

"You've just succinctly expressed the prevalent point of view in today's museum world, Chris, and as a result of it we have sorry efforts like a Punk Music and Contemporary Art exhibition at the Met—the Met!—and ladies' underwear at the Paris Decorative Arts Museum, and . . ." He sighed his disgust. "These things are designed to entice *whom*, exactly? No, I see it very differently. I don't want the art museum demystified. Our 'product,' if you choose to call it that, as Clark indeed does, *is* the mystery, the wonder of art. That is what the art museum, and the art museum alone, has to offer, our singular distinction. Alix, would you agree with that?"

"Prentice," Margery said firmly, "are you planning to stop badgering these poor young women long enough to let them have something to eat?" She turned to them. "He thinks he's still at the lectern, you see. It's all very sad. Now, just you try these potato croquettes and see if you can tell me what they're stuffed with."

. . .

"That was really nice," Chris said as they drove back uptown, "but I'm ready for some plain, *un*fancy, solid American food for dinner."

"Me too. How about a pizza?"

"Perfect, can't get any more American than that."

"I know a good place, and on the way we can drive right through the intersection I was talking about before. In fact, we're about to now."

"The epicenter, the heart of the heart of downtown?"

"The very place."

"Is that it up ahead, where those tour busses are lined up along the curb?"

"That's it."

A few seconds later Chris burst out laughing. "The *heart* of Palm Springs?" Chris shouted with more laughter. "I would say they're a little off in their anatomy."

133

Alix laughed along with her. They were on Tahquitz, approaching Palm Canyon and coming up behind an enormous, billowing skirt that revealed a curvy, four-foot-wide, panties-clad rear end. This was Palm Springs's number-one tourist draw of the moment, the brilliantly colored "Forever Marilyn" statue, nearly thirty feet tall, in her most iconic pose, from *The Seven Year Itch*, where she stands caught in the updraft from a New York City subway grate, futilely trying (but not very hard) to hold down her ballooning skirt.

"It's only on loan to Palm Springs," Alix told her. "They're trying to buy it, though. I heard they offered one point two million, and they're waiting to hear."

"It's beautiful, in a strange way," Chris said, looking up at Marilyn's laughing face as they passed. "She looks so happy. Makes you smile, doesn't it? Look at all those people, they're all smiling." She twisted to look back as they passed it and crossed Palm Canyon. "So it's for sale," she said thoughtfully as she straightened. "One point two million, was that what you said?"

Alix fixed her with a stern glance. "No, you can *not* have it. As your trusted and respected counselor and guide, I forbid it. I'm letting you get away with the portrait miniatures, but there's such a thing as going too far."

"Well, I think it's a wonderful idea, and I intend to talk you into it."

Alix responded with a phrase she'd learned from the many times she'd heard Tiny mutter it: "*Quando voleranno gli asini.*" When donkeys fly.

14

Two miles north and west of Giuseppe's Pizza and Pasta, where Chris and Alix were starting on their final slices of linguica and mushroom pizza, Mickey Buckner was sitting behind the wheel of his snazzy new Mazda MX-5 Miata, relieved to be only a block from home. He shouldn't have been driving at all and he knew it, not after consuming the better part of two sixty-ounce pitchers of beer at the Village Pub. He already had one DUI conviction on his record, and that had been a miserable enough experience. God knew what would happen if he got a second, and he had no interest in finding out. But he hadn't liked inconveniencing one of his less intemperate friends for a lift, or having to come back and retrieve his car in the morning (and where would he leave it, anyway?), and it all seemed like too much to deal with. So here he was.

He was being extremely careful, and not only because of that DUI, but because the shiny red automobile was only a few weeks old, and he had every intention of keeping it dingless for years to come. And so the route he'd chosen was mostly along quiet streets. He drove slowly and cautiously, coming to a complete, standing stop at every intersection that had a stop sign, and a rolling stop at the ones that didn't (first prudently checking behind him).

Which was why he was now paused at this particular intersection, the signless junction of Santa Rosa Drive and South Patencio Road, peering up and down Patencio to make sure it was safe to cross this last barrier between him and home, only a block away. To his right, nothing to be concerned about. About thirty feet up Patencio, a man that he had seen crossing Santa Rosa as he drove up to the corner was continuing his unhurried stroll northward, away from him, head down and hands in his pockets. As most people did in these quiet old residential neighborhoods, he was walking in the roadway itself; the sidewalks, where they existed at all, were too troublesome to bother with, being broken up every few yards by lawns and walls.

The other way, to Mickey's left, fifty feet or so down Patencio, a green compact was very slowly approaching—a 2012 Ford Focus. (Mickey owned a garage. He knew cars.) It was well into twilight, but the Ford didn't have its lights on, which made Mickey realize that he didn't either.

He reached to turn them on, but before his hand got there, he was startled by the sudden gunning of the Ford's engine. At the same time its brights flicked on and a second later it came screaming across the intersection five feet in front of his hood. The walking man only had time to begin to turn around before the car plowed into him with an appalling *whunk!* and mowed him down. Or rather, mowed him *up.* He went flying straight up in the air—ten feet, it seemed to a stunned Mickey—with his arms windmilling, came down on the Ford's windshield and roof, bounced over the passenger side, and apparently got hooked on something so that he was dragged down the roadway for ten or fifteen yards, arms, legs—and head—flopping. The Ford, still at high speed, jigged sharply left, then right, to throw him free, and he was flung off to slam into the white-painted stone wall that fronted a house at the next corner. There his limp body collapsed forward into a flattened human heap like nothing Mickey had ever seen before.

The man was bent completely double, as if he'd been trying to touch his toes and had overdone it. His fingers extended well beyond his toes and his face rested against the ground between his knees. Nobody but a contortionist could take a position like that, and Mickey didn't think he was a contortionist. For a normal person's body to pancake that way, his back had to be broken, his spine snapped, muscles and ligaments severed. And his head, his head was all . . .

Mickey barely got his own head out the window before half a gallon of beer came pouring out of him, mixed with what was left of a large order of fish and chips. Then he just sat there, shaking. He had just been witness, probably the only witness, to an assassination; what else could it be? The speeding Ford had never slowed (other than to shake loose its victim), let alone stopped, but had roared off, to swing right at the following corner with tires squealing, and rear end fishtailing.

But what was he supposed to do? Call 9-1-1, right? He knew in his heart that was the right thing, and he was a good citizen, he really was, but in his current condition he'd be crazy to talk to anyone who could and would report it to the police. Call anonymously and hang up before any questions could be asked? But could they trace the cell phone to him? He didn't know. A public telephone was out of the question because who knew where they were anymore? Maybe call in the morning? But then they'd want to know why he'd waited. Surely, it was his duty to call them. He could identify the make and even the year of the car. Most important, he could tell them that it had been no accident, no unfortunate split second of driver inattention. Still . . .

While he dithered, two men came running toward the broken body from around the far corner. He knew them, not by name but by sight, and he sprang into action before they had a chance to see him there. He put the car into reverse and barreled rapidly and expertly backward—he'd had plenty of experience at it at work—turned right at the next corner, and headed back to downtown. He needed to do some quiet thinking, to figure out what he should do. And he needed a drink, just a short one to calm himself down. He headed toward a quiet, dark bar he knew just off South Indian Canyon Drive, where the bartender left you alone unless you wanted to be talked to. He parked on the street and walked in, surprised to find himself more unsteady on his feet than he'd been at the wheel. The only people at the counter were a gay couple at one end, and they were too engaged with each other to notice him. All the same he chose the stool at the other end of the bar.

"Give me a Coors Light, Charley," he said. "No, wait, make that a Scotch on the rocks, double." Why not? The beer had all come up, hadn't it? The alcohol had been flushed out of his system. He needed to settle down, to get things straight in his head. A Scotch, slowly sipped, would help him with that. Still, moderation was required. "On second thought, put in a splash of water, Charley."

Half an hour later he'd decided what to do, and it hadn't been all that hard, not once he'd relaxed a little and taken the time to think things through. Really, there wasn't even anything to argue about with himself. What was there for him to go to the police about? He'd seen enough TV shows to know they'd figure out what had happened from the tire tracks, and the position of the body and other forensic stuff: the fact that the Ford had jumped into high speed from a standing start, had hit the poor bastard mostly from behind, had jigged left and right to shake him loose, and then sped on. And they'd know which way it had headed from more tire marks at the corner of Baristo.

He'd be able to tell them that it was a green 2012 Ford Focus, of course, which was important, only *was* it a green 2012 Ford Focus? Was he ready to swear to that? It had been dusk and he'd glimpsed it for no more than three or four confused seconds. Mightn't it have been something similar, a Fiesta, or a Chevy Cruze, or even a Toyota FT-CH? Could he even say with certainty that it was green and not blue or black? What if he gave them information that turned out to be wrong and some innocent person was arrested?

He couldn't give them the license plate number, not a single digit or letter of it, and he had no idea of what the driver looked like, or whether it was a man or woman—it could have been a chimpanzee for all he knew—or how many people were in the car. He'd just plain never noticed. It had been too sudden, too fast, too dark. So, all things considered, what could he tell them that would actually be helpful? Not a damn thing. So what was the point of going to them at all? There wasn't any.

Jesus Christ, what a load off his back.

"Charley," he said, "I'll go ahead and have that Coors Light now, I think. So tell me, whaddaya think, are the Chargers gonna do any better next year or not?"

15

By the time Alix got back to the Villa Louisa it was dark. The evening's outdoor movies were getting under way on the back lawn. With a dozen other like-minded people, she got a cup of decaf coffee from the nearby urn that had been set up, settled into one of the lounge chairs, and watched a loopy old Marx Brothers short, followed by an equally dopey 1930s Barbara Stanwyck seaboard comedy, and thoroughly enjoyed both of them. At the close, when a clerk came out to shut the projector down, he was nice enough to ask if she'd be more comfortable if he went with her when she opened the door to her bungalow.

Although she hadn't been thinking about it until he brought it up, she took him up on the offer, and then, as an afterthought, asked him to change the code on her lock and make another new key card for her.

He approved. "Better safe then sorry."

With those words in mind, she double-checked the windows and doors to make sure they were locked, and pulled the blinds. Once into her pajamas, she browsed in a rickety old bookcase along the wall, found a dog-eared Agatha Christie that looked as if it might have been left by Miss Crawford herself, and took it to bed with her, hoping it would ease her into sleep. It did; when she surfaced in the middle of a pleasant dream some nine hours later, awakened by her own laughter, the book still lay open on her chest, turned to page two. Feeling rested and relaxed, she tried to remember what the dream had been about. It had involved Prentice Vandervere and Harpo Marx. They had been going through some kind of lunatic routine with Harpo booping away on his horn to distract Prentice, who was trying to deliver a learned lecture from—

A sudden recollection sat her up, blinking. Not of anything from the dream, but of something Prentice had mentioned over cocktails the previous evening. It had been while they were talking about the Pollock. Alix had observed how much Mrs. B must have wanted the Pollock to have given up nine prize paintings from her father's personal collection to pay for it. Prentice's biting reply had been along the lines of: "Well, you know Clark. He can be very persuasive when he wants to be."

At the time it hadn't registered. Only now did she realize what it meant. When she and Clark had been discussing the Pollock the other morning, Clark had led her into thinking the painting was a favorite of Mrs. B's. *Her pride and joy*, he'd called it, which, according to what Prentice had said, had to be an outright lie. More than that, Clark had mentioned nothing about his own part in bringing it to the Brethwaite, nothing to suggest that the picture was in reality a recent acquisition (which it must have been, since Clark had been there barely four months). Without ever saying so explicitly, he'd managed to leave her with the impression that the Pollock had been in the museum's possession a long time.

Her mind was racing now. A lot of things had suddenly clicked into place. Or if that was overstating it, then at least she now had some plausible explanations for last night's attack and for Clark's behavior. Or if even that was overstating it, then at least she had some possible rationales for them. What if the painting *was* a forgery? What would happen to his job and his reputation if that were to come out, considering the assets the museum had given up to acquire it? Couldn't that be why he asked Alix to postpone telling Mrs. B about her suspicions?

Well, yes, but would he really try to kill her over it? It was hard to believe, but suppose she took the speculations a little further: What if he *knew* it was a forgery and had known it all along? What if he'd somehow engineered the sale to the Brethwaite, knowing it? Why would he have done that if it didn't benefit him in some way? It would hardly be something new in the art market: A person who orchestrates a sale and for his efforts is paid a "finder's fee," or a "referral fee" (or in plainer language, a kickback). If the sale is important, as the Pollock sale was, such a fee can run into six figures; excellent news for Clark.

Except, of course, that having any knowing part in selling a forgery was as illegal as hell, and if it were to come out that it *was* a fake, he would be facing criminal trial, civil suits, and serious jail time. Now *there,* she thought with a long exhalation—she'd been holding her breath without knowing it—was the rationale for murder that she'd been looking for, and a plausible one at that.

Plausible enough to call Detective Cruz? Maybe not. Did she really believe it herself? She wasn't even sure about that. The only solid, physical fact that she could produce to Cruz or to herself was Clark's puffy, red nose, and she knew Chris was right about that. As evidence went, it was ludicrous. It could just as easily mean he was Santa Claus. Still, she owed it to herself to go to the detective with it. For all she knew, Clark would come after her again. After all, from his point of view, nothing had changed. If there was a reason to go after her the other night, it was still there. And if what she was hypothesizing was right, he had to do it soon, before the time they had set for Alix to go to Mrs. B if she still had doubts about the painting. And that would be Tuesday, three days from now.

Yes, call Cruz. Definitely.

She found the card he'd left with her, dialed his number, got his voice mail, and left a message saying she had some ideas about who it was that might have attacked her. She wasn't any more specific than that because somehow she felt sillier and more paranoid naming Clark over the telephone than she would in talking to Cruz face-to-face. She would be at the museum most of the day if he wanted to talk to her there, she said, or she'd be happy to come to the police station if he preferred that.

· · ·

The detective's car pulled into the Brethwaite's parking lot an hour later, just as Alix was getting out of hers. "Okay if we talk outside?" she said. "More private."

"On a day like this? What could be better? Lead on." He seemed to be in the same mellow mood he'd been in the other night, but he looked a lot fresher, with a crisp, blue-checked sport shirt, a newly shaven jaw, and the breezy smell of aftershave still clinging to him.

She took him around to the north terrace, the one that looked out over the wind turbines and the desert, and asked if he'd like some coffee. When he said yes, she went inside to get it from the break room, and on the way back she stopped at the workroom, where the paintings were being prepared for transfer to the auction house. Alfie Wellington and Drew Temple were at one long table, assembling the backs of two of the braced, made-to-measure crates. Each segment had numbers and letters on it to show which piece attached to which, and where. Jerry was at a smaller trestle table next to them, where he had one of the paintings lying face up and was applying a protective "X" of masking tape to the glass pane that fronted it. This was the first step in the final packing process. After that it would be wrapped in newsprint. Then would come bubble wrap, and then the insertion into the partly assembled crate, probably with a few handfuls of foam peanuts thrown in to fill up any empty spaces. Finally, the front of the crate would be screwed on by hand, through the screw holes that had been drilled in advance.

"When do they ship?" she asked Jerry.

"Some today, the rest Monday. That is, if these two clowns can get their act together and manage to do more than one crate an hour."

"If you're unhappy with our work," Drew said, "just say so. It was my impression we were doing you a favor."

"Touchy, touchy," Jerry sang.

"What Jerry fails to allow for," Alfie said to Alix, "is that we're mere volunteers, untrained in the subtleties of this intricate task."

"Yeah," Jerry said, "you have to know not only the whole alphabet, but the numbers too, all the way up to twelve."

Alix saw now that the object he was working on wasn't a painting, but the panel with the twelve miniatures. She leaned over to look at it more closely, then tipped it toward her to eliminate the glare on the glass crystals. She found elements in the portraits she hadn't seen before; not just the wonderfully executed details—the silky, elegantly knotted white cravat on the boy, the little girl's upswept, extravagant head of curls—but the overall texture, the surface quality of the paintings. They shone with a golden glow, almost as if they were backlit.

"Jerry," she said pensively, "these two Dunkerleys—how sure are you they're really—"

"Stop!" Jerry cried. "Alix, please, for God's sake, have mercy; don't tell me, not at this point, that these are fake *Dunkerleys*!"

Alix laughed. "No, but you know, I wouldn't mind getting a magnifying glass from my workroom—"

"Absolutely not!" he cried theatrically, snatching up the panel and clasping it to his breast. "Won't someone here *please* control this woman?"

"Seriously," Alix said, "my friend will probably take your advice and bid on it at the auction, and I'm helping her, so I'm doing some research. You said the other day there was a pretty solid provenance on these two. It'd be helpful to have a look at that. Any problem with that?"

"Nope. They've already been sent to Endicott, but I'll be there next week, and I'll e-mail you copies. Remind me if you don't hear from me by, oh, say, a week from Monday."

"Will do. Thanks, Jerry."

"Or you can stop by San Francisco if you want to see the originals." He held the panel up not far from his face. "I'll tell you, I like these things a lot myself—all of them, not just the Dunkerleys—just beautiful. I wouldn't mind placing a bid on this thing myself."

"What? What?" Alfie called, looking up from his screwdriver. "Set the valuation of an object and then bid on it yourself? I believe that's frowned upon in the business. Although now that I think about it, I must say—"

"Moot point," said Jerry, "since I couldn't afford it anyway."

"Well, that's your own fault, dummy. You're the valuator, aren't you? You should have set the value at something you *could* afford."

"Damn, why didn't I think of that? I wonder if it's too late to re-set it to something I could manage."

"I doubt if twelve ninety-five is quite what Clark has in mind," Drew said, straight-faced.

"Enough screwing around, gentlemen," Alfie said after another slug from his trusty mug. "Drew, you and I better get on with the job.

Putting crates together might turn out to be a useful skill for a couple of ex-curators."

"We are not amused," said Drew, his nose longer than ever.

. . .

Detective Cruz accepted his coffee with thanks, and they both sat on one of the benches, this one with a cheery little bronze plaque on it that said, "In loving memory of our dear husband and father, Max L. Borowski. We shall miss you greatly."

"Don't you love these little signs?" Cruz said. "Sure lighten the mood." He took a mug from her and held it in both hands, elbows on his knees. "So. What do you have to tell me?"

She told him, not leaving out even the most tenuous elements of her reasoning. It was made more awkward than it might have been because he was utterly silent, as he'd been the other night when Officer Campbell was interviewing her, so she was doing lots of explicating and rationalizing. Throughout, his fleshy face wore an intent expression that she couldn't place. Skepticism, she would have expected, but this was something else. Wariness? Outright disbelief?

The more she talked, the more inscrutable his look got. Was he trying his best not to *laugh*? "Look," she said with some frustration, "I know as well as you do that this all sounds crazy, and I wouldn't be coming to you with it if I wasn't concerned that he might try it again. Or try something else. I would have thought it was your job—"

"Whoa, hold your horses. Let me set your mind at ease on that point. I can tell you with complete assurance that Mr. Calder will *not* be coming after you again."

"I don't understand. Have you arrested him?"

"Alix, he's dead."

"*What?*" The news was so out of the blue that this came out more squawk than speech. "*Clark? He's dead?* But I was talking to him just yesterday afternoon . . . I know," she said in response to the detective's wisp of a smile, "that's what everybody says. It's just—"

"Just that someone who's going to die any time soon ought to have the decency to look it, and in most kinds of death they do. But not this kind."

She caught her lower lip on her teeth and expelled a breath, stalling for time to collect herself. "How did he die?" she asked in a whisper.

"Hit by a car a few blocks from where he lived."

"An accident?" But something about Cruz's manner told her otherwise.

"Hit-and-run," he said. He paused, as if considering whether or not to say more, then went ahead. "And not an accident."

"Are you telling me he was murdered?"

"That's what the forensics point to. Of course, there's still an autopsy to be done, and lab work, but I can't see how they're going to change that."

"My God."

"Listen, Alix—what you were telling me about the Pollock . . . is it possible that that could have something to do with this?"

"With someone murdering *him*? No, I don't see any connection there. Most of what I told you wasn't much more than wild surmise anyway, so no . . . but . . ."

His eyebrows went up. "But?"

"Well," she said, "he wasn't very much liked, at least not around here. You probably know that already."

"We know practically nothing about him, we've just started. What can you tell me? Why wasn't he liked?"

"Well, basically, he's pretty new here and he's really been shaking up the organization. For one thing, his new plan is going to mean that some of the curators' jobs are going to be cut. And some of them are even—"

She hesitated, chewing her lip, and the experienced Cruz adroitly read her mind. "I know. You don't like the idea of being an informer, you don't want to get anyone in trouble, you're not accusing anyone, and so on. I'd feel the same way. But think of it like this: Anything you can tell us, we're going to find out anyway, but the quicker we learn it, the sooner we can start excluding people as suspects, and the better our chances of quickly narrowing in on whoever did do it."

More lip chewing. "Look, detective—"

"Call me Jake, will you? It's only fair; I've been calling you Alix."

"Thank you. But look, I haven't even been here a week. I barely know these people's names. I've hardly brushed the surface. How about this: You talk to the people directly involved, the curatorial staff—well, and Mrs. Brethwaite, the director—and then if you still have questions that you think I can help with, I'll do my best."

She didn't expect him to accept that, but he did. "All right," he said comfortably. He reminded her of a big cat now, lapping up his coffee and clearly luxuriating in the combination of sun and crisp morning air.

"Oh, let me ask you one other question now," he said, as if it had just occurred to him. "Where would you have been last night at six thirty, seven?"

Alix had once been addicted to *Law and Order*, and she remembered wondering how it felt to be asked that question: *Where were you last night?* Now she knew. Not good.

"I would have been having dinner with my friend. Chris LeMay. At Giuseppe's Pizza and Pasta, on East Palm Canyon."

"Would anybody be able to verify that? Other than her?"

"Well, I'm not . . . oh, that's right, Chris was kidding around with the guy behind the counter. I know he'd remember *her*."

"That's good. You understand, I had to ask that question. Well . . . other than that, is there anything else you can think of that might lead somewhere?"

She began to shake her head. "No . . . Oh, wait a minute, maybe I do have something. Chris and I went to see him yesterday morning—she wanted to buy some drawings before they went to auction—and we overheard him on the phone having an argument with someone. He was getting pretty upset."

He lifted a hand. "You know, I think it might be better if we talked down at the station at this point. You amenable to that?"

"Sure. When?"

"No time like the present."

"Let's go. I'll follow you."

Instead, Cruz offered to drive her to police headquarters and then back to the museum, and she accepted. For the first few minutes of the drive they were both quiet, cogitating and reflecting, and then Alix said, more to break the silence than anything else: "How many detectives does the department have?"

"Four, why?"

"Well, I was starting to think maybe you were the only one. You're the only one I've seen."

"No, there are four of us, and we all have plenty to do. I've been the lead on the Phantom Burglar for months, which is why I showed up at your bungalow the other night, and as for Clark, the All-Knowing Skull, applying a subtle and complex algorithm, selected me for this one too. I'm partnering with a guy named Pat Malloy, but he's out in the field this morning, so it'll just be me today."

She was frowning. "The all-knowing—?"

"We're here," he said before she could finish.

. . .

They parked at a curb lined with departmental black-and-whites—
three patrol cars and three motorcycles (and two Segways)—and to
get to the long, low headquarters building they had to cross a small
plaza that was centered by a bronze memorial statue. Beside a semi-
abstract open car door, two life-sized, realistically sculpted officers
were on the ground: one, obviously grievously wounded, on his back,
the other kneeling at his side, tending him, with his cell phone to his
face. "Help is on the way" read the identifying plaque, and Alix
thought it was stirring and particularly well done.

"That's beautiful," she said, stopping in front of it. "It's extremely
moving."

She caught a narrow, darting look from Cruz, which didn't surprise her. Almost every layperson seemed to assume that any *real* art
expert would ex post facto look down her nose at sentimental, old-
fashioned representational art. But when he saw that she meant it, he
thawed. "It is, isn't it? Gets me every time I walk by it."

"Is it based on a real incident?"

"No, it's a memorial to two of our officers killed in the line of
duty at different times. But trust me, there have been plenty of real
incidents just like this."

"I don't doubt it. Anyway, it's beautiful."

"Certainly is." If she hadn't been certain that Cruz liked her
before, she was now.

Once through the entrance lobby, he led her into a corridor lined
with office cubicles, each of which held a compact, cluttered desk, a
couple of rolling chairs, a corkboard bulletin board with the usual

jumble of memos, photos, cartoons, and paper scraps pinned to it, and a metal filing cabinet, all in a space that was no more than eight by eight. She hoped—but doubted—that Cruz had something larger in which to work because he would have had a hard time squeezing himself into one of these.

"You were about to ask about that skull thing before? That's him right there, the All-Knowing Skull."

He was pointing at a plastic Halloween fright skull, the kind that has eyeballs dangling out of their sockets on springs. Someone had mounted a pair of nerdy, Clark Kent-ish spectacles on this one, which sat atop one of the partitions separating the cubicles, its popped and bouncy eyeballs looking down into one of them. "The way it works is this. It's moved once a week to face a different cubicle. And when a new case comes up, whoever's cubicle it's looking into at the time, he's the assigned—the lead investigator. It happened to be gazing into mine when the first Phantom burglary occurred, and into mine again when Calder got himself killed."

Alix looked sideways at him. "I know you're kidding."

"I am not kidding. What's more, I think it's a great system. It's fair, it's impartial, and it's understandable."

She shook her head, laughing. "I suppose so, but I have to say, you people certainly have your own way of doing things."

"I prefer to think of us as trendsetters. Come on, I want to hear more about this argument you heard." He took her to an interview room, as utilitarian a space as could be imagined: a small plastic-topped table, three chairs, and a wastepaper basket. The matte white walls were blank except for a rectangle about the size of a light switch plate mounted at eye level on one of them. In its center was what appeared to be a lens.

"A camera?" Alix asked. "Are we video-recording this?"

Cruz nodded. "Any objection?"

"None, record away."

Cruz tested the recording system, then stated the date, time, place, and participants. "Okay, Alix, suppose you just tell us what you started to tell me at the museum."

Alix took a moment to order her thoughts. "Yesterday morning my friend Chris LeMay and I went to see Clark about Chris buying one of the auction items before it actually went to auction, and as we got there we overheard him having what sounded like an argument with someone on the phone."

"About . . . ?" Cruz asked.

"Well, we really weren't listening that hard. It's just that there's no door on his office. But we heard enough to know it was something about an arrangement of some kind that the other person wanted to change. 'A deal is a deal,' I remember Clark saying. And he wasn't happy about it. But the person on the other end must have been pushing him, because Clark, um, let's see . . ." After a second it came to her. "Oh, that's right. The other guy—well, I don't know if it was a guy or not—the other person asked for seven at first and Clark said that was out of the question, and then after listening for another minute he said all right, six was possible, and that seemed to settle it. He didn't like it, though."

"Six what? Hundred dollars, thousand dollars, *million* dollars?"

She shrugged. "Six dollars, for all I know. Or six paintings, or six tickets to a baseball game. I have no idea. You understand, we weren't really listening, we were just . . . overhearing." She thought for another few seconds. "And that's about it. Oh, no, wait a minute. He called him by name! It was . . . it was . . ." She grimaced, raking her mind. " . . . Seymour . . . Milton . . . something like that, something

old-fashioned . . . Stanley . . . Morton . . . no, *Melvin*, that was it!"
she cried triumphantly.

"Melvin," Cruz echoed. "Mean anything to you?"

"Nothing. Sorry."

"Nothing to be sorry about, but is there anything else you
remember? Even if it doesn't seem like anything?"

"Yes, I think—"

"Hold it," Jake said, reaching into a shirt pocket for his cell phone,
which must have been on vibrate, because Alix had heard nothing.
"Yeah, Spike, sure," he said into it. "No kidding, is that right?
Damn . . . Look, I kind of have my hands full right now. Could you
maybe give this to Booker? He's familiar with it all. Okay, thanks."

When he closed the phone there was a wry little smile on his
face. "Guess what. Another burglary, just a few minutes ago. With
the Phantom's M.O. plastered all over it."

"Ah." Alix's wry smile matched his. "So would I be correct in
thinking that Clark is now off the hook as far as being the Phantom
Burglar goes?"

"I'd have to say you're right about that. And that it makes what
you were saying before a lot more probable."

So she wasn't paranoid after all. That raised her spirits. "Does that
mean you think he did come after me because I said the Pollock—"

Jake lifted his hand. "Let's not get back into that right now, Alix.
I need to think about it some more. For the moment, let's stay with
his murder. You were about to tell me about something else you
remember."

"That's right. The person he was talking to on the phone—just
before he hung up, Clark said, 'All right, Melvin, see you there.' As if
they were going to get together, or at least be in the same place at the

same time. I don't think he said when, so I guess he could have been talking about some meeting or conference a year from now."

"Or last night."

"Yes." She shrugged. "And really, I think that's everything."

"Thank you, Alix," Cruz said, but he looked disappointed, as if he'd been hoping there'd be more meat in what she had to say. "If you remember any more at all, even a couple of words, you'll call me?"

"I will. And I'll talk to my friend Chris and see if she remembers anything I forgot."

"Thanks for coming in, then," he said rising. "Let's get you back to the museum. I have to get over there myself. Want to talk to the staff."

"Jake, if it's all the same to you, could you drop me off downtown instead, on the way? I'm meeting Chris there."

16

Chris was presumably still working in her room when Jake dropped Alix off. Chris had recently discovered IRMA, the Geneva-based International Register of Missing Art, and had offered to help them modernize their digitized database, which was huge but antiquated and hard to access. They had snapped her up, of course, and she had brought the project with her; her intention was to put in a few morning hours at it on her laptop at the Colony Palms. The two women had agreed to meet for a ten-thirty break at the Coffee Bean, on the northeast corner of North Palm Canyon Drive and East Tahquitz Canyon Way, which was about midway between the Colony Palms and the Villa Louisa and within easy walking distance of each.

This was of course right at the "heart of the heart" of downtown. Directly across the street from the coffee shop was the Marilyn Forever statue, once again surrounded by camera-clicking tourists and their busses. But this side of Palm Canyon Drive was quieter, and Alix, arriving first, had no trouble finding an umbrellaed sidewalk table to which to carry her iced tea lemonade.

A few feet to her left, and no more than a hundred feet from Marilyn, was a far smaller (merely life-sized) patinaed bronze sculpture of a seated Lucille Ball. Lucy occupied the left half of a bronze bench, leaving the right side free for people to have their pictures taken sitting beside her, within the curve of her outstretched arm, which lay across the top of the bench. This relatively modest statuary, probably once the highlight of this particular corner, was now half-hidden behind boxed shrubbery and under the Coffee Bean's awnings. The bench wasn't getting many takers, probably because Lucy, dwarfed and diminished by the statue across the street, understandably looked as if she were just a little put out.

Chris wasn't due for another fifteen minutes, and being early for anything was not part of her genetic makeup. That gave Alix some time on her own, for which she was grateful. Things were getting crazier by the hour and she needed some quiet time to sort things out. Clark Calder. She hadn't known him from the Man in the Moon until a few days ago; she hadn't even known he existed. Yet two nights ago he had inexplicably tried to murder her (she no longer had any doubts about that), and last night he himself had been murdered. The first was bizarre enough by itself; the second was even more so. Could it possibly be that the Pollock was at the root of both, after all? But if not, what other connection did she have to—

Five lively orchestral tones, emanating from her bag, startled her out of her ruminations: *deet-deet-da-dah-dah*, the opening notes of the "Toreador Song" chorus from *Carmen*. This was the ring tone she'd assigned to contacts whose calls might be important, that were to be picked up on the spot, if possible.

As always, after the initial startlement came a smile. Alix's mother had been a dedicated opera fan with season tickets to the Met. She had taken the willing Alix with her often, and sometimes Geoff as well. Geoff enjoyed opera, but there had always been a subversive streak to him, and (out of her mother's hearing) he often taught her little parodies of the lyrics of the most famous arias. Pure doggerel, but they had made a twelve-year-old girl laugh, and they still made a thirty-year-old smile. She still remembered his version of the "Toreador Song."

Torayador-ay,
Don't spit on the floor-ay.
Use the cuspidor-ay.
That is what it's for . . . HAY!

There were only three numbers with this ring tone: Geoff's for one, and Chris's, and the person's whose call this turned out to be: Jamie Wozniak, the operations specialist for the FBI's Art Crime Team.

"Hi, there, Jamie," she said, incipient laughter still playing around her lips. Jamie's calls were always welcome. Usually, they meant that an interesting consulting job was in the offing if she was in the market for one.

Not this time. "I have news for you," she said, sounding excited herself, which was unusual for the imperturbable Jamie. "We've found the SOB."

"Which SOB would that be?" Alix asked, her mind back on Clark.

"The one who's been dissing you on the Web, of course. The Art World Insider himself, the dastardly blogger, Peter Bakeworthy."

"You found him?" A sudden thought chilled her. "Jamie, you promised—you *swore*—you wouldn't get Ted involved."

"And I kept my promise. I just pushed a few buttons on my own. I do have certain competencies, you know."

"But I thought it was next to impossible, that it took months—"

"Alix . . ."

"—and even if you did get the PSI or the UPS, or whatever it is—"

"Alix . . ."

"—it still took a court order, and in order to get a court order—"

"*Alix!*"

Alix blinked. "Sorry. What?"

157

"Thank you. It *is* hard, and it generally does take months—for the average person. But permit me to point out that we *are* the FBI, after all."

"Good point." Alix laughed, having settled down a little. "So then—who is Peter Bakeworthy, really?"

"His name is Clark Calder, and he—"

Alix had thought she had used up her capacity for astonishment for one day, but not so. "*Clark Calder?*"

"Yes, you know him?"

"Yes, sure. He's—he was—the senior curator here at the Brethwaite."

"Well, apparently you did something to get on his nerves."

"Obviously. He tried to kill me a couple of nights ago."

"He—?"

"Only now somebody's killed *him*."

Alix imagined she could hear the perplexity at the other end. Jamie, she thought, was waiting for a punch line to follow.

"I'm serious, Jamie. It's true,"

A shocked "My God," was all Jamie could muster. And then, a second later, a shrill: "What is going on out there? Are you okay? Are you *safe*?"

"Yes, I'm fine, don't worry about me. But as for what's going on, I'm totally in the dark, and so are the police. I hardly knew the man and barely interacted with him at all. The only thing we argued about—differed about; you couldn't even call it an argument—was this Pollock the museum has—" A new thought hit her. "Jamie, wait. Clark couldn't have been the only one whose nerves I've gotten on. There's somebody else. There has to be. Those book reviews—he couldn't have been responsible for them."

"Why not?"

"Because I've only known him for a week—not even a week. Those reviews go back months."

"That may be, but he was responsible for them anyway."

"I can't believe it," Alix murmured. "Are you sure?"

"Oh, we're sure."

"But *how*? Clark wasn't stupid. He'd know to cover up his tracks."

"He *did* cover them up, Alix. As far as we know, he didn't submit anything from his own computer. Almost all of them turned out to have been sent from hotel or public library computers, in batches. So what I did was to look at the hotel guest lists to search for people that were registered there either that night or the previous one, and only one name came up more than once. That was Clark Calder, and he showed up five times. Hell of a coincidence, huh?"

Alix couldn't come up with anything in reply. She was still resisting the idea of Clark's being behind them. It just made no sense.

"And listen to this," Jamie went on. "The last few reviews—and the new blog—all came from the library in Palm Springs, on Sunrise Way."

That settled it. Alix gave in. "Wow," she said softly.

"So what are you going to do?" Jamie asked when nothing more appeared to be forthcoming. "Can I help?"

"I don't know. I have to think about this, Jamie. This is very . . . mystifying. Thanks so much for doing all that work, and for letting me know."

"Alix, take care of yourself. If you need anything from us—"

"I know, and I appreciate it. I'll be in touch. 'Bye."

While Alix had been on the phone, Chris had shown up, had offered a carefree salute and a mouthed "Be right out," and gone inside to get her morning caffe latte. She was comparatively underdressed for once, in a silver-threaded blue summer sweater, trim leopard-spot ankle pants that emphasized her long legs, and three-inch heels. Big, white-rimmed Lolita sunglasses. And only two or three jangly bracelets on her wrist. Her work clothes, apparently, Alix thought with a smile.

When she emerged she had a formidable turkey and cheddar sandwich on her tray as well as the latte. "Forgot to have breakfast," she explained as she settled down at the table. "I'm starving. So what was that phone call about? Is something wrong? You look a little weird."

"I'm not surprised. That call was a little weird and then some," Alix said slowly. "That was my friend Jamie from the art squad. They found out who it is that's been trashing me on the Web." She sat scowling, trying make what Jamie had told her fit in with everything else that had been happening.

Chris, not the most patient of women, let five seconds go by. "And are you planning to let me in on it, or is it a secret?"

"It was Clark."

Chris had half the sandwich on the way to her mouth, but she laid it carefully down and took a moment before speaking. "Clark, the man we talked to yesterday. The head curator at the Brethwaite."

A nod from Alix. "Yes."

"The one you think tried to kill you."

Nod.

"And he's the one that sent out that awful blog? The FBI says so?"

Alix sighed. "Chris, would you like me to write it down for you?"

"I'm sorry, it's just that it's all so incredible. I didn't believe you when you said it was him the other night, but now . . . I don't know." She shook her head. "But what in the world can he have against you?"

"I'm trying to figure that out."

Chris took an abstracted nibble of turkey and cheddar and pondered. "Gotta be the Pollock," she announced. "If it *is* a fake, and

160

what Prentice said is true—that the museum paid millions for it on his advice—he's in big trouble. He's trying to discredit you to protect himself."

Alix shook her head. "That was the first thing that occurred to me too, but no, that's not it."

"And why is that not it?"

"Because, according to Jamie, those bogus book reviews are Clark's doing too, and they've been going on for, what is it, two months, three months?"

"But you didn't even know him two months ago. You didn't know him last week."

"Exactly."

"And you have no idea at all—"

"No, none."

"Well, you just have to confront him then, don't you? Do you want me to come with you?" She looked pleased with the possibility of combat. And ready. And willing. All Alix had to do was to give the word and Chris would forget her sandwich and join her on the field of battle right now, this minute; that was the message that came across.

"That would be harder than you think," Alix said. "There's something you don't know."

"Which is?"

"Clark's dead. Last night. A hit-and-run. The police say it's murder."

Chris was one of the few women Alix knew who could whistle, and she emitted a low one now. "Jeeeezus. How—I mean, what—"

It took twenty minutes of muted explanation to sketch in all the details, and when Alix had answered all the questions to which she had answers, she said, "I guess I'd better call this detective, though, and tell him about Clark's hassling me on the Web."

161

"You sure you want to do that just yet?" Chris warned. "It's kind of incriminating, when you think about it. Gives you a damn good motive for wanting him dead."

"But that's why I want to tell him. Better coming from me than letting him find out for himself, which he surely would."

However, Cruz was out of the office at the moment—at the museum, Alix remembered—and he'd be in and out all day, so she left a message asking him to call her when he had the chance. She was still uttering the last few words when Chris abruptly said, "Alix, you need to get away from this craziness for a while. Let's take the car and get out in the desert on some of these back roads, away from people, see some scenery, eat at one of those date-shake places they have out here. The Salton Sea's only about forty miles from here and I've never seen it, have you? Doesn't that sound good?"

Alix hadn't seen it either and it did sound good. "Great idea," she said, flipping the phone closed. "We can just enjoy ourselves and put the whole thing out of our minds until tomorrow."

"And don't forget," Chris said, "there's a bright side to Clark's getting murdered too."

"There is?"

"There certainly is. No more nasty things about you on the Internet—except the ones you deserve, of course."

"Good point. And now I don't have to worry about anybody lurking out there trying to murder me anymore. That's even better."

. . .

It was growing increasingly clear that he would have to kill her too.

The thought repelled him. Running down Clark had been bad enough—awful—the dreadful, unforgettable sound of it, the sight of that disfigured face up against the windshield—blood, shattered teeth—the fright, the freezing horror when the body got caught on the mirror, or on something, and he couldn't shake it off at first, so that it flopped and banged against the side window a few inches from his face. Horrible.

He was not a killer, he didn't see himself as a killer, he had never before killed anyone or even thought about it; not seriously, not until the day before yesterday. And now, not twenty-four hours after killing Clark, he was sitting here priming himself for a second murder. Unbelievable. But he knew the kind of person Alix London was, and he couldn't chance letting her live. There was so very much at stake: the rest of his life.

But it would have to be done differently. Clark's murder had been unplanned and wildly dangerous (although, thank God, there had been no witnesses), a frustrated reaction to Clark's arrogance and stupid, stupid intransigence. With Alix it would have to be safer, better thought out— and especially, accomplished somehow at a distance. He didn't think he could stand another experience like the one he'd had with Clark.

Think.

. . .

For once Jake Cruz had the pleasure of sitting behind a desk that matched his size—it matched *him* too, wide and heavy, with thick bowling-pin legs; a sturdy and reliable piece of work, but starting to show signs of wear. Made of solid oak supposedly crafted from the timbers of a British warship captured on Lake Erie during the War of 1812, it had once belonged to L. Morgan Brethwaite. Now it sat in the museum director's office, where Lillian Brethwaite had used it ever since assuming that job. Unfortunately, the massive chair that went with it had been too big for Mrs. B—her toes barely touched the floor—so it had been replaced with a smaller one, an austere, unpadded wooden banker's chair, the arms of which had been digging into Jake's hips for the past hour and a half.

He was just finishing up the last of his interviews with the cura-torial staff. Madge Temple had proved the most cooperative, or at least the talkiest, of the bunch and he was having trouble getting her out of there. He tried one more time.

"Well, I think that wraps it up, Ms. Temple. Thanks very much for your help." He indicated the card he'd given her on his previous attempt to shake himself loose. "You'll call me if anything comes to mind?"

The expression on Madge's face, a bit porky but still engagingly gaminlike, suggested that she found this amusing, but then she had seemed to find the entire interview amusing, to find *him* amusing. "Now why," she said as if to an invisible personage off to her right, "do I have the impression he's trying to get rid of me?"

Jake managed a chuckle. "Well, actually, I do need to get—"

"I'm going, I'm going. Back to the grindstone." But at the door, she turned. "Oh, one question, though. Is it all right to tell my hus-band how this went—what we talked about—or am I sworn to secrecy?"

"Perfectly all right, no problem at all."

As if, Cruz thought, it would have made any difference if he'd told her she had to keep it to herself. Either way, Drew Temple would have heard it all before the hour was out—he was probably hearing about it right now—and anybody else she could corral would hear it too, no doubt considerably embellished, by the end of the day.

He really didn't have any objection. All four interviews had gone over the same ground and everybody's information had corroborated everybody else's. He was pretty certain that all had been reasonably honest and forthcoming in answering his questions, possibly because they knew that any issues they tried to evade—anything potentially disadvantageous to themselves—would be happily served up by one or more of the others. But then his purpose hadn't been to probe very deeply; he was simply trying to get a grasp of the situation at the museum vis-à-vis Clark.

He eased himself out of the chair and stood at a window massaging the dent in his left hip. So what had he learned? He'd learned that if Clark Calder's plans were implemented, every one of them had something to lose.

a) Drew and Madge Temple's separate departments—Decorative Arts and Costumes and Furnishings—were to be combined into one Costumes and Decorative Arts department under Madge. Drew would be demoted to assistant curator and would henceforth report to his wife, an outcome at which the sour-faced, pointy-nosed Drew took extreme umbrage and thought unfair, inappropriate, unseemly, and deeply flawed. Madge, after due reflection, wasn't exactly nuts about it either. It held little promise of improved domestic relations.

b) A similar problem confronted the stately Prentice Vandervere and the rosy-cheeked, palpably tipsy Alfie Wellington. Vandervere's department, Paintings, was to be combined with Wellington's Prints and Drawings into a single department, necessitating the elimination of one of the two curator positions. According to Clark, the decision as to which of the two men was to be put in charge, and which to be downgraded or possibly let go, had not yet been made. There was general agreement that Clark's main intention here was to humiliate Prentice, with whom he'd been at odds from the beginning. The only one who let Clark off was Prentice himself. "I really am an old codger now," he said, "and perhaps the job would be a bit too much for me."

Jake thought otherwise. The old guy was sharper than *he* was, and miles ahead of Alfie Wellington, whose brains had been well suffused in *marinade au bourbon* and who had years ago lost whatever ambition he'd once had. Alfie himself feared—hated—either possible outcome. He didn't want a more important job, and he didn't want to lose his current position. He just wanted things to stay the comfortable way they were. (*Not so different from me, really*, Jake thought.)

Okay then, what did it all amount to? Yes, they all had reason to not like Calder very much, as Alix had said, and perhaps even to wish him dead. But kill him? What for? Mrs. Brethwaite had already approved the plans, so what good would it do any of them to get rid of Clark?

But like any seasoned cop, he well knew that logic went only so far in explaining motives for murder. Or human behavior in general.

17

The afternoon turned out to be just what Alix and Chris had hoped. It was a straight shot toward the Salton Sea on Highway 111, through flat, open desert, and the ride went quickly. They had the windows down, and the warm, dry breeze felt cleansing and revitalizing. They were almost to the sea, passing through the small town of Mecca, when Chris, leafing through a travel guide Alix had brought with her from Seattle, came up with another idea. "How about a hike instead? There's this place, Painted Canyon, just a couple of miles up a dirt road." She read aloud: "Spectacular wind-and-water-carved rock formations, narrow, shaded canyons hemmed in by walls streaked with rose, pink, red, purple, and green mineral deposits, with bighorn sheep on the—"

"I'm convinced. Where's the road?"

"Turn left there," Chris said, pointing.

. . .

They saw no bighorn sheep, but the rest was as advertised. They strolled for almost three hours on the sandy, flat bottom of a canyon—*cleft* would be a better word, just a few yards wide in some places, and towered over on either side by sheer, eighty-foot cliffs lit with faint pastel colors. The day had grown hot, but down at the canyon bottom, shaded by the walls, it was cool and comfortable, at least for the first hour, before the sun had reached its height, and Alix imagined she could still smell the river that had created this place so many eons ago. They saw only two small groups of hikers (serious ones with sturdy, worn boots and multiple liter bottles of water). Most of the time they had the place to themselves.

They stopped at one pretty place with sweeping views a long way up and down the winding canyon, where Alix said: "Do you realize there is nothing visible here that was made by humans or altered in any way by humans? This is no different from the way it would have looked a million years ago."

"Which reminds me," said Chris, master of the non sequitur, "I'm hungry. And thirsty."

.   .   .

While Alix and Chris had been exploring Painted Canyon, things had been hopping along at the police department. Jake Cruz had come back from his interviews at the museum with an intriguing new idea forming in his mind. Not long after he arrived at the station he went looking for his partner on the Calder case, Pat Malloy. He found him in his cubicle, peering hard at his computer screen. His desk was alarmingly cluttered with file folders. In his left hand was one of them, in the other his computer mouse, and between his teeth, like a pirate dagger, was a ballpoint pen. The screen at which he was looking so intently showed four different windows. The existence of the big corkboard beside his desk could only be taken on faith, so completely swathed was it in push-pinned papers, sketches, and photos.

"You busy?" Jake asked.

"Now why would you ask that?" Malloy said around the pen, continuing to scowl at the screen. "I was just sitting around trying to come up with something to pass the time. Thinking about taking a nap, maybe."

"Well, instead of that, how about coming with me to the video room? I want to show you something."

Malloy removed the ballpoint from his mouth. "Mm, okay, I *guess* I could put the snooze off till after lunch, but tell me what we're going to see."

"Interview with the London woman."

"I watched it while you were gone, Jake. I just finished ten minutes ago. I could practically recite it to you."

"Humor me."

"Okay, if it's that important," Malloy said, "but we can do it right here. I put it on a flash drive . . . somewhere." He was rummaging with both hands in a drawer that was as cluttered as the desktop.

"Are you kidding me? I can barely fit into my own so-called office when I'm all by myself. I'm not about to squeeze into this place with you. I've already set it up in the video room. Come on, buddy, up and at 'em."

The video room was two doors down from the interrogation room and was mostly used for watching live interviews. Once upon a time it had been the evidence room, but that had been moved downstairs to a larger space. The plaque on the door still said "Evidence Room," however. One of these days somebody would get around to changing it, but since it was used only by the detectives and they all knew what it was, nobody had bothered.

"Okay, now," Jake said, settling himself. "I've got it right at the place I want you to look at. Or more specifically, to listen to."

On the screen, Alix was speaking:

"'A deal is a deal,' I remember Clark saying. And he wasn't happy about it. But the other person must have been pushing him, because Clark, um, let's see. . . . Oh, that's right. The other

guy—well, I don't know if it was a guy or not—the other person asked for seven at first and Clark said that was out of the question, and then after listening for another minute he said all right, six was possible, and that seemed to settle it. He didn't like it, though."

"Six what? Hundred dollars, thousand dollars?" Jake's voice from off-screen. "Million dollars?"

"Six dollars, for all I know. Or six paintings, or six tickets to a baseball game. I have no idea. You understand, we weren't really listening, we were just . . . overhearing. And that's about it. Oh, no, wait a minute. He called him by name! It was . . . it was . . . Seymour . . . Milton . . . something like that, something old-fashioned . . . Stanley . . . Morton . . . no, Melvin, that was it!"

"Melvin. Mean anything to you?"

"Nothing. Sorry."

"Nothing to be sorry about, but is there anything else you remember? Even if it doesn't seem like anything?"

"Yes, I think--"

Jake fast-forwarded through his phone call's interruption until Alix continued.

"The person he was talking to on the phone--just before he hung up," he said, 'All right, Melvin, see you there.' As if they were going to get together, or at least to be in the same place. I don't think he

said when, so I guess he could have been talking about some meeting or conference a year from now."

"Or last night."

Jake stopped the video. Alix's face remained on the screen, caught with her mouth half-open and her eyes half-closed. "Now I'm going to repeat something she said and try to make it pretty much the way she said it. Tell me if I get it right."

Malloy looked hard at him. "Jake, this is slightly weird."

"Just listen: 'All right, Melvyn's. See you there.' Did I get it?"

"On the nose. You're very smart. Can I please go take my nap now?"

"Pat, I didn't say the same thing, I said: 'All right, Melvyn's. See you there.' M-e-l-v-y-n-s."

"You've got to be joking," Malloy said with a jerk of his head. "How the hell do *you* know how she spelled it? How would *she* know how Calder spelled it? They sound exactly the same."

"That's my point, don't you see? How do we know—how would *she* know—whether he was talking *to* a person named Melvin, or *about* a place called Melvyn's?"

"Like the restaurant, you mean?"

"Like the restaurant."

Melvyn's was the restaurant at the Ingleside Inn, a famous holdover from the Golden Age, when it had hosted just about every famous personality from Clark Gable to Salvador Dali to Norman Vincent Peale, and was still bringing in the tourist crowds with recent well-publicized sightings of the likes of Tori Spelling, Diahann Carroll, and Kirsten Dunst. It was also a pretty decent place to eat, and its Casablanca Lounge was a good place to have a quiet, secluded drink, as long as you got there on the early side.

"Possible," Malloy allowed. "So you think what they were talking about was getting together at Melvyn's."

"That's right. *Melvyn's. See you there.* Period, not a comma. Sounds exactly like *Melvin, see you there,* because the 's' carries over."

Malloy was nodding along. "Possible," he said again. "And that gets us where?"

"Wait, let me finish. Melvyn's is on West Ramon Road, near South Cahuilla. Calder was killed on Patencio, just north of Santa Rosa, which—"

"—would be two or three blocks northwest of there."

"—and three or four south of San Jacinto, which is where he was leasing," Jake said. "And if you look at a map you'll see it's on the most likely route he would have taken if he was walking home from Melvyn's."

"And the ME says he had to have been struck from behind by a car heading north, which means he could very well have been heading home from there. I hate to say it, Jake, but I think you've got something here."

"Ah, the light dawns," said a grinning Jake, "but let's take it a little further. That business with 'seven' being impossible and 'six' being okay? What if it didn't refer to six hundred or six thousand or six million anything? What if—"

"—it referred to six o'clock? Maybe even six o'clock last night?"

"Right. Calder was killed a little before seven—we've got those two guys who heard the hit and came running out. That would fit perfectly with a brief meeting—say half an hour—at Melvyn's, wouldn't it?"

"It would, Detective Cruz. Very nice."

"Thank you, Detective Malloy. Would you say the next step would be to see if we could get a lead on just who it was he was meeting with?"

"Sure would. We've got a good picture of Calder. I could take it over to the Ingleside and see if anybody remembers him and is able to give us a description of who he was with. In fact, if you want, I'll take it over right now."

"Pat, at this time of the day, you're not going to find whoever staffs Melvyn's at six p.m. Better save it till later in the afternoon. But there's something else you can do now."

"Hallelujah," said Malloy dryly. "I was praying you'd come up with something to kill all this time I've got hanging over me."

"Those two guys who ran out? We know from them that there was another car near the corner where he was hit, and it backed up and got out of there in a hurry, which tells us that this was a guy who saw what happened and wanted nothing to do with it, so he's somebody we'd dearly love to talk to. From the information the two of them provided, the lab has come up with the probable make and model: a Mazda MX-5 Miata, 2010 or 2011. Red."

Malloy nodded again. "That might conceivably help. Not your common everyday car."

"What's more, they're pretty sure they've been seeing it around the neighborhood, so it's a good bet whoever owns it lives nearby."

"Interesting thought. Which way was it headed again? Before it backed away, I mean."

"It was on Santa Rosa, about to cross Patencio going west. So I'd suggest that the place to start looking for it would be to start hitting doorbells on the very next block of Santa Rosa, and circle out from there for a few more blocks. Find a photo of a red Miata and show it around, see if anybody knows who owns one."

"Okay." Malloy stood up. "Just might get us somewhere." He reached for the remote and closed down the image of Alix's face, frozen into its heavy-lidded, open-mouthed expression; it shrank to a little white squib and disappeared.

"Pretty girl," he said. "Shame to leave her there looking like a goofus."

18

It was an eventful afternoon at the museum as well. In the conference room, the director was conducting a hastily called meeting with her curators. The mood was sober. There were no pastries, no coffee.

As usual, Mrs. B was doing the talking. Discussion would not ensue until she signaled that it was welcome, which sometimes happened, sometimes not.

"This will be brief," she announced. "If any of you wish to call it a day when we're done, please do. I intend to do the same. Now. You all know about last night's awful events as well as I do, and if I'm not mistaken all of you have spoken with the police. I see no point in our dwelling on the matter here. I do want to explain what will happen now, however."

She had her long, strong, capable-looking fingers clasped in front of her, with her eyes circling the table from left to right, fixing first on one person for a brief, intense moment, then swinging to the next, and so on around the table. Then she would do it again. An observer would have no trouble telling who was the temporary subject of that flinty gaze just by looking at him or her. There would be a subtle change—a stiffening, an immobility. A frozen second or two and it would leave and move on to the next in line. It was like watching a sonic-boom shock wave shimmer around the table.

"Most of the modifications Clark was in the process of introducing will remain in effect, with the exception of the personnel changes.

As of this moment, those will *not* be implemented. The curators will all remain in their current positions: Prentice as head of Paintings; Alfred, Drawings and Prints; Madge, Costumes and Furnishings; Drew, Decorative Arts. I hope that is to your liking."

Several let-out breaths could be heard around the table, and then Drew said, "I would like some clarity on the meaning of 'as of this moment.' Are you saying we should take this as a conditional, temporary adjustment, and that Clark's changes might still be made, or was it just a figure of speech?"

"Simply a figure of speech, Drew. There are no plans to revisit the matter. Are there any further questions?"

Jerry Swanson raised his index finger. "I'm a little confused as to what I'm doing here, Mrs. B. I'm running a little behind on the crating, and I would really like to get back to work."

"You're here, Mr. Swanson, because I require your assurance that Clark's death will in no way impede the auction. I wish it to proceed exactly as planned and right on schedule. Do you anticipate any difficulties there?"

"None whatever," Jerry said grandly. "In fact, I would like to take this opportunity to commend you on your decision, which I find to be practical, astute, and essential."

Mrs. B was not big on humor in general, and irony (if that's what this was) was particularly unappreciated, especially at so inappropriate a time. "*Do* you," she said. No question mark, but the dismissive nuance went right by Jerry.

"You bet I do. If we scrapped the auction now, just think of what might happen! Good God, Endicott might even dock my salary!" He gave her his broadest, brashest grin. Not being an employee of the museum, he was more inclined to be flippant with her than were the others.

His grin was not returned. Mrs. B. looked at him with narrowed eyes. Few people could stand up to one of Lillian Brethwaite's raking glares, and even Jerry was not among them. The grin vanished. "Um, so will I be working—directly with you, then, Mrs. B? Now that Clark is, uh, gone?"

"No, I have more than I can deal with as it is. You will be working with our senior curator."

"That'll be something to see," Madge deadpanned sotto voce, to Alfie, who sat on her right, "what with the guy dead and all."

Alfie leaned sideways to whisper back. "Kind of an improvement, though, wouldn't you say? All things considered?"

If Mrs. B heard, she chose to ignore it. She turned to Prentice. "Prentice, I've given this matter considerable thought. Your duties as curator of Paintings should be quite light for the foreseeable future. I would appreciate it if you would consider assuming the duties of senior curator, at least for the present."

"Yay," Alfie said, with a single, soft clap of his hands.

"With a commensurate salary increase, of course," continued Mrs. B. "I would like you to begin by—"

"I appreciate the offer, but I'm not sure I want to take that on," Prentice said. "I've put in my time in managerial positions, and I'm extremely happy to be free of such responsibilities now. I really doubt that I'd be the best person for this."

"Now you're being modest, and I think you know it. What would you say to trying it for, say, a month—through the completion of the auction process? If you don't find it to your liking at the end of that time, I'll come up with something else. But I honestly suspect you'd find the challenges interesting."

Prentice's slightly twisted posture exuded discomfort. "Perhaps, but—"

"Prentice, to be perfectly frank, it's the auction that I'm most concerned with. The arrangements were consuming most of Clark's time, and I simply don't have that kind of time to devote to it. Or, I might add, the necessary competencies."

"And to be equally frank on my part, Mrs. B . . . Lillian . . . I have found myself in disagreement with almost every proposal made by Clark since the day he came, not least the idea of the auction, which I am very sorry to see taking shape. For me to participate in—to be *responsible* for—something I find repugnant would be . . . would be . . ."

While he searched for an adequate word, Jerry spoke up, directing his remarks to Mrs. B. "Actually, the time-consuming part on the museum's end is pretty much over. Everything's in place. Should be smooth sailing from here on in. I'm pretty sure I can handle things day to day, and only come to you if something new comes up, which I doubt is going to happen."

"Yes, well," said Mrs. B. She turned earnestly back to Prentice. "This auction is more important to the future of the museum than even you realize. It would be a personal favor to me if you take it on. Prentice . . . I *need* your help." Her gaze dropped to her clasped hands. She was embarrassed.

Madge, Drew, and Alfie exchanged shocked glances. Mrs. B embarrassed? Mrs. B *coaxing*? This was incredible. " . . . wonders never end?" Drew could be heard murmuring.

The director's uncharacteristic pleading had gotten through to Prentice. "Lillian, I'll do what you ask," he said with a faint sigh. "I'll see the auction through. But then I would like to return solely to Paintings."

"*Thank* you, Prentice. I am much relieved."

"Jerry," Prentice said, "I'll need you to bring me up to speed."

"Sure," Jerry said.

"It may be harder than you think. I've worked at keeping clear of it, you see. I couldn't even tell you all of the paintings that are being sold—I didn't want to know. So that's where your education effort should start, I suppose."

"No problem, I'll run you off a list the second we're out of here."

"Naturally, I'll need to spend some time with the actual paintings themselves as well. I trust that won't delay matters?"

Jerry frowned. "Uh-oh."

"It creates a problem?"

"Well . . . no, not really. Most of them have already been crated, but they're still in the workroom. I guess we can get them back open again if you really think it's necessary."

"I'm afraid I do. I'm sorry for the additional trouble. I'll help you with them."

"Aw, no, that's okay, it's not that hard. But the other thing is, a few of them have already been shipped to San Francisco. Five of them, I think, but none of the major pieces. The stars of the show are all still here."

"Ah. Well, let's start with those, then. When would be a good time to begin?"

"Any time, prof. Right now, if you want."

"And that," said Mrs. B, in better spirits than she was when the meeting had begun, "would seem to be a perfect place to call a halt to these proceedings. Thank you all. Prentice, thank you again."

Mrs. B left first, and then Prentice and Jerry went out together, leaving Madge, Drew, and Alfie still at the table.

"Well, there's a load off our minds," Drew said, actually looking happy for once. "Sanity has been restored."

"And not a moment to soon," Alfie agreed. "Indeed, a historic meeting."

"I'll say," Madge chimed in. "He actually called her 'Lillian,' did you hear? *Twice!* And she never blinked."

"The times, they are a-changin'," Alfie sang with what he must have thought was a Bob Dylan twang.

19

None of the eating places that Alix and Chris saw in Mecca caught their fancy, so they stopped at a gas station convenience store and bought some mixed nuts and cold apple juice to tide them over as they drove back, keeping their eyes open for places that appealed to them.

"There!" yelled Chris near Indio, about halfway back to Palm Springs. "What could be more perfect than that?"

She was pointing at the gigantic wooden figure—crude and two-dimensional, but even taller than Marilyn—of a blue knight brandishing a prominent yellow shield (on which was inscribed "Shields"), and pointing imperiously across the road at the long, low, shedlike front of Shields Date Garden and Cafe. It was like one of those roadside attractions that had once upon a time symbolized the long, open stretches of Route 66. Various makeshift placards and signs informed visitors that Shields had been right there since 1924, that their world-famous Medjool date shakes were to be had inside and that the café featured date pancakes, date burgers, and jalapeño- and prosciutto-stuffed dates. Also that "the world's longest-running movie," *The Romance and Sex Life of the Date*, was showing continuously in the theater, as it had been doing for the last half-century and more.

Once inside, they both had chicken club sandwiches in the café, followed by date shakes consumed on stools at the old-fashioned soda fountain, and strolled for a while in the surprisingly large and beautiful date gardens, among old trees and ponds. Afterward, they wandered through the store, where Chris bought a half dozen boxes of stuffed and candied dates and had them shipped to Seattle. They even watched *The Romance and Sex Life of the Date*, which they agreed had been informative, moderately interesting, and definitely G-rated. All told, they spent another three hours at Shields.

"You were right," Alix said contentedly as they climbed back in the car. "Couldn't have been more perfect. I couldn't feel less stressed."

"Genuine funk," said Chris. "That's what was so nice and relaxing about the place. Not this cheesy, phony funk you see everywhere else these days."

By the time they got back downtown it was getting dark and Chris joined Alix to end the day at the Villa Louisa for the evening's outdoor movie, *And Then There Were None*, a 1940s version of Agatha Christie's tale about a party of people staying at a mysterious mansion, where they are bafflingly eliminated one by one. Chris and Alix got there as one of the employees was winding up his sonorous, over-the-top introduction: "Where will the killer strike next?" he was declaiming. "Who will live? Who will die?"

"And who," came an equally booming voice out of the darkness, "will care?" Everyone laughed, and it was that sort of mood in which the movie was then watched, with viewers, Alix and Chris included, occasionally throwing in droll asides of their own to general laughter and applause.

All in all, thought Alix , she'd had a lovely day—especially given the way it had started.

· · ·

In the morning she took a grumbling, barely awake Chris to the airport for her seven a.m. ShareJet flight to Seattle and then drove to the museum, where she planned to put in a solid day's work on the Sargent.

Unlike Jackson Pollock, John Singer Sargent was a painter with whose work she very definitely "connected," and she was both pleased and humbled to have been given the chance to restore *Mrs. Jay Chandler Winthrop* to something like the clarity and brightness it would have had on the day it came from his easel in 1893. "America's greatest portraitist," as he was often called, was born in Florence, trained in Paris, and lived most of his life in London, where he died. But he did make frequent trips to America to take on some of the portrait commissions that poured in from across the sea. And what portraits they were—masterly and lush, in the rich portraiture tradition of Velasquez or Hals. And as with those gentlemen, his finest and most famous ones were of the aristocracy of the day. With Velasquez it had been the Spanish royalty, with Hals the civic dignitaries and rich burghers of Haarlem, and with Sargent the wealthy socialites of London, Boston, and Paris. But with all three painters, whoever the subject might be, he or she was rendered with a liveliness and humanity that could enthrall a viewer from another century, another universe.

Eager to get started, she had planned ahead and brought a 20-ounce Starbucks caffe latte with her so that she could get to the painting without having to stop in the break room, which she suspected would be buzzing about Clark's murder, something in which she had no desire to participate. Having successfully accomplished this, she was pleased to see that the binocular microscope had been brought up for her from the storeroom, and there were four slit-open cartons from art supply houses on the worktable: the material she'd ordered a couple of days ago.

Earlier, she'd removed the frame and made her usual careful examination of the painting, front and back. The wooden stretcher (the framework to which the canvas is attached—by tacks, in this case) was unwarped and in excellent condition. No repair work required there. The front, while by no means in terrible condition, was in need of some TLC. A layer of grime coated the surface, and under it the old varnish had yellowed and darkened. The result was a flattening of Sargent's three-dimensional effects and a muting of his colors. Alix was sure that the cleaning process would reveal a vivid, living portrait that no one had seen for at least fifty years, and she was looking forward to her coming ah-ha moment, usually accompanied by a shiver of pure pleasure, when Sargent's original, vivid colors first peeped through, clean and bright.

But before that, a few minor repairs were necessary. Over the decades a dozen tiny frayed areas—"pinpoint losses"—had opened up in the canvas's weave. These defects, although barely visible, had to be fixed so that there was no risk of them opening wider during the cleaning or in the future. For this purpose she would apply a dab of gelatin adhesive to each spot to firm up the edges of the hole and hold them in place; a restorer's version of Super Glue.

She took a couple of gulps of coffee, set the cardboard cup a safe distance away, used distilled water to mix a ten percent solution of the adhesive, picked up one of her thinnest brushes, and got to work, starting in the upper left corner, a dimly gleaming sconce on the wall behind the sitter. Except for the movements of her arm and the occasional emergence of the tip of her tongue, she remained stone-still.

In an hour it was done. Before she could go on to the next step, the adhesive needed to set, so it was a good time to get started on the Eakins; one of his later boxing scenes. And after that the Mary Cassatt still life, which would probably be the trickiest.

And so the day passed, without incident, without trauma. Without, in fact, speaking more than a few desultory sentences to anyone. When she took a mug of coffee and a couple of packaged oatmeal cookies out to the atrium for a late-afternoon break, she found Jerry and the curators, minus Prentice, having a break of their own around a couple of pulled-together picnic tables. Responding to their amiable waves, she sat down with them at the end of a bench.

Alfie Wellington was expressing worry about a visit the following afternoon from someone who'd called the museum, saying she was sure she'd found a drawing by Gherardo Cibo while going through her father's house after his death. With Prentice away for a couple of days, Mrs. B had asked Alfie to take a look when she came in with it for an "expert" opinion.

"And I never even heard of the man," Alfie moaned. "Everything I know about him I learned from Wikipedia, and that was this morning. How am I supposed to tell her if it's the real thing or not?"

"Doesn't matter a whole lot," Jerry said. "The only place *anybody* ever heard of him is Italy. Worth twenty thousand, tops, probably a lot less."

"That's not the point, Jerry. It's important to the woman, you know?"

"I know something about Cibo," Alix volunteered. "Sixteenth century, Genoese, worked a lot in brown ink and watercolors. Rocky landscapes, that kind of thing?"

Alfie turned to her with hope in his eyes. "Yes, exactly, that's him. Could you maybe help me out then? Talk to her with me?"

"I really don't know that much, but if you think I could help, sure, maybe I could."

"Bless you, child! Tomorrow at two? No?" he added, seeing a change in her expression. "Bad time?"

"It's only that I hoped to get away tomorrow afternoon. I'll be ready to take a real break and get out by then, and I was planning on taking the tram up to Mt. Jacinto. But if you really—"

"No, that's all right. I'll ask her to leave it with us until the next day."

"That'd be great."

Alix had joined them a little reluctantly, thinking they'd be buzzing about Clark's murder, but she was happy to see that that subject had apparently been exhausted. Word of her having been attacked, however, reported in yesterday's paper, had gotten around. Still, they were considerate of her feelings and privacy; no intrusive questions (even from Madge), just friendly expressions of concern and sympathy, and a few general expressions of worried wonderment at the series of drastic events besetting their small, obscure, arty coterie. After fifteen minutes Alix went back to her workplace, where she finally consumed those two oatmeal cookies while sitting back and studying the Eakins.

All in all, it was a long, peaceful day of solitary, productive, and deeply satisfying work. Just before she left for the Villa Louisa, Richard, Mrs. B's secretary, sent her a typically formal e-mail informing her that she was invited to a seven o'clock reception the next evening at "Palm Springs's finest restaurant," Le Vallauris, to celebrate Prentice's appointment as senior curator, and she was welcome to bring a companion. The only other thing that took her away from the paintings, besides a couple of quick meals, was a brief trip to Mammoth Auto Rentals to trade her compact for a Subaru hatchback. (She realized she'd be hauling things back and forth to the museum; thus the hatchback.)

And tomorrow she was hoping for an even nicer day. A little more close work, demanding but satisfying, in the morning, followed by a bracing dose of mountain snow in the afternoon.

· · ·

And just like that, he had a plan.

He would have to make sure he wasn't seen, of course, but who was going to see him at three o'clock in the morning in an unlit parking lot?

If anybody was around, he'd just wait them out. The whole thing would take maybe five minutes, during most of which he'd be out of sight under the car anyway.

The plan wasn't foolproof; far from it. It was, in fact, a pretty iffy proposition, but it was worth a shot. He thought of it as something like a first offer: great if it worked, but if it didn't he had plenty of time to come up with something else. He had come to feel a lot more secure and confident in himself over the last few days. Clark had been killed last Friday. Here it was Monday, and as far as he could tell, the police had gotten nowhere. From what the papers said, they were still treating it as an accidental hit-and-run. And why would they not?

The big advantages of his plan were that he'd be miles away when it happened, so that he would be spared the nastiness of it, and that there was no conceivable way that it could possibly be tied to him. The big problem was that nobody was going to mistake this one for an accident. It couldn't be anything but an attempt at murder, but even that didn't worry him. The police were bound to proceed on the supremely logical assumption that whoever had attacked her in her room just a few days earlier was responsible.

And that would turn out to be as dead as any dead end could be.

20

In the bustling heart of seventeenth-century Antwerp stood the workshop of Peter Paul Rubens, one of the few painters of that time (or any other time) who didn't find it necessary to die in order to become famous. So famous, in fact, and so successful that the portrait commissions pouring in were more than any one man, even the prolific Rubens, could handle. His solution was to enlist his dozens of apprentices in the task. The newer ones would do the prep work—the sizing, the priming; the more experienced ones would rough in the "easy" parts of the picture—the background, the furniture, the simpler parts of the clothing; and Maestro Rubens would step in to do the hands, the face . . . and, of course, the signature. Even in his own time, his studio was sometimes referred to as a "factory."

Today, four hundred years later, a smaller but remarkably similar operation was taking place in Seattle, in a handsome loft on the top floor of a not-so-handsome warehouse in the gritty industrial district south of downtown. The warehouse's lower floors housed the Venezia Trading Company, the primary business of Geoffrey London, Alix's father, and on those two floors Geoff, Tiny, and two other employees filled orders from hotel chains for cheap, cheaply framed prints of sunsets, card-playing dogs, and eighteenth-century naval battles, "Louis XVI" lamps with metal loops welded to the bases so they could be bolted to night tables, and, naturally, that perennial favorite, the Aztec-style synthetic onyx soap dish.

The third-floor loft was something else altogether. In addition to providing Geoff's modernized, sleekly furnished living quarters, it included a studio in which Rubens's methods still lived. Apprentices (aka Geoff's employees) laid out the basic elements of paintings that were assigned to them, and the maestro (aka Geoff) applied the finishing touches. This was no school, however; this was the locus of a new business venture that he had begun as a sideline, but which was now showing signs of seriously taking off. Geoff had hit on a remarkable way to capitalize both on his renown as an eminent restorer and his greater fame as a notorious forger, in both of which he took equal pride. And to do it legally.

"Genuine Fakes by Geoffrey London," was the slogan of his website, MasterArtForger.com, which promised that:

> *whether you would like to own your own scrupulously reproduced, favorite painting by Renoir or Picasso, or a 'new' one specially painted for you, Genuine Fakes will be happy to provide it. Or how about a portrait of your spouse 'done by' van Gogh or Modigliani?*
>
> *All paintings are signed by Mr. London and are framed in a manner appropriate to the artist and the time. If you prefer your older paintings aged and crackled, this can be done for a small additional fee.*

Even with prices that ran from five to fifteen thousand dollars, Geoff, like Rubens, had all the business he could handle.

As it happened, the painting on which he was at work this morning was to be a "Rubens" in the making, the nearly finished portrait of the next wife (number four) of one Kazimierz Czechowics, an elderly Polish shoe manufacturer who was also something of an art connoisseur. Czechowics had requested that the portrait be done in the manner and even in the scandalously scoop-necked attire of Ruben's bosomy *Portrait of Susanna Fourment*, with particular attention to Kazimierz's fiancée's cleavage (of which he had proudly provided a loving photograph).

Czechowics had bought the $15,000 full-service package, which meant that, as far as possible, the techniques and materials were to be those that Rubens himself would have employed. And so one of Geoff's newer workers had cut and assembled the oak planks that would be the backing, had applied a chalk and animal-skin-glue ground, and then covered it with dark brown primer. (Whereas almost all of the Old Masters used white primer, which would then be allowed to show through where the artist wanted lighter shades, Rubens often did it the other way around, using light pigments for the highlights and allowing the primer to show through where he wanted darker colors.)

Tiny had then taken over, using paint thinned with turpentine (another Rubens innovation) and then painting the blue-gray background and the less detailed areas of the fabrics.

The rest was Geoff's responsibility. He was now applying highlights to the woman's forehead, using a slender sable brush to lay down thin, parallel, side-by-side strokes with a mix of white and Naples yellow. Emulating Rubens's even, masterful flesh-tone brush strokes was the most demanding part of the entire job, and Geoff was uncomfortably aware that his hand wasn't as steady as it once was. He could feel the sweat pooling under his arms. It was a relief to know that once he got through this, all that was left was the application of a few red and blue accents around the eyes. After that it was back to his "apprentices" for the resin-oil varnish, and—

The phone in the living area rang; his private number, known only to a few. He made an irritated noise and jerked his head, but took care not to jiggle the brush. He kept his focus on the work. This close to finishing, there was no way—

The answering machine came on. "Geoff, this is Sophie over at SAM. I've got some interesting material on Pollock to show you—"

He threw down the brush and ran for the phone.

"—that I think you'll find—"

He grabbed the phone. "I'll be right over."

"Meet me in the library upstairs."

· · ·

Twenty-five minutes later Geoff hurried through the Second Avenue doors to SAM, as the locals familiarly referred to the Seattle Art Museum. He chose this entry instead of the main one on First Avenue to spare himself the stomach upset of having to look at the grim Hammering Man, the fifty-foot-high sculpture of dead-black metal that "adorned" the front of the museum but would have been more at home on display in the Gulag. Once, during the night, some pranksters had attached a huge ball and chain to the ankle of the somber figure, but they were quickly removed. In Geoff's opinion, it would have been a good idea to leave them there, because then at least the thing would have had the virtue of being funny. But the powers that be didn't agree with him, and the big guy continued to hammer slowly, clumsily, maddeningly away, unencumbered by ball or chain, every fifteen seconds of every livelong day (except Labor Day, when they gave him his once-a-year holiday). Since Geoff couldn't do anything about it, he had decided his best course was to avoid looking at the thing. It was a decision that had served him well.

He took the elevator to the fifth floor, where he found Sophie Chiu awaiting him in the art research library. Sophie, the associate curator for Modern and Contemporary Art, was a constitutionally anxious person, but the buoyant level of enthusiasm that went along with it made her a delight to speak to and a source of inspiration. Bird-like and darting, with painful-looking, chewed-down fingernails, she was quick to offer help and quick to supply it, and the fastest-talking person he knew. She was sitting at a table near a south-facing window, with photographs, stapled printed material, and opened periodicals spread out in front of her. Among them were a couple of the pictures Geoff had given her of the Brethwaite's Pollock, which he had taken when he was wandering around with Tiny, out of Alix's sight.

"Geoffrey, come!" she whisper-shouted at him as soon as he walked in. Sophie's favorite tense was the imperative, and she used it well; a commanding person despite her size.

He hadn't quite sat down before she was waving a sheet of paper in his face. "Look!"

He saw five or six scrawled, apparently enlarged signatures covering the page. "Pollock signatures, are they?" he said.

"Yes, and don't you dare give me that famous dubious look of yours, or use that tone either. These are the answer to your problem." She whapped the sheet with the flat of her hand, bringing a sternly disapproving look from the bearded man at the next table. Sophie brought her "whisper" down a notch. "I looked at about ten million 'scholarly' monographs on how to recognize a genuine Pollock—factural dimensionality, linear elegance, compositional centricity, blah, blah, blah. Opinions all, subjective and unconfirmable. But this"—another whap, another frown from the next table, this time unnoticed by Sophie—"this analysis of his signature—"

Sophie wasn't easy to break in on, but Geoff finally managed it. "Sophie, tell me that you're not really talking about handwriting analysis. *Graphology?* Please."

"No, I'm talking about handwriting *identification*, and that's a whole 'nother ball of fish."

Geoff smiled. Among the pleasures of conversation with Sophie were her occasional malapropisms. "Sorry," he mumbled. "Please continue."

"Trust me, Geoffrey, this is *science*. And so for that matter is graphology when it's the real thing. There are quack doctors too, you know, but that doesn't prove medicine in general is a scam. Honestly, I don't know how anyone can be so judgmental about things he doesn't know anything about."

"Perhaps, but permit me to—"

"Just listen for five minutes for once in your life, will you? No, better yet, *read* for five minutes." She handed him a photocopied article, and put a finger on the middle of the second page. "Don't bother with the beginning. You can start here."

"No, I will read the entire article," Geoff declared, "even if it should take me *ten* minutes. You should consider it a personal tribute to my confidence in your judgment." He settled himself to read. With frequent breaks to glance at the page of signatures and compare it with the signature on his own photograph of the Brethwaite Pollock, it took him exactly eleven-and-a-half minutes, at the end of which he raised his head, looking pensive and impressed. "I am a changed man, Sophie. You're right; this is meaty stuff."

In the article, a forensic handwriting expert named Patricia Siegel described how she'd evaluated an earlier questionable Pollock by comparing its signature with those on a wide range of undisputed Pollocks. Using photos of these undisputed signatures, she cogently showed how the great variability, the erratic "irritability" of his stroke, while seeming at first to confuse the issue, was itself an important identifying element. Pollock's stroke was *reliably* uneven, with jerky, spontaneous movements, flooded letters, stops and starts, and blurred lines. The signature on the suspect painting, by contrast, while superficially resembling Pollock's, was carefully "drawn," the stroke pressure evenly applied throughout (indicating painstaking forethought and execution—the antithesis of a natural, spontaneous signature).

There was more, much more: In the authentic signatures, the *k* in "Jackson" was always just a little smaller than the *k* in "Pollock";

the height of the *J* in "Jackson" was relatively short compared to the *k* in the same word; and on and on, little unconscious tics that even a careful forger was unlikely to note. Pollock himself could hardly have been aware of them.

The whole thing was brief, direct, and extremely convincing. Geoff took a final look at his own photograph, held it next to the ones that illustrated the article, and raised his head. "Hmp," he said thoughtfully.

"So what do you think?" Sophie asked.

"What do I think? I thank my lucky stars this kind of analysis wasn't available in the bad old days. I wouldn't have had a very long career as a forger."

"You didn't have a very long career as a forger."

"True," he said with a smile, "and a good thing too, I should say."

"But I meant, what do you think about the painting, your painting, Alix's painting?"

"I think this lady's on to something, Sophie. It's a fake. The signature's false."

"That's what I thought too." She sat back with a look of satisfaction. "So tell me what happens next."

"Next I copy this article and e-mail it to Alix. Can I take it with me?"

"Not necessary. Give it to me. I'll have it scanned into a PDF and sent to your phone. And you can pop it over to her while you're right here."

"Oh, I don't think there's that much of a hurry. I can just   "

But she had already snatched it from his hand and was on her way to the door, waving the article over her head. "A rolling stone gathers no moths."

21

Deet-deet-da-dah-dah.

Alix had just gotten to the museum when her ring tone sounded, and once again, it made her jump. The thing was, her cell phone was rarely working because she almost never remembered to turn it on. Or more honestly, because she almost always remembered *not* to turn it on. Since the majority of her calls involved technical things, she knew it made sense to be able to check on whatever the subject was before attempting to wax wise on it. So she preferred to let the device save them up for her and then to return the calls in a bunch once a day. Or so.

But yesterday she'd neglected to turn it off after calling Chris to make sure she was up and ready to go to the airport, and so it had remained on.

Deet-deet-da-dah-dah. The high-priority signal. She was opening the phone when Geoff's voice came on. "Alix, I've e-mailed you—"

"Hi, Geoff, I'm here."

"Ah, good. I e-mailed you some material a few minutes ago—"

"Oh, I haven't checked my e-mail yet this morning."

"I'm shocked. This is one you *will* want to check, however. It pertains to the authenticity—or the lack thereof—of the Pollock."

"I thought I asked you not to—"

"Well, and so you did, but I didn't see what harm it could do for me to exercise my initiative a little, and I think you'll be pleased that I did."

Indeed she was. Once Geoff explained what he'd learned from Sophie Chiu, Alix knew at once they were on to something, and once she read the article and looked at the photos, she was convinced. The handwriting deductions didn't quite make it to the level of *proof*; outside of chemical or physical forensic evidence, art authentication at base was always a question of human judgment—and therefore always arguable. (In the world of art evaluation, it was a given that what *can* be argued, *will* be argued.) And even physical or chemical evidence didn't speak for itself. It had to be interpreted. Human judgment again.

According to Clark, there *had* been a forensic analysis in which the painting's authenticity had been firmly established, but she'd never seen it for herself, so she didn't know how trustworthy it was. It was past time, she thought, to bring this all to Mrs. B's attention—not something she looked forward to—but first, she wanted to look at the painting for herself one more time. She printed the article to take with her and circled around to the next level (to get from anywhere to anywhere in the Brethwaite, you had no choice but to travel in a circular arc), where the picture was displayed, wondering for the hundredth time what it was that she had seen in it that had made her suspicious in the first place. Or had her connoisseur's eye now evolved to the point where she could intuit falsity in a *signature*? No, impossible. The propensity for a talent might be innate, but to amount to anything it needed to be honed by experience and training, and when it came to signatures she had none of either. She barely registered them. Until she'd seen the photos Geoff sent, she'd had no idea what Pollock's signature looked like. If you had asked her yesterday whether *Untitled 1952* was unsigned as well as untitled (or was *Untitled* a title, technically?), she couldn't have said—

She stopped so abruptly she came close to toppling over her own feet. In front of the painting, a man stood quietly with his back to her. Tall, erect, square-shouldered, unmistakably handsome even when seen from behind.

Ted.

If anything, a year without sight or sound of him had intensified the effect he had on her, and coming on him so suddenly, so unexpectedly, had almost knocked her legs from under her. The feelings that now roiled in her head were muddled and contradictory. She was thrilled to see him, yes. But she was humiliated too, and angry—did he think she was some fluttery, fainting Victorian heroine who needed a big, brave hero to come and rescue her from danger? Damn him.

She was annoyed with Jamie too, for telling him about what had been happening. Why didn't anyone pay attention to what she asked of them—especially what she asked them *not* to do? First her father and the Pollock (she thought unreasonably), and now Jamie. Anger notwithstanding, she yearned to run to Ted, felt physically pulled toward him, and yet she knew that, had he not already seen her, she would have turned and run the other way. She wanted him there and she wanted him not there.

"Ted—what are you *doing* here?" It wasn't something she consciously decided to say. It just popped out, so charged with anger, surprise, excitement, and God knew what else that he jumped, then spun to face her.

"Alix! I was just . . . I'm here about this picture . . . to talk to Ms. Brethwaite . . . it's a case I'm working on . . . it's got nothing to do with you . . . well, except tangentially, of course . . ."

She couldn't believe it; the cool-as-a-cucumber Ted Ellesworth, Mr. Unflappable, was *flustered*—every bit as much as she was. But why should *he* be flustered? Was it that he was simply embarrassed to see her face-to-face after so baldly going out of his way to avoid her all this time? Had he hoped to get in and out of Palm Springs without running into her?

In any case, he recovered his wits before she did. "I think I'd better start one more time," he said with an apologetic smile. "Hello, Alix, it's nice to see you again. How are you?"

"I'm fine, Ted. It's nice to see you too."

Did he feel as stupid as she did? They sounded like a couple of characters in a dusty old novel of manners. Now what?

They had moved closer while speaking and now stood looking awkwardly at one another. Alix was afraid that he was going to offer to shake hands, but he did better than that, although not that much better. He placed one hand on each shoulder and gave her an almost-hug; bodies almost touching, cheeks almost touching, but nothing *really* touching, the kind of hug two reserved and proper friends might share on unexpectedly running into each other. But, oh, my, it felt wonderful. For an instant her cheek brushed the rough fabric of his tweedy sport coat, and she smelled newly mown hay. And there was just a hint of the cedary aftershave she had forgotten all about but now remembered with a bittersweet pang.

"Alix," he said, releasing her (after a moment longer than necessary, or was that wishful thinking?), "I'm due for an appointment with Mrs. Brethwaite right now, but I hope we can get together and catch up later on."

I hope so too! "I should have some free time this afternoon," she said offhandedly. "Perhaps—no, wait, you're going to talk to her about this painting? The Pollock?"

"Among other things, yes."

"You think it's a fake?"

"I think it might be."

"I think it *is*. And I was just on my way to talk to her about it myself."

"Really?" He turned to study the painting again. "What makes you think so?"

"Admittedly, only a gut feeling to start with—"

"Never mind 'only.' I know about your gut feelings."

"—but then just this morning my fa—that is, I found this study of Pollock's signature—" She thought it best not to insert Geoff into the conversation. Ted still had a few reservations about him. (Understandable, she thought; she had a few herself.) "—that compares his—"

"Wait, hold it, why don't you come with me? This fits exactly into what I need to talk to her about."

"Good idea. She's not going to like hearing this. I could use some protection. She can be a pretty scary old lady."

He leaned close, tapped his jacket, and whispered confidentially, "No fear. I'm packing."

. . .

"I'm sorry, Agent Ellesworth, she'll be delayed a bit, perhaps another fifteen minutes," said Mrs. B's secretary, Richard. "She asked me to apologize on her behalf. If you'd care to have a seat—"

"Why don't we wait in my office instead?" Alix suggested to Ted. "You can give us a call when she's ready, Richard."

Richard looked dubiously at her. "I'm sorry, Ms. London. The director was quite clear. Her appointment is with Agent Ellesworth. If you would like to schedule—"

"Alix will be attending too," Ted said. "At my request."

The corners of Richard's mouth turned very slightly down. "Of course. As you wish. However, Ms. London, your 'office,' as you refer to it, will be in use. The security staff will be conferencing there. It *is* the conference room, you know."

"Do you know, I believe you may have mentioned that before, but thank you for reminding me. We'll be out in the central courtyard, then."

· · ·

"Let me explain what I'm doing here," Ted said as they sat down opposite each other at one of the picnic tables. "You're familiar with Lord & Keen?"

"I know who they are, of course. Major New York dealer. They specialize in American Modern, if I'm not mistaken. I think I read they're in some kind of trouble, didn't I?"

"They are, indeed. Several suits have been filed against them, and unless I'm wildly wrong they're going to be in a lot more trouble before very long. They will be if I have anything to do with it."

The prominent ninety-year-old dealership had been the subject of an investigation for several months, he explained. Evidence was mounting that they had knowingly passed off as many as two dozen forgeries of works by artists like Rothko, O'Keeffe, DeKooning—

"And Pollock," Alix said.

"And Pollock. This particular one, in fact, was bought from them."

"And so you're here to check it out, see if it's the real thing or not?"

"Alix, if what I wanted was an opinion on a painting's authenticity, there's somebody else I'd be far more likely to rely on, especially considering that she happened to be right here in the vicinity."

"Thank you, I'm flattered, but why exactly *are* you here then? Not that I'm not happy to see you, because I am. Or was that a double negative?"

Something about his attitude or his bearing had cheered her up and loosened her tongue. He was . . . friendly, maybe more than friendly. Was it possible that things between them could still be repaired? Had he perhaps forgotten about her performance at that wretched lunch or at least come around to putting it into perspective, seeing it as a sort of temporary, post-traumatic reaction to her nearly getting killed in Albania? That was certainly how she'd come to look at the way she'd behaved, and the way she planned to put it to him if/when the time was ever ripe. She realized she was suddenly feeling absurdly happy.

"I'm glad to see you too, believe me," Ted said, "but if you want to know why I'm here, maybe you should stop asking questions and just listen and let me talk for a couple of minutes?"

She propped her chin on her clasped fingers, elbows on the wooden table. "Talk away. I'm all ears."

Apparently, all of the fakes had been done by one man: a twenty-nine-year-old Taiwanese immigrant, believe it or not, who had been here illegally for four years, lived in a no-deposit, $75-a-week boarding-house (who knew such things still existed?) near the Newark docks, and spoke little English. This frightened man had cooperated when first interviewed, but all he could tell them was that he'd been paid a thousand dollars cash plus expenses for each painting, by a person whose name he didn't know. He claimed he had no idea where the paintings went and Ted had believed him. He had disappeared after the first interview, and there had never been a second. Unfortunately, a full list of his fakes hadn't yet been compiled.

"You don't think he was—?" Alix said.

"Killed? Yeah, maybe he was killed or hidden away, or there could have been some kind of accident. But remember, he was an illegal, he was scared, and when the FBI started showing some interest, he disappeared. Not exactly unusual."

Lord & Keen themselves had at first declared that all the paintings in question had received their usual thorough review before being offered for sale; they had been submitted to recognized authorities who had confirmed they were what they were purported to be. Then later, when two of the paintings—a Whistler and an O'Keeffe—had subsequently been determined to be fakes, the dealership had claimed to be as aggrieved as the buyers and had immediately taken the pictures back and made full reimbursements. They had also removed the "authorities" they'd used from their list of consultants.

Ted didn't buy any of it, and more recently, as the net around them tightened, Lord & Keen had been refusing to speak with the FBI at all and they had hired a top-notch criminal law firm to keep it that way. Ted and his team, undeterred, were now looking into things from the other end of the chain, slowly going through the list of institutions and individuals that had bought major works from them in the last several years, and contacting them one by one to get whatever information they could about their purchases. The Brethwaite, having bought the Pollock from them, was on the list, but Ted hadn't expected to get to Palm Springs for several more weeks.

"And yet here you are," Alix said.

"Sure, because of what happened with Clark Calder."

"So Jamie told you, after all," she said tightly. "I assume she also told you he attacked me a couple of nights ago."

"She did." Ted eyed her. "And this annoys you."

"Yes, after I explicitly asked her not to!"

"And what exactly is so annoying about her telling me that somebody attacked you?"

"What's so annoying about it! It's just that I expected . . . that I thought . . . that I didn't want you to think you had to . . . well, that I . . . Rats," she finished, scrambling for words and trying to remember just why she'd been so adamant about keeping him out of her life. She certainly wasn't sorry to have him here beside her now.

"I see. Well, that certainly clears things up," he said, looking her steadily in the eye. She fought to keep her own gaze level. "But I'm a little annoyed myself, Alix. In the first place, I would have thought that if somebody tried to kill you, you might have let me know, don't you think? Regardless of what you happen to think of me personally—"

What I think of you personally. So the things she'd said at that lunch *were* still on his mind. Well, what else could she realistically expect?

"—I do have some pretty good resources at my command."

"But it had nothing to do with what I think of you personally," she blurted, screwing up her courage. Here was her opening, a chance to explain, to apologize, to get a start on making things right. "In fact, if I'm going to be honest, my feelings toward you—"

He wasn't even listening. "And second, I didn't know anything about what was going on down here until yesterday. Jamie didn't tell me until after we heard about him getting killed."

This struck her as dishonest. "Oh, really? You knew about that? You follow the local news from Palm Springs, do you?"

"No, we don't," he said coolly, "but we've been following the news about Clark Calder ever since we connected him to the purchase of a major Lord & Keen painting back when he was with a museum in Austin."

"Oh," she said lamely. When would she learn that trying to be snide never worked for her? She always wound up with her foot in her mouth.

"In fact, it was the fake Whistler I was talking about a minute ago."

She thought about that. "So . . . assuming this one is a fake too, it's the second time he's been at least circumstantially involved with Lord & Keen in a forgery?"

"A lot more than circumstantially. He was the senior curator on the Whistler as well, and the one who was primarily responsible for arranging the sale."

"I believe that was the case here too," Alix said.

"It *was* the case. I talked to Mrs. Brethwaite on the phone last night and she confirmed it."

"Wow."

"And now he's been killed."

She nodded.

"And a few nights ago he tried to kill you. Aside from any concern I might have for you—and whether you believe it or not, I do have considerable concern—it was obvious that something was going on with the guy and it was time for me to check it out."

Believe it or not, I do have considerable concern? That got Alix's mind reversing direction and taking off in a dozen new ones, but now wasn't the time to pursue them. "Well, it certainly looks to me as if he was the one who broke in, but I don't have any evidence. And the police don't agree with me."

"Oh, it was him, all right, and the police do agree. Before I came here I spent half an hour with the detective working on it—"

"Jake Cruz."

"Right, good guy. They came up with some prints on the plastic shoe cover your man left behind, and they matched the ones on an old employment record of Calder's. The blood on the inside of the mask is undergoing DNA testing too, but with the fingerprints, it's a foregone conclusion."

"So I was right," she mused. "Ted, I still don't understand how you got here so fast. Clark was killed the night before last. You just heard about it yesterday. Yet here you are, you've already talked to Jake Cruz—"

"Red-eye from Dulles. Flew all night, got here at the break of dawn. My eyeballs don't always look like this, you know."

Your eyeballs are beautiful, she thought inanely, barely suppressing an idiotic little grin.

They turned at the sound of one of the glass double doors that opened into the courtyard.

"Mrs. B will see you now," said Richard, doing his usual Jeeves impersonation.

22

"And that's about where we stand on things, Lillian," Ted said, having gone over what he'd just been telling Alix. Astonishingly, Mrs. B had asked him to call her Lillian inside of two minutes, a privilege that no one else at the museum had been accorded. Not even Clark. Not even (as far as Alix knew) Prentice.

They were in the director's office, Mrs. B looking tiny behind her big oak desk, but no less raptorlike; a sort of mini-bird-of-prey. She was wearing another mannish outfit: a black, buttoned-up Nehru jacket over a stark white shirt with a band collar. It made her look like a priest—but not the mellow Bing Crosby kind. More along the lines, say, of Torquemada.

Alix and Ted were across the entire breadth of the room from her, primly seated at opposite ends of a heavily brocaded Second Empire sofa that could have held four.

"And you think our Pollock is one of these forgeries," Mrs. B said without expression.

"At this point I'm not sure what I think about that. I believe Alix has some new information for us, but let's save it for a minute." They were so far from each other that they were practically shouting.

"Bringing us more good news, no doubt, eh, Miss London? I can hardly wait." Mrs. B had swung her head to focus those sharp, hooded eyes on Alix.

Alix felt like a butterfly pinned to a specimen chart and resented it. "I'm simply doing what any honest—" she began hotly, but Ted interceded.

"How did you meet Clark Calder, Lillian?"

"It was at a conference of private museum directors a few months ago. Clark had just resigned from the Austin Museum of American Art, and he was full of exciting new concepts that I thought could help us get out of the financial bind we'd gotten ourselves into. And bring us into the twenty-first century at the same time. We're rather a fusty old bunch here, you see, and set in our ways. And I include myself in that. Clark . . ." She shook her head, thinking back. "Clark seemed like a much-needed breath of fresh air at the time."

"Did you check with the Austin museum about his tenure there?"

"Of course I did."

"And?"

"And I received a letter from their personnel director giving the date he began, the positions he held, and the date he resigned. Nothing more—some sort of privacy agreement they have with their employees. So I based my decision on my personal judgment, which, until that time, at any rate, had usually been quite reliable."

"Austin doesn't have a privacy agreement with its employees, Lillian—just with Clark," Ted said. "A mutual non-disclosure agreement. He doesn't talk about them, they don't talk about him. And yes, technically he did resign—but it wasn't voluntary."

It was his recommending and overseeing the purchase of the fake Whistler that had gotten him into trouble. The museum was greatly embarrassed when the painting was proven to be a fake, of course, and they were anxious to put the affair behind them. The picture itself was gone—Lord & Keen had taken it back—but they wanted Clark gone too, and with as little fuss as possible. So he agreed to resign "without prejudice"—and with a small financial settlement—and both sides had signed on to the non-disclosure agreement.

"Good heavens," said Mrs. B. "You'd think they'd have told me."

"They couldn't. They were bound by the agreement."

"Nonsense. They told you, didn't they?"

"Sure, but things are different when it comes to a criminal investigation."

"Of course they are," Mrs. B snapped. "Don't you think I know that? But when it's something of this magnitude—"

"My God," said Alix.

They both swiveled to stare at her. Four eyebrows went up in unison.

"Ted," she said. "That fake Whistler at the museum in Austin—do you happen to remember what it was a picture of?"

"Yeah, I think I remember—where are you going with this, Alix?"

"Was it one of his Nocturnes?"

"I believe it was; one of the ones with the fireworks. At that park in London. In Knightsbridge, I think."

"No, Chelsea. Cremorne Gardens. My God."

"That's right, Cremorne Gardens. How do you know that?"

"My G—"

"If she says it one more time," Mrs. B rasped, "I will strangle her right here and now, with my own hands, I swear it."

"Never mind, I'll do it for you," Ted said. "Alix, damn it, what's going on?"

Alix spoke dully, stunned by what she'd just realized. "I know why Clark was writing those reviews."

"What?" Mrs. B asked.

"I know why he tried to kill me."

"*What?*" Mrs. B was two-thirds out of her chair, her palms flat on the desk.

Alix had forgotten that the director was out of the loop when it came to the recent determinations that Clark had been both the blogger and the intruder—she wouldn't even have known about Alix's suspicions—so this took a few minutes of explanation, at the end of which Mrs. B flopped back into her chair, looking totally at a loss for once in her life, but then after a second she called: "Richard! We need some coffee in here!"

Bustling sounds in the outer room indicated that he had heard and was obeying.

"The thing is," Alix went on, still a bit dreamily, "he lost his job at Austin because of me."

"Alix," Ted said, "that was five months ago, long before you even knew who he was."

"Yes, that's right, but I *did* know—I still know—Millie Somers, one of the associate directors. She's an old friend from Harvard, and when I was in Austin on something else six or seven months ago, I stopped in to see her and she showed me around the place. Well—it's getting to be a familiar story now—and that Whistler Nocturne struck me the wrong way and I said something to Millie about it. From what you've been telling us, inside of a month or two, the picture was gone and so was Clark."

"And you think it was on account of your comments," Ted said thoughtfully.

"I know it was. Millie told me so. Well, she didn't tell me about firing anyone, but on the strength of what I'd said, they had some forensic testing done, and it turned out that one of the pigments was titanium white—"

"Which wasn't developed until what, the 1940s?" Ted said.

"Nineteen thirty, actually, but it still eliminates James McNeil Whistler as the painter unless he did it thirty years after he died."

Richard came in with the coffee and set it on the desk. These weren't the thick, white open-source mugs that hung on a pegboard in the break room, or the very slightly finer ones used for staff meetings. These were slender, elegant, willow-patterned cups, so thin-walled they were translucent. Alix was afraid she was going to break one just by picking it up. Matching saucers came with them, as fragile as the cups.

"So you think those reviews were . . . what?" Ted asked Alix. "Revenge? Spite?"

"That's exactly what I think. I got him in trouble, he wanted to bring me down too." She shook her head. "And I didn't even know he existed."

Mrs. B was very slowly stirring two packets of Sweet'N Low into her cup. She seemed really shaken. "But to try to *kill* you? It was all over and done with . . . it just seems . . ."

"No, not over that," Alix said. "Over the Pollock. He knew I thought that was a fake too. He thought I was going to do it to him *again*."

"Cost him his job, you mean?" She shook her head. "Let me be frank. The Brethwaite is at best a second-tier museum in a small city in the middle of the desert. I don't find it persuasive that he would have resorted to murder in order to keep his job here. There must have been more than that to it."

"There was," Ted said. "This would have been the second time he'd engineered the sale of a fake, an extremely expensive fake, from Lord & Keen. He had to know there was an investigation going on, and he'd know that a fake Pollock would bring us down on him like a ton of bricks. There's no way it could be an innocent coincidence. He was working with them, he was part of the operation, and he knew he'd be going down with them. Is that what you were thinking, Alix?"

"I hadn't really thought it through that far yet, but yes, I do think that."

"Lillian," Ted said, "a few minutes ago you said Calder seemed like a breath of fresh air *at the time*. Did that imply that your opinion of him changed later on?"

Mrs. B seemed to hesitate.

Alix jumped up. "This is none of my business. I'll wait outside until you want me again."

Mrs. B waved her back into her seat. "Nonsense, you sit yourself right back down. I have no objection to your hearing this." She raised her cup and seemed surprised to find that it was empty. "Richard!" she called, "We could use a warm-up."

Alix had had only a couple of sips and Ted's cup was still brim-full. They both refused fresh cups. Mrs. B used the three or four seconds it took for her secretary to appear with the pot, and the few more that it took to stir in sweetener, to put her thoughts in order—or to decide what to say and what not to say.

"He *was* a breath of fresh air," she began after inhaling the coffee's fragrance and sipping, "and he had ideas that had never been heard in these parts, ideas that made sense and still do. But . . ." The cup was carefully placed on its saucer. "But, as attractive as he was, he wore on one after a few months, you see."

After about two minutes, in my case, Alix thought.

"He was always . . . what is the phrase? . . . pushing the envelope, overstepping his limits. What he was trying to do was important, but his attitude needlessly offended the staff and had begun to get on my nerves too." She laughed, the first time Alix had heard her do it; a funny little old person's *hee-hee* that didn't fit her at all. "Possibly, these aren't the sort of things I should be saying while the police are still hunting for his murderer."

"Oh, I don't think Detective Cruz suspects *you*, Lillian," Ted said with a friendly chuckle of his own. With Ted it was impossible to tell if he was being genuinely friendly or was playing her along, cop-style. And why not the latter, Alix suddenly thought. Why *wouldn't* Jake have her on his suspect list? Whatever close relationship she and Clark might have had in the past had obviously soured. Alix had seen that when Mrs. B had cut him down to size on his graphic novel idea, and now Mrs. B herself had said as much.

"Alix," Ted said, "perhaps this is the time for you to tell us about the Pollock."

Alix did, showing them the illustrations of Pollock's real signature and the fake ones, and she could see that both of them were impressed—and, in Mrs. B's case, also angry and a little sick.

"If you had your suspicions from the start," she said sternly, "don't you think you should have come to me with them?"

"I do now, Mrs. B—"

"Oh, call me Lillian, will you, for Christ's sake."

"Thank you—but at the time that's all they were, suspicions. More gut-level than brain-level, so I went to Clark instead. He said he'd be setting up a meeting for me with you, but first he wanted to gather the records for me to look at—the forensic testing report, the—"

"What forensic testing report? There never was an independent forensic assessment. We just went with Lord & Keen's evaluations."

After all of Clark's lies, one would think that one more wouldn't surprise her, but this Alix hadn't anticipated. This was yet another reason he wanted her dead and wanted it done in such a hurry. It had been on Thursday that he'd promised to show her the forensic report in a few days—the following Tuesday (tomorrow, actually; how astonishingly much had happened in so few days)—and he knew he couldn't deliver because it didn't exist. So she had to go before Tuesday came around. He'd made his attempt on her that very Thursday night and had had no chance to try again because he was on the other end of a murder himself the very next night; a successful one, this time.

A quick glance and a dip of the chin from Ted showed that he was thinking the same thing. The sharp-eyed Lillian spotted both glances but misread them.

"I know what you're thinking," she said. "What kind of ninny would spend a fortune on a piece of art without being absolutely certain that it was the real thing? At this moment I am having exactly the same thought."

"If it makes you feel any better," Ted said, "the museum in Austin didn't do any independent forensic checking on their Whistler either— not until Alix showed up and alerted them. It happens all the time, Lillian. I don't have any statistics to back me up, but I'd bet that most art purchases, individual and institutional, are made without getting an independent forensic lab in on the act. Especially when the seller is somebody as reputable—as supposedly reputable—as Lord & Keen."

"That may be, but knowing that others were equally stupid does not make me feel any better. I suppose I was somewhat under Clark's sway at the time, but I can't really blame him for it. In the end, it was my decision."

She rubbed her temples; thumb squeezing one side, two fingers the other. When she lowered her hand, there were red dents left in her skin where her fingertips had pressed. Her eyes were closed. The white band collar, snug about her neck when they'd come in, now hung loose, as if her neck had shriveled since then.

Alix would never have expected to feel sorry for the Iron Lady, but she was sorry for her now. "Lillian," she said gently, "what Ted said is true. This is something I know about. Most buyers don't demand scientific testing. As with you, they fall in love with something; they want so much for it to be the real thing that they don't want to take a chance that it might not be. It's like wives or husbands hiring private detectives to spy on their spouses. They don't do it at the beginning, when they're in love and full of wonderful thoughts about the future. They only do it after the relationship has gone bad—when it's too late."

"Thank you for that, child." Lillian smiled sweetly at her. Good heavens, the woman was becoming more human by the minute. "But I still feel like the chump of the century. Ted, will we be able to recover our money from Lord & Keen?"

"I hope so, Lillian, but I can't promise. There's going to be a long line of people wanting the same thing. I suggest you have that picture examined by a reputable forensic lab right now, get their report as soon as possible, and get yourself at the head of that line."

"I can put you in touch with the best of them, if you want," Alix said.

Lillian sadly nodded her acceptance of the offer and turned to look out the window on her left. "Ah, me," she sighed.

. . .

Ted and Alix started talking at the same time as they exited the museum, en route to the parking area. "I have a question," Alix said. "I have an idea," Ted said, and then, after they both laughed: "What's your question?"

"About Clark getting murdered. Are you assuming it had to have something to do with the Pollock too?"

"With the Pollock in particular? I'm not sure, but I'm betting it's got something to do with his flimflam operations with Lord & Keen in general. There were a lot of transactions, and we don't yet know how many of them he was involved with. But even if you take just the Pollock and Austin's Whistler, you're talking about a tremendous amount of money changing hands—well over twenty million between the two of them. I think Jake needs to look into that. He might be focusing too much on Clark's relations with the museum people here."

"So do I need to tell him about all that, or will you?"

"I will."

"Thank you. So what's your idea?"

"About what?"

"A minute ago you said you had an idea."

"Oh, right," Ted said. "I was just thinking, let's go have some lunch."

Alix smiled. "I don't know. The last lunch we had together didn't work out all that well."

He gave her a polite, pro forma smile in return. Did he really not understand what she meant, or was he tactfully pretending not to? Either way, it seemed to bode well.

"Sure," she said, "let's. I know some nice places just a few minutes away."

"No, I have a better idea. Do you have to get right back, or can you take a few hours off?"

Where was this leading? Was she kidding herself or was he trying to set them on a new footing, or rather back on their old footing? Or was she reading more into this than was there? Ted was the hardest damn man to read that she'd ever met. Well, she supposed, the thing to do was to go with the flow and see where things led. "No, I can take a few hours. In fact, I can take the whole afternoon," she ventured a bit more boldly. "I'm not on an hourly schedule. I have a due date to get the work done, and I've allowed myself plenty of time."

"Good. Because I was also thinking that you've had a stressful few days here, and it'd do you good to get away from things for a while. See some different scenery."

Alix laughed. "That's exactly what Chris said we should do yesterday."

"And did you?"

"Yes, she thought it would relax me, put things into perspective."

"And did it?"

"Yes, actually, it did. We went to this lovely desert canyon. We could certainly go back there, if that sounds good to you. It's not that far."

He was shaking his head. "No, I'm not nuts about the desert, to tell you the truth. I like green, I like to see *water* in my rivers, and I wouldn't mind getting out of the heat. Aren't there some oases around here?"

"Yes, but what would you think of taking the aerial tramway up to Mt. Jacinto instead? You'll see more white than green, but it's supposed to be beautiful, and it's what I was hoping to do today anyway. It'll certainly get us out of the heat, and there's a restaurant at the top, so we can get something to eat there."

"Perfect, let's get going."

"Did you bring any warmer clothes?"

"My bags are still in my car. I've got a couple of sweaters. I'll put one on."

"I'd put them both on, if I were you. And we can swing by the Villa Louisa so I can get a coat. I'll drive. I know the way." She smiled up at him. (Had he always been this tall?) "This'll be fun—we can have ourselves a snowball fight, and then go in for a hot lunch. No, let's change the order. I'm starving."

"Either way, sounds exciting." He smiled at her. "And enjoyable."

23

Getting to the tramway took a straight four-mile shot up North Palm Canyon Drive to where the streets thinned out, and empty lots started to outnumber houses, and the desert began to intrude. Then a turn onto the two-lane Tramway Road for another four miles, the first half through unlovely, boulder-strewn desert, and then up along the floor of a valley that ascended through increasing scrub and even a few clumps of greenery, to the aerial tramway's base station at 2,600 feet. The famous rotating tram itself would then lift them to almost nine thousand feet, where it was winter ten months of the year.

While Ted put in a call to his office to apprise his people of the latest developments, Alix's mind had already soared to the top of the mountain. There was a cocktail lounge up there, she knew, adjacent to the restaurant, and it went without saying that such a place could be counted on to have a roaring log fire going. They would have a good lunch, have their snowball fight, and then come back inside, into the lounge, laughing and pink-cheeked from the cold. They would sit in a warm place, relaxed and pleasantly tired, staring quietly into the fire and listening to the crackle of the wood, slowly sipping Irish coffees, or maybe Ted would be having a cognac. And Alix would quietly say, "You know, Ted, about that lunch we had in DC—I said some things . . ."

But . . .

. . . they never got that far. They didn't even make it to the tram. A ten-inch-long Coachella Valley fringe-toed lizard had plans of its own.

What the lizard had in mind was the securing of a fat, blue-blacked beetle for its midday meal. The beetle was minding its own business on the sun-drenched pavement of the road a few inches from the edge. The lizard, immobile except for its shifting, conical eyes, watched from a foot away, its scaly brown-and-tan-speckled skin making it almost invisible against the desert landscape. It took two seconds for its primitive brain to make the necessary distance and direction calculations, and then the ribbonlike tongue snapped forward, almost too fast to see, and unfurling as it went. Whether the beetle saw it coming at the last millisecond or just happened to move at that precise moment is uncertain, but move it did. The tongue missed, the beetle flew clumsily off with a brittle *whirr-rr-rr* of its wings, the humiliated lizard pretended the whole thing had never happened and slunk away into the desert to seek its lunch elsewhere, and that was the end of it.

But . . .

. . . not for Pete Menendez, a weary commercial plumber heading back to Palm Springs in his van after an all-night maintenance job at the visitor center atop the mountain, who caught the sudden roadside movement out of the corner of his eye. Half-asleep at the time, he overreacted, jerking the steering wheel hard left to avoid the whatever-it-was on the road. The car instantly obeyed, lurching over the double yellow line, into the opposing lane of traffic, and directly into the path of an oncoming Subaru hatchback. Paralyzed with shock, he could only stare, popeyed, as the hatchback seemed to *leap* out of his way and into the lane he had come from and then flash away behind him.

After another frozen second, his ability to move returned and he quickly pulled the wheel right, dragging the van back into its proper lane.

"Hoo boy," he breathed once he got his breath back, and then, relieved and chastened, went on his way with decreased speed and increased alertness, making it home without further problems.

But . . .

. . . leaving a lulu behind for the hatchback. With Alix London at the wheel, it had been zipping along at 70 miles an hour, the California limit. She would have been going even faster if there hadn't been a rather hard-nosed law enforcement type in the seat beside her. The road was uncrowded and rail-straight for the most part, the day clear, the desert empty and flat. And Alix did love to drive fast. A weakness, to be sure, but (as Alix saw it) one without undue risk, since she was not your average driver. She knew what she was doing. She had been trained, after all, by a former race car driver—the middle-aged son of the expert restorer who had mentored her during her apprenticeship in Italy. The son, Giancarlo Santullo, had put a lot of emphasis on safety; no wonder, since he was allowing her the unprecedented privilege of weekend soloing on the nearby Amalfi coast in his prized Lamborghini Gallardo LP 560, the car with which he'd once finished second in his class at Le Mans. Eager to get her hands on the wheel of the gorgeous Lamborghini, Alix took to the lessons with enthusiasm and application.

So she knew a lot about driving and a lot about cars and engines, she was an extremely attentive driver, even an expert one, and her reflexes were quick. Those reflexes were called into action the split second that Menendez's van began its swerve into her lane. She was aware of the danger even before she was aware that she was aware. Without anything that might be called conscious thought, her brain made much the same kind of instant calculations that the fringe-toed lizard's brain had made, of which she was no more conscious than the lizard had been. The two vehicles were about three hundred feet apart. She was going 70, Menendez about 50, so they were closing at a rate of around 120 miles an hour—almost 200 feet per second. That gave her a little over one second to react. Both instinct and expertise agreed on the necessary strategy: Get the hell out of the way and do it in a hurry. They came up with contradictory tactics, however.

Instinct: *Jam on the brakes and yank that steering wheel left.* Expertise: *No, dear, not at this speed. Both stopping and turning require friction—traction—between tires and pavement, and there is only so much of it to go around. Try to both steer and brake at 70 miles an hour, and you won't get much of either. You'd better decide which it's going to be . . . and do it fast.*

Alix went with expertise and chose steering, which got her into the opposite lane, the lane the van had come from, and out of its way, but it was a close thing. The right side of the van caught the passenger-side mirror of the Subaru and snapped it cleanly off. Alix never felt the impact, any more than Menendez had, but the Subaru did. There was a shockingly loud *bam!* and the passenger-side curtain airbag popped open, whacking Ted in the ear and bringing a yelp from him.

Alix, meanwhile, was still going almost 70—the whole thing had taken only that single second—and their troubles were far from over. They were in the wrong lane, but that was the least of it; the nearest oncoming car was half a mile away. More pressingly, a few yards ahead was a jog in the road, first to the right and then back to the left, about thirty degrees each way. Under ordinary circumstances, an inconsequential squiggle, even at her current speed. What did make it a problem was that her quick dodging of the pickup had left them traveling on a diagonal path relative to the road, a sharp one, perhaps forty-five degrees leftward. If not for that upcoming jog she would have been able to straighten the car and then get it back where it belonged, but when the forty-five degrees she was already fighting were tacked on to the jog's thirty, they added up to a curve she couldn't possibly negotiate. They would lurch off the road and very likely turn over.

Better . . . safer . . . *not* to attempt to turn, but to brake, keeping the wheels straight, and let the car follow its present diagonal momentum off the road and into the desert, where the added friction of the gravelly sand would help bring it to a safe stop before it got very far. There was a long, sloping ridge four or five feet high running parallel to the road only thirty or forty yards away (suddenly the desert didn't seem so flat any more), but Alix thought she could stop before they reached it, or if not, then she would maneuver along its flank until she could stop, with nothing more than a little cosmetic damage to the Subaru, and—knock on wood—none at all to them.

She pressed hard on the brake pedal, and felt with gratitude the momentary catch that marked the point at which the antilock system kicked in to prevent a locked-wheel skid. Which was fine. What wasn't fine was the "momentary" part. It was like stepping on an overfilled balloon. A split second of resistance, then *pop!*—and then nothing. The pedal broke through and her foot rode without resistance all the way down to the floorboard. Not only was the antilock system kaput; there were no brakes at all.

She couldn't stop the car. She couldn't even slow it down.

"No brakes," she managed to grind out as they jounced off the road and onto the rocky desert floor.

"Fun and games," she thought she heard Ted mutter.

She did her best to turn before they reached the ridge but it was hopeless. Even with her twisting the wheel as hard as she could, the hatchback flew straight up the slope. An instant later they were airborne, seemingly weightless. All she could do was hang on to the wheel, terrified, powerless, and waiting tensely for the impact when they hit the ground again.

The slope had acted much like a well-placed ramp in a movie, where a car—usually a police car, for some reason—racing down an alley is suddenly launched into the air, only to come down on an equally well-placed pile of cardboard cartons or packing crates, or maybe a rickety wooden outbuilding. The difference was that there weren't any sheds or packing crates here, just rock-studded desert.

Fortunately, the car hadn't nosed over in flight. It plopped down on its underside. Hard. *Bam!Bam!Bam!Bam!* Who knew modern cars had so many airbags, coming from so many different directions? However many were left, they all went off now, pushing Ted's and Alix's faces into suffocating air pillows, but only for a moment. The bags immediately deflated, leaving them free to move, but Alix had no control over the car, which took three clanking, bone-rattling bounces and then finally rocked to a halt, leaving the two of them shaken up but apparently unhurt.

Alix switched off the ignition. The automobile was now filled with the airbags' powdery, sulfurous residue. It was on their clothes and in their nostrils, but they continued simply to sit there without moving, not even opening the windows.

"You all right?" Ted asked after a while.

"I think so," she said, exploring her molars with her tongue and not finding any cracks. "You?"

"Same," he said. "My brain might have shaken a little loose, though. I don't think anybody's going to notice."

"Afraid we're not going to make that lunch," Alix said after a few more seconds.

"No." Another couple of beats. "Well, at least I was half-right."

"About what?"

"This afternoon. Didn't I say it'd be exciting?"

24

They sat for another minute without moving, and then Alix switched on the ignition long enough to open the windows. Neither of them was quite ready to be up and about yet, but they needed the fresh air.

"Alix," Ted said, "what the hell just happened?"

"We lost our brakes."

"Yes, but I mean *why* did we lose them?"

"How would I know? I'm no expert, Ted."

"You know a lot more about cars than I do. That makes you the consultive expert of the moment. Why do brakes fail?"

"Oh, a whole lot of things. I don't know . . . Low hydraulic fluid levels, overheated brake pads, or worn calipers, or the rotors could fail, or *any* of the parts could fail."

"Any ideas on which it was?"

"None of the above," she said. "Not all of a sudden, like that. There would have been signs ahead of time—squeaks, spongy stops, something. And there weren't any; I would have noticed. Besides, I got this car from Marathon; they're a big agency, they would have checked it before they let it out. And I doubt if I've driven twenty miles since then. So then . . ." A shrug.

"That's what I thought," he said solemnly. Clearly, his mind was working toward the same conclusion hers was. They each knew what the other was thinking, but neither wanted to say it. It was Ted who took the leap. "So then . . . what? Did someone cut the brake line or something?"

"Like in those old movies?"

"Frankly, I've only seen it in old movies myself, but that doesn't mean it doesn't happen outside of them."

"Actually, it does."

"It does happen?"

"No, it does mean it *doesn't* happen."

This was too much for Ted to handle in his present woolly state. "It does mean it doesn't . . . "

"Happen outside of them. Old movies."

They were both more or less aware that the conversation they were having was not only faintly ridiculous but a little surreal. They'd just been through as hair-raising and dangerous an experience as one could expect to live through and emerge with all bones intact, and yet their conversation was calm and quiet, without expression, and they sat not looking at each other but still staring blindly through the windshield. They probably weren't technically in a state of shock, but they were pretty numb.

"And the reason it happens only in old movies," she said, "is because, back in the forties and fifties, there was a single brake line that came out of the master cylinder, which then split into four different lines, one to each wheel. So all you had to do was cut that single line, and the brakes on all four wheels failed."

"And now?"

"Now there are either four separate lines that come out of the master cylinder, or two lines that then split into two each—I think that's what these Subarus have. So cutting a single line would still leave the brake pads operating on at least two wheels—and we had *nothing*, believe me."

"Are the brake lines easy to find? Would you have to take the engine apart to get at them?"

"What? No, you could just pop the hood or else get underneath without doing even that. Why?"

"Well, what would stop somebody from cutting *all* the lines? Might have taken a lot of work in the old days, but a cordless hacksaw or shears would make pretty quick work of today."

"I suppose that's true," she said thoughtfully. "Still, I'd say it's impossible in this case."

"So then, what did happen?"

She shrugged.

They sat for another few moments, continuing to surface from their dazes. "I have a brilliant idea," Ted announced.

"Mm?"

"Let's get out of the car and look under the hood and *see* if they've been cut or not."

"Would you even recognize what a brake line looks like?"

"No, but I bet you would."

They both laughed, and that seemed to ease them out of their zombie-like states. Alix pulled the inside hood release and they climbed out of the car, each with a few grunts acknowledging bruises they hadn't been aware of. The car was even worse off than they'd realized, with a twisted frame, a broken front axle, four flats, and pieces that led all the way back to the road, like the bread crumb trail in *Hansel and Gretel*, only this one was made of broken lights, bumper parts, hubcaps, and assorted pieces of undercarriage.

The hood had buckled, but the outside catch still worked. Once Ted wrestled the hood open and got it propped, Alix leaned over and looked into the engine compartment. Ted leaned over and looked at Alix.

"They *are* cut," she murmured incredulously. "Both of them. Somebody actually cut them. I can't . . . I don't . . ." She shook her head.

"Show me," he said.

She indicated two pre-bent metal tubes, each about the thickness of a pencil, that emerged from a steel cylinder—the master cylinder—and disappeared into the recesses of the interior in different directions. Both of them had inch-wide gaps in them a foot or so after they came from the cylinder, where they would have been easy to reach, either from above or below.

Alix was scowling down at them. "I see it, but I don't believe it. I'm telling you, this couldn't have caused it."

"Alix, I don't understand." Ted was showing a glimmer of impatience. "These tubes, they transmit the brake fluid, the hydraulic fluid, to the, what are they, the brake pads—"

"To the calipers, actually, which transmit the force to the pads, which press on the drums or the discs, which—"

"All right, all right. The end product is, it's the pressure from the fluid that stops the wheels from turning, right? So if the lines are cut, the hydraulic fluid doesn't get through and the wheels keep going round and round and the car doesn't slow down. That would be the *point* of cutting them, wouldn't it? And that's what happened to us. So what am I missing here?"

"Well, think about it. When would the lines have been cut?"

"I don't know. What's that got to do with it?"

"Whenever it was, obviously it had to be before we started out from the museum, correct?"

"Obviously. Probably during the night. Where do you park it?"

"On the lot at the hotel, and there's no lighting, so it wouldn't have been that hard to get at without being seen, so let's assume that's when it was done. And it had to be last night, not before. I only got this car yesterday."

"Okay. Last night. So?"

"So how did I get to the museum this morning? How did I stop when I got there?"

"All right, maybe somehow it was done after you were parked at the museum. I know that's more unlikely, but—"

"So then how did we get all the way out here before the brakes finally failed? I stopped at the Villa to change, I slowed to turn onto Palm Canyon, I stopped for the light at Amado, stopped for the light at San Rafael just before we turned onto this road, slowed down probably two dozen times on the way. Did I do all that without any brake fluid? No way."

"Ah." Ted leaned back against the side of the car, nodding. "I see what you're saying," he said slowly. "Damn. Well, we'll—"

He broke off for the third or fourth time to give a smile and an A-OK sign to a passing driver who had slowed to offer assistance. Funny, Alix thought, the van, the vehicle that had been directly involved, had gone on its way without a backward glance, as far as it was possible to tell, but now, almost everybody driving by was showing concern.

"I better make a couple of calls," Ted said, taking out his cell phone. "Marathon, you said the agency was? They'll want to send out a tow."

While he did that Alix scowled hard at the cut lines—and there was no question about their having been purposely, maliciously severed. Brake lines were made of heavy-gauge stainless steel; they simply did not burst or tear on their own. That got her thinking . . .

"Okay, they're on their way," Ted said. "And let me call Jake too. He'll probably want to come out himself if he's available."

"Oh, I don't know about that. This would be a new case. The All-Knowing Skull may have other ideas on who to send."

He looked at her, one eyebrow raised. "I have no idea what that means, but I want Jake, and I'm betting I can get him out here."

"You know, I feel like I'm personally keeping the Palm Springs Police Department in business," Alix said. "I wonder what they used to do before I showed up."

Ted smiled at her. "Things do seem to have a way of, er, becoming interesting when you're around, don't they?"

"It's a knack I'd be glad to give away if I could. Listen, let's go back to where the car was when the brakes failed. There's something I want to look for."

They walked back to the approximate spot and Ted made his call to Jake while Alix systematically scoured first the road itself (nothing) and then the swaths of desert on either side of it. There were more waves and smiles to motorists on their way to and from the tram.

"Oho!" she cried, just as Ted finished his call. She bent to snatch what looked like a three- or four-inch length of narrow green hose or tubing from the ground a few feet from the edge of the road.

"Jake's on his way," Ted said. "Oho, what? What is that thing?"

"Come, I'll show you." She tightened her fist around it. "I knew it!"

He had to trot to keep up with her as she ran excitedly back to the car, and when they reached it, its hood still propped up, she held up the flexible green tubing like a magician showing off a trick, said "Watch this!" and fitted it onto one of the cut ends of the nearer brake line, then bent the tubing into a U-shape and fit its free end onto the other segment of the brake line, thereby closing up the gap.

"I think I'm sort of seeing where you're going with this . . ." Ted said, "but I'm still a little . . ."

"Well, I couldn't figure out why there was a *gap* in the lines. That takes two cuts instead of one, and one cut would have done the job. And then it occurred to me . . ."

The hydraulic fluid in the lines is put under tremendous pressure when the brake pedal is depressed, she explained. A stainless steel brake line can take that pressure without bursting—or swelling, which would also lower the pressure in the line. Rubber tubing can take some pressure too, but only up to a point. Whoever did this was counting on the rubber segments standing up to relatively soft stops, but bursting or popping loose at the first really hard stop—when the car was moving fast and had to stop quickly; when it was a matter of life and death, in other words. And that was exactly what happened.

"So," Ted said, "he was just hoping you'd eventually run into a serious situation, a critical situation, when you really needed the brakes . . . and they wouldn't be there. The fact that it happened now, right here, was just coincidence?"

"Unless you think that guy that ran us off the road was in on it, yes, but I can't imagine that."

More waves and we're-okay-thanks smiles to a couple of drivers.

"Ted, this thing is all very clever, but it's not exactly a surefire way to get rid of someone, you know. After all, we're still here."

"Yeah, thanks to some fancy driving on your part. But what you said about its being pretty iffy is true. I'm assuming this was a kind of first try. If it didn't work, or didn't happen at all, he'd try something a little more certain. Which means he couldn't be in that much of a hurry to . . . to deal with you; that he's got time enough to make another try."

"To kill me, you mean—we may as well say it, don't you think? It would also mean that I can expect another try at it. That should make the next few days even more exciting."

Ted let out a pent-up breath. "Whew. This is all really hard to believe."

"What? That someone's trying to kill me? If you ask me, it's getting to be pretty old hat. Seems to happen just about every other day."

"No, not that someone's trying to kill you—that *two* people have been trying to kill you."

"Two people? How do you figure—" She slapped her forehead. "Oh, my God, I must still be in shock or something. Of course it's two people. If Clark was the first one—"

"He *was* the first one," Ted reminded her.

"But he sure can't be number two, can he?"

"Not very likely, I'd say. *Hi there, we're fine, thanks for checking.* So then, who? Do you have any idea at all?"

"No, there *isn't* anybody. Clark was the only one with a stake in the Pollock."

"Then maybe it's not about the Pollock, maybe it was never about the Pollock, maybe it's about something else."

"Ted, honestly, there *isn't* anything else. I've just been doing my work, keeping to myself. I mean, maybe I've ticked off somebody without meaning to—"

"Naw," Ted said. "You? Surely you jest."

Alix gave him a sour smile. "—but there certainly hasn't been anything to get myself killed over."

"Alix, maybe it's got nothing to do with the museum at all. Maybe . . ." Ted was looking down the road over her shoulder at a dark blue, unmarked sedan approaching from the city. "Here comes the man you need to be talking to about this, and there's the tow truck right behind him."

229

A moment later, Jake Cruz pulled over, stopped beside the road, and stared at their car.

"Jesus H. Christ, did you get hit by a train? I never knew there was a crossing here."

"It felt like we got hit by a train, Jake," Ted said, "but, believe me, it could have been a lot worse. Thank God it was Alix behind the wheel and not me."

Alix shrugged it off, but in fact she was pleased.

The tow truck pulled up then, a big flatbed tow, and Jake had to move his car back to make room.

The overalled, booted driver climbed down and stood there, gnawing on an unlit cigar and sizing up his job.

"It's a bit of a mess, isn't it?" Ted said, being friendly.

"Seen worse," was the nonchalant reply. "You folks going to need a ride back?"

"No," said Jake, coming up. "I'll take them." And then to the driver. "H'lo, Ed."

"Well, hi there, detective. We sure meet in some lovely places."

"Yeah. Just good luck, I guess. Give us a minute with the car, will you, before you take it."

"My pleasure," Ed said, climbing back up to his seat and taking out a cigarette lighter. "I'm on hourly for this one."

Jake did most of his own car maintenance, so it took just a few minutes for Alix to explain her deductions about the brake line tampering.

"Well, that's a new one," was his only response.

After that, they went over the same ground that Ted and Alix had covered—who would want to kill her/why would anyone want to kill her/what did it have to do with Clark/what did it have to do with the Pollock? But other than concluding that the bad guy was very likely the same one who'd killed Clark—there was such a thing as too many coincidences, after all, and in a town that typically saw three or four murders a year, this was one too many—they made no progress. As to what the connection was between the two, and whether they were related to Clark's attempt on Alix, they couldn't come up even with a hypothesis.

Jake used a tissue to pull off the green tubing and looked into one end. "Some kind of oil in there, so you're probably right. Kind of sorry you handled it, though. Maybe we can still get some latents off it."

"According to what Alix said, there must be a second one lying around, though," Ted said. "Shouldn't be too hard to find."

"Yeah, I'll have a couple of guys out. But this is obviously a pretty slick character. Be surprised if he left any prints." He called to the driver. "All yours, Ed. This is a police case now. You know the drill."

Ed waved his cigar in acknowledgement. "I'll take care of it, chief."

On the way back to Palm Springs, Ted sat in front with Jake, Alix in the back, and after a few more unproductive surmises about what had happened, Ted changed the subject. Slightly.

"How're you coming on Calder's murder, Jake?"

"Ah, well, there I can report some progress—thanks to your telling us about what he was planning to do that night."

Alix, watching the barren, brown desert glide by, didn't see the flick of his head that indicated he was talking to her, and only realized it from the silence that followed.

"My telling you?" she asked. "What did I tell you?"

"Don't you remember?" Jake asked, clearly enjoying himself. "You told us you heard him on the phone, arranging a meeting at Melvyn's Lounge. You even told us when: six o'clock. You don't remember?"

"No, I didn't. I never said that. I said . . ." Her eyes opened wide. "You mean 'Melvyn's' is the name of a place? *That's* what he meant?" She replayed his words in her mind. "Well, sure, that could be, I guess, but how in the world did you come up with it?"

"Just the usual superior police work. We're detectives, we detect. But the thing is, my partner went over there, to Melvyn's, and showed Calder's picture to the waitress, and she remembered him—she wondered if he was a movie star. She also remembered that he was there with another guy, a guy in a baseball cap, and they were getting pretty annoyed with each other over something. Couldn't really give us anything like a helpful description of the other guy, but she thought she could probably ID him if she saw him again."

"Which is good," Ted said. "All you need to do is come up with the other guy."

"On whom we are closing in with implacable rapidity. My partner in excellence tracked down somebody who actually witnessed the hit-and-run, but took off at the time. The guy's an auto mechanic, and he was able to tell us a lot, including the make, model, and year of the car. And color. A 2012 Ford Focus. Green."

"That sounds like real progress, Jake," Alix said. "Congratulations."

"Well, it is progress, but do you have any idea how many 2012 Ford Focuses are registered in San Berdoo County alone? And if you throw in L.A. and Orange right next door, sheesh. But we're working at it. Ah, civilization."

They had reached the end of Tramway Road—the end of the desert—and Jake turned them south onto North Palm Canyon. They traveled only a few blocks before turning onto East Vista Chino, which took them away from downtown. "Where are we going?" Alix asked.

"We need to stop off at the police department, get a statement. We'll need a few words from you too, Ted. Shouldn't take long, given that the scene of the crime wasn't really a scene of a crime—for all we know, the guy who did it was a hundred miles away—so there's not much to get from you. Which brings me to my next point: Wherever he is, he's still loose, and that means Alix is going to need some protection. We're a little tight on personnel, but I know Lieutenant Mitchell would okay—"

"How about holding off on that, at least while I'm here, Jake," Ted said. "I'll be happy to stick close to her."

"That okay with you, Alix?" Jake asked.

Okay for Ted to stick close to her? Was he kidding? "Sure, I guess so," she said offhandedly.

Ted turned in his seat. "I've already booked the bungalow next to yours at Villa Louisa, Alix."

"You—?"

"I called while you were hunting for that tube. So I'll be right next door if you need me, even in the middle of the night."

Jake's head cocked just perceptibly at that, and Alix felt the blood rise to her cheeks. A double entendre? From Ted? No, impossible, the guy was too straitlaced for double entendres. For Alix, who was thought by some to be a tad straitlaced herself, it was a considerable part of his manly charm.

"Listen, Jake," Ted said as they turned into the parking lot at police headquarters, "I had a thought. About that Ford?"

"Shoot." Jake pulled the key from the ignition and turned toward him. "I can definitely use a thought."

"Well, Ford Focuses are the most popular rental cars in the country. So before you go checking on every single one in the United States, why don't you call around to the local rental outfits and see if maybe someone brought back a green 2012 in the last couple of days with damage on it? From what I saw in those photos of Calder's injuries, there's no way the car got away without injuries of its own."

"Now that is a *hell* of a thought," Jake said, and then slowly nodded. "You feebs. Never mind what they say, you really are pretty smart guys."

25

Their interviews with Jake and his partner took longer than expected—until almost seven o'clock—and when they were done, Jake drove them to the museum parking lot, where Ted still had his car. This was at Ted's request. "No point in your getting another rental," he volunteered, when Alix had implied that that was her intention. "Wherever you're going, I'm driving you, like it or not."

Jake nodded his approval.

"I guess I can live with it," she said, borrowing one of Ted's own rather ambiguous phrases, "if I have to." Had she meant it to be taken as grudging acquiescence? A meaningless throwaway line? An ironic joke? She didn't know herself. Well, let him wonder too. It was, after all, his laconic, unrevealing response at that cursed luncheon at the National Gallery, when she turned down his offer to continue working with him. *I can live with that.*

Ted in a nutshell.

This time he didn't respond at all, so she was in the dark as to his reaction, assuming he'd had any.

"I need food," Ted declared when they'd gotten out of Jake's car. "I've been listening to my stomach rumble for the last half hour. Any suggestions as to where to go?"

"Well—"

"*Not* up on the mountain, if you don't mind. Maybe some other time."

"No, I most certainly wasn't thinking that," she said, laughing, "but . . . well, one of the curators—Prentice Vandervere, an old professor of mine and one of the most respected—"

"I know who Prentice Vandervere is. We've gone to him a few times with questions. I have a lot of respect for him. Be an honor to meet him."

"Oh, good. Prentice is the new senior curator at the museum and Lillian's putting on a reception for him at Le Vallauris—"

"A reception? Kind of gauche, wouldn't you say, what with her previous senior curator's body barely cold."

"Well, yes, I suppose it is, but she's not the most sentimental person in the world, you know. I think she's come to regret ever having had anything to do with Clark, and she's anxious to put everything about him behind her. Anyway, Le Vallauris is supposed to be the best restaurant in the city. Reception started at seven, a few minutes ago. I'm invited, and I'm welcome to bring someone if I like, so I was thinking—"

"Don't bother thinking, you don't have any choice. You're bringing me. Where you go, I go. That's the deal."

"Oh, darn," she said, and smiled at him. And he smiled back.

. . .

On the brief drive to the restaurant, something occurred to her. "Ted, I just had a thought. What if whoever cut those lines didn't do it just on the off chance that I might have to stomp on the brakes in some highly unlikely life-and-death situation while I was tooling around Palm Springs? What if he knew I'd be driving on that straight, flat, clear, uncrowded road today? He'd know nobody drives under fifty miles an hour on that thing. Wouldn't that improve his odds of my having to put that kind of pressure on the brakes?"

"Sure, but how could anybody know? We didn't decide on it ourselves till just before we left."

"Not exactly. I'd wanted to take the tram this afternoon anyway, even before I knew you'd be here. I told you that, remember?"

"No, I don't, but why does that matter?"

"Because I also told the people at the museum. Yesterday, when we were taking a break in the atrium. All the curators except Prentice, and then Jerry too."

"Why would you do that?"

"Why wouldn't I? We were just chatting. I didn't think I was risking my life. The restaurant parking lot is there."

He was nodding as he drove into it. "You raise a good point, Alix. That's worth thinking about. And are you sure those are the only people you told?"

"Absolutely. My God, do you think it's one of them?"

"Maybe so." He was nodding. "Maybe so."

"So what do we do now?"

"We go in there and get something to eat. And maybe you point out those people so I can have a look at them. But first, eat."

· · ·

If Le Vallauris wasn't the classiest restaurant in the city, it was sure putting on a good imitation, complete with an elegant host who glided from group to group inquiring in a charming French accent as to how things were, and waiters in black tie—not college-age kids, but smooth, efficient older men; professionals.

The Brethwaite reception was on the back patio of the old Spanish Revival house that held the main dining rooms, and very like a garden in Old Spain it was, with rose-pink flagstones underfoot, a dense green canopy of fig leaves overhead, and a luscious floral perfume in the air, at least some of which was from the vases of fresh flowers on the tables. The far corner of this pleasant place was cordoned off for the museum people, with a buffet table, a private bar, and a few small cocktail tables. Most of the attendees were standing in little groups within easy range of the buffet, employing the standard two-fisted cocktail party stance: wine or highball glass in one hand, and a canapé or two in the other.

The curators were all there, of course (with the surprising exception of Prentice), along with Jerry, Lillian, and Richard, and one or two others that Alix had seen around, but the rest were unfamiliar—spouses, or friends, or employees she hadn't run into. The men were almost all in sport coats, the women in dresses. Alix, still wearing the cords and hiking shoes she'd put on for the mountains, was distinctly underdressed and she hesitated at the entrance. Ted, seeing her reaction, pulled off his tie (his jacket and the sweaters he'd worn for the tram were back in the car), rolled his shirt sleeves up to his elbows, and opened his shirt collar a few buttons to put her more at ease.

What the hell, Alix thought, and walked in with him.

Even Lillian had dressed up for the occasion. Apparently recovered from her downhearted humor of the morning, she was again erect and regal in a lacy, jacketed, knee-length cocktail dress—very sweet and feminine, but there was also a vintage tiara glittering in her hair, in case anyone had any doubts about who was queen of the hive.

When she saw them, she waved them in and went on with what she was saying.

"—have noticed that our guest of honor isn't here. That's because he's been in San Francisco on business, you see, and his plane is just arriving about now. He should be here shortly. When he does arrive, he will have quite an announcement to make. Oh, and the auction catalogues have arrived, so everyone is welcome pick up a copy. They're over there on that table." She pointed to her left. "In the meantime, please continue to enjoy yourselves. The smoked salmon is quite marvelous."

"I'll drink to that," a red-faced Alfie said happily, lifting his glass.

"What *wouldn't* he drink to?" Drew Temple muttered as he came up to Ted, looking as usual both depressed and sullen—and spoiling for a fight. "I hear you're with the FBI, is that right?"

"Is that a question or an accusation?" Ted said, but he said it pleasantly.

"I have a question I want to ask you," Drew said, not so pleasantly. "What I want to know is why the federal government thinks it's perfectly all right—"

Ted's cell phone bipped. He held up one hand to stop Drew while he extracted it with the other. "Yes, Jamie, hello," he said, and then, to Drew: "You'll have to excuse me. I have to take this." And then again, into the phone: "It's a little noisy here, let me find someplace quieter." He shrugged another apology to Drew and threw a funny, saved-by-the-bell look toward Alix as he moved off with the phone to his ear.

Alix went in the direction that Lillian had pointed to find a catalogue, first stopping at the bar to get a glass of white wine. The catalogues, a dozen or so of them, were in a cardboard carton on a small table provided for people to set down their used glasses and plates. The catalogue covers looked nice: glossy, understated, and attractively done.

Endicott Fine Art Auction Galleries, Ltd.
San Francisco
presents
Treasures of the L. Morgan Brethwaite Museum
7 P.M., March 14, 2014

But it was the carton itself, a US Postal Service mailing carton with an Endicott Galleries return address, that caught her eye. The postmark strip in the upper right corner showed that it had been mailed from San Francisco on February 8, Saturday, the day before yesterday. *Saturday?* But that would mean . . .

It would mean that she and Chris had been lied to by Clark when Chris had said she was interested in buying the panel of miniatures before they went to auction. He'd told her that it was impossible because the catalogues had already been mailed. That had been on Friday, but now Alix knew that in reality they hadn't gone out until the following day. That supposedly disappointing "conversation" he'd had on the phone with the printer—the whole thing had been a sham. There'd been nobody on the other end. He just didn't want to sell it.

He'd jumped at Chris's offer on the Marsden Hartleys just a few hours before, yet when it came to selling the miniatures, he'd concocted an excuse for why it couldn't be done. Why would he do that? Clearly, he'd seen some kind of profit for himself in *not* selling them—at least at that point. Selling them later, then? Getting possession of them at the auction, then reselling them later for a lot more? But why would they have earned a lot more later?

Her mind was churning away. Those two portraits that Chris had liked so much—the little boy and the little girl in the bottom row—wasn't it possible that they weren't painted by the obscure Joseph Dunkerley, but by the illustrious John Singleton Copley, as Alix had initially sensed? (But had never followed up on, damn it.) If Clark had somehow known that, he would certainly have known that two matched Copleys would bring millions, not the thousands of dollars a pair of Dunkerleys would command, and would certainly have wanted them for himself . . . at Dunkerley prices.

But where did that lead? He knew he couldn't get away with bidding on a lot from his own museum, which meant he would need to have somebody do it for him: a proxy. So there had to be a second person involved. The person he'd been arguing with on the phone, perhaps? The person who'd met him at Melvyn's? The person who'd run him down just a few minutes later?

She paged through the top copy of the catalogues, searching for . . . well, she wasn't really sure of what she was searching for. The Marsden Hartleys that Chris had bought were not in it; that was as expected. The panel of miniatures *was* in it. That was also as expected. She looked hard at its photograph, but the resolution wasn't nearly good enough to—

"Oho, I see your attention has been caught by the miniatures."

Prentice, tall, elegant, kindly, smiling, stood beside her, having apparently come in without being noticed.

"Yes, they're beautiful."

"I've just come back from Endicott," he said. "I wanted to see all the pieces for myself, and I'm very glad I did." Unusually for Prentice, his suit coat was rumpled, probably from wearing it on the plane. Prentice Vandervere would probably be the last man in America who still flew in coat and tie. He was definitely elated about something tonight. "Alix, you're not particularly well acquainted with the field of miniatures, if I recall correctly."

"No, I'm not."

"Well, look at these two on the bottom right, the boy and girl."

"The Dunkerleys."

"Oh, I'm not so sure about that."

Alix felt a little flutter in her chest. If Prentice was about to tell her that he had identified them as Copleys, that would settle it. "You're not?" She was surprised to find herself short of breath.

"You can't tell from the photograph here, but you've looked at the actual panel, haven't you? Do you remember how luminous these two were, glowing almost as if they were lit from behind?"

"I do, yes." Her excitement continued to grow.

"That's because they were painted, not on ivory as was almost every other miniature of the time," Prentice told her, "but on a ground of gold leaf laid on copper. It was a technique unique to one particular American artist, a very *fine* artist, and the fact that he used it was completely unknown to his contemporaries, and not even suspected until just a few years ago." He paused to heighten the suspense. "I wonder if you have any idea who that artist was."

She knew, all right, but she wasn't about to spoil his pleasure in the moment. "No, I don't. Who?"

"Copley! The great John Singleton Copley! I knew it the moment I looked at them!"

Alix was glad she hadn't blurted the name. She suspected it had been a long time since he'd been this happy. "Copley!" she said. "That's wonderful! But I thought there was a solid provenance that established them as Dunkerleys."

"Provenance? No, no such thing, not at any rate as you and I understand the term. I've been through the records. An aide to Mr. Brethwaite bought them for him in 1971—at a country auction in New Hampshire. That's the extent of their provenance as Dunkerleys. They've been moldering away in the basement of the house ever since, never considered important enough to come up into the light, which was why I'd never seen them before, although I castigate myself now for never seriously exploring our storage areas. Isn't that something? Copley!"

"Yes, wonderful." Her mind was doing more than churning now. Barely remembered events and half-formed ideas were beginning to sharpen and rearrange themselves, to line up and connect. The killing of Clark, the rigging of her car's brake system—they had nothing to do with the Pollock. That was over and done. It was the *Copleys* that were at their root. It all added up.

And what it added up to was Jerry Swanson.

Consider: It was Jerry who had lied to her about the existence of a credible provenance on the miniatures, much as Clark had earlier lied about the existence of forensic testing on the Pollock. And just as Clark had thought it necessary to rid himself of her before she found out otherwise, so had Jerry when it came to the Copleys. And when she'd tried to take a closer look at them while they were being packed, he'd practically torn them out of her hands, making a joke out of it.

But it was no joke. Clearly, Jerry knew, just as Clark had, that they *were* Copleys. The two of them were in it together—a swindle, a scam to get ownership of them for a fraction of their worth by bidding for them at the auction, and then later selling them for millions after "discovering" that (gasp!) they were actually Copleys. But neither of them would be allowed to bid at the auction, so there had to be yet a third person involved, a proxy who would buy the lot for them without revealing their names.

That was a lot of convoluted thinking, but it had only consumed a few seconds, and Prentice, normally so suave and contained, was continuing to prattle away.

"I've managed to establish that they're 1759 portraits of two of the children of Andrew Oliver, a lieutenant governor of Massachusetts, and they haven't been seen since 1811, when they were auctioned by his heirs at Christie's London to an unnamed buyer. And now, here they turn up in *our* basement! Imagine—a lost Copley—*two* lost Copleys—after two hundred years. Lillian has already requested their removal from this particular auction of course, but I entertain no illusions about them remaining at the Brethwaite for long. For one thing, they're too small to monetize very many eyeballs, heh-heh, but more importantly, this really isn't the place for them. I anticipate enormous interest from museums that already have significant miniature collections—Boston, New York, New Haven—and I have no doubt that the price they bring would more than resolve the financial predicament that has so worried Lillian. But the big thing, the wonderful thing, is two beautiful little Copleys that had been lost to the world for . . ."

Click, click, click, pieces were popping up and dropping into place faster than she could keep up with them: how Jerry had once mentioned that he did his own car maintenance and thus had to have a pretty good knowledge of engines and brake systems; how he had been present yesterday when she announced that she'd be driving the desert road to the tram; how—

"I'm sorry, Prentice," she said abruptly. "I have to—excuse me." She ran to find Ted, leaving Prentice with his forehead puckered in surprise.

"Alix?"

Ted was standing at the far end of the patio near the iron-grill fence, just slipping his cell phone into a pocket. He looked as if he was thinking hard.

"Ted! I know who it is! Who killed Clark, who meddled with the brakes on our car! I don't have it altogether clear yet in my mind, but it was . . . it has to be—"

He mumbled something—a question. Alix thought she'd misheard. "What did you say?"

"I asked if you were talking about the valuator from Endicott, Jerry Swanson."

"Yes! How do you know?"

"I *don't* know. I'm guessing, trying to put the pieces together based on what I heard from Jamie just now. I'm still trying."

They were whispering, working hard to keep from stealing peeks at Jerry, who was fifteen or twenty feet from them, engaged in a spirited conversation with Madge. Still, he seemed to somehow sense their interest, because he gave Madge a couple of quick nods and began to sidle away.

Ted took a step toward him. "Mr. Swanson? Sir? Could you hold on a minute, please? I'd—"

Jerry froze for a split second, then broke and ran for the open gateway that led from the patio out into the parking lot and the street. Three steps was all he managed before colliding with an elderly, frail-looking waiter balancing a loaded tray on one shoulder. Down went the waiter with a desolate gasp, down came the tray with a din of clanging cutlery and shattering china, and down went Jerry, sprawling forward to his hands and knees. He was up quickly, again bolting for the gate.

There he flew straight into yet another obstacle, but this time the person on the other end was neither slight nor elderly. Detective Jake Cruz seemed to fill the entire gateway and proved, at least as far as Jerry was concerned, to be an Immovable Object, against which the pudgy Jerry was no Irresistible Force. Jerry bounced off his chest like a beach ball coming off a stone wall, and landed on the seat of his pants.

"Why, hello there, Mr. Swanson," Jake said, looking down at him. "How nice. We were just looking for you."

Jerry just sat there with his mouth open, looking balefully up at Jake. He had lost his black-plastic-rimmed glasses, and now his face looked all doughy and featureless. It looked as if it wouldn't take very much to make him cry. Jake stepped out of the gateway and from behind him came a uniformed officer and a man in a polo shirt and slacks; Jake's partner, Alix assumed.

"Stay where you are, please, don't move," the partner said sharply while the officer came around Jerry. Kneeling behind him, reaching to his utility belt with one hand for his handcuffs, he quickly interlocked his other arm with Jerry's and pressed on Jerry's shoulder, at which Jerry, forced forward, grimaced—"Hey! Ow!"—but a moment later the pressure was released and he was hauled to his feet, his hands now cuffed behind him. Nobody's head had ever hung lower.

A pat down produced no weapons (Alix would have been surprised if any had turned up; a killer Jerry might be, but not the kind who would do it face-to-face with a knife or a gun), and he was hustled off. Every head on the patio swiveled to follow them. Some people were appalled, but most looked thrilled, already working on the way they would be telling the story tomorrow. Alix heard more than one whispered, appreciative "wow" floating in the air around her.

. . .

Soon enough the soft "wows" began to morph into increasingly excited buzzing, at which point Alix and Ted ducked out through the gate.

"Where are we going?" Alix asked as they walked toward Ted's car. "Somewhere to eat, I hope?" Neither of them had had anything since breakfast.

"You bet your life, somewhere to eat. We sure haven't had any success at it so far today, have we? Any suggestions?"

"Well, we just walked out of the best restaurant in town. We could see if there's a table in one of the dining rooms, away from the others."

With a nod of concurrence, he took her elbow and steered her away from the cars and around the building to the front entrance.

There they were told by the hostess that they were in luck. A private event had been canceled, and several tables had been made available. One was still left. Would they like it?

"Would we like it!" Ted said with a grin.

A few minutes later they were seated beneath a lovely old Flemish tapestry, a forest scene turned a romantic, faded russet with age. An operatic aria played softly over the speaker system. *Bellini*, Alix thought. Norma. *"Casta Diva."* She even thought she recognized Callas. How lovely. Could she really have been watching the arrest of a murderer five minutes ago—someone who'd actually tried to kill *her*? Hard to believe that that wild scene—like something out of an opera buffa, what with people running into each other and falling down all over the place—had barely finished taking place no more than twenty yards from this beautiful, quiet corner.

A bottle of Oregon Chardonnay had been set into an ice bucket on the thick linen tablecloth, had received Ted's approval, and was now being poured for the two of them. Smiling, they clinked glasses, took their first sips, murmured their appreciative *mmm*s, set the glasses down, and sat back looking at each other.

"Ted," Alix said, "you want to tell me what that was all about back there?"

"Obviously, Jake concluded that Jerry was his man and acted accordingly."

"Yes, obviously, but did you know it was going to happen? Did you have anything to do with it?"

"No, nothing. I was as surprised as you were."

"But . . . do you mean to say all of us—you, me, Jake—came to the same conclusion at the same time? That seems a little—"

"Yes, it does, but apparently that's exactly what happened. Jake must have some pretty good evidence against Swanson, but he sure hasn't let me in on it. Neither have you, for that matter. How did you come up with Jerry?"

They paused while the gray-haired waiter put down their first course, a salad of roasted, cubed beets and chopped pistachios that had been formed into a neat cylinder, topped with feta cheese, and stacked on a base of thinly sliced apple rings arranged into a circle.

"Beautiful," Alix said.

"Thank you, madame, I hope you enjoy it." Another French accent. He didn't actually back away from the table, but somehow gave the impression of doing it.

The explanation of her reasoning took them through the salad course.

"That makes a lot of sense," Ted said, pouring them more wine. "You'll want to tell Jake all about it too."

"I will. Your turn now. How did you narrow it down to Jerry?"

"I didn't narrow it down to his being the guy who killed Clark and damn near did us in too, if that's what you mean. That only popped into my mind when you came running up. I was coming at it from another angle entirely. I was focusing on the auction."

Among the things he had done, he told her, was to get a list of registered bidders from Endicott. On that list he had spotted a familiar name: Ferenc Herczog, a mysterious Hungarian or Bulgarian or Romanian or Slovakian emigré who appeared to make his living acting as a proxy at art auctions around the world for buyers who chose to remain anonymous. Nothing illegal about that, but some of Mr. Herczog's clients had not been among the most elite ranks of art collectors. Some had been downright shady. In the past, Herczog had been helpful to the FBI, sometimes through inducement, more often through—let's not say bullying or harassment, but rather through the patient explanation of the possible consequences attendant upon cooperation or the lack thereof.

In this case, it took only twenty minutes of such patient explanation by Joe "Lurch" Mazurski, Ted's scariest agent, to get the name of the secretive buyer Herczog was representing. And that name—

"—was Jerry Swanson," Alix said. "The valuator buying the object on which he himself had set the value."

"Right. A definite no-no. Jamie had just told me that when you came up, at which point the connection to what's been going on around here more or less made itself."

The waiter was back with their main course, big bowls of steamed mussels with crushed tomatoes.

Alix tilted back her head to get a good whiff of the fragrance and sighed. "*Mm.* Garlic. Saffron. This smells too good to spoil with theories about scamming and murder and such. Besides, enough is enough. What do you say we just *eat*?"

"Best idea I've heard today," Ted said, and they tore into their portions, making a primitive feast of it. Fingers soon came into play. Additional linen napkins were requested, and a second order of rolls was used to sop up the juices.

There was laughter and good conversation (none of which Alix could remember afterward), and more wine was drunk, although it came as a surprise to both of them when their waiter tipped the bottle up to pour and it turned out to be empty.

"May I bring you more?"

They were both quick to turn down the offer. Alix liked wine, but she wasn't much of a drinker; this was more than she'd had in a long time, and she thought the same was true for Ted. They smiled at each other over their coffees, and Alix began to think that perhaps things between them had repaired themselves on their own, and maybe this night was heading somewhere, somewhere good.

But when they got to the Villa Louisa a little after ten, still glowing from the wine, they said brief good nights, warm but polite—no touching—and went to their separate doors some ten feet away from each other. Alix hadn't invited him in for coffee or a nightcap and he hadn't either suggested it or stood around waiting for it.

Having closed her door behind her, she leaned giddily back against it, letting the room swim around her, and broke out laughing.

What a couple of hopeless prudes they were.

26

Ted had promised to join Alix at the hotel's breakfast buffet at nine the next morning, but instead she got a call from him (on the hotel phone, since hers wasn't turned on) just before she was ready to leave her room.

"I'm at the police station. I talked to Jake, told him what the two of us came up with last night. Jake's got the guy in the interview room now, and I'm sitting a couple of doors down with Lieutenant Mitchell, watching it live. I don't expect to get back till eleven or so, so you're on your own for breakfast, but I thought we could do something after that. I'm not flying back till tomorrow, and I should have the rest of the day free."

He paused, waiting for her to say something, and she said it. "That's wonderful. How about giving the mountains another try?" Alix could hear the tension in her own voice. She was scared to death she was going to spoil everything again.

"That sounds good," Ted said, and she thought she heard a similar unease from his end of the line. "Are you sure you can afford to take another day off from the museum, though?"

"You bet. I've given myself plenty of time to get the work done." *And even if I hadn't . . .*

. . .

During most of the drive to the tram, they talked—that is, Ted talked—about what had transpired at the police station. Possibly it was because she'd been through an excitement overload in the last few days and her nervous system was fed up with it, or maybe because, with everything that had been happening to her in the last year, this kind of thing was starting to seem routine. Either way, she found herself strangely impatient with it, as if it had all happened a long time ago to someone else; so impatient that she was having a hard time focusing. She was able to grasp the main points, however.

The key for Jake had been Ted's suggestion that he check with the local rental agencies to see if anyone had turned in a damaged Ford Focus in the last couple of days. A survey of the Palm Springs agencies produced nothing, but when they extended it to the surrounding communities, they hit pay dirt at Hansen Motors in Cathedral City. A green 2012 Ford Focus had been returned the previous night with a battered front end; according to the driver, he had hit a deer. The client's name: Jerry Swanson.

Fortunately, the car was still on the lot, awaiting repair and repainting. It had been run through a car wash, probably more than once, and cleaned by Hansen after Jerry had brought it in. But blood is one of the most difficult substances in the world to remove completely from any surface. Chemical testing can reveal it at dilutions of one part in fifteen million. If it was the car that had killed Clark, there would be human blood on it, and it would be detected.

Jake and his partner hadn't waited for that, however. They got a photograph of Jerry from Endicott Galleries and took it to Melvyn's, where they showed it to the cocktail waitress, along with several photos of similar-looking men. The waitress unhesitatingly fingered Jerry as the man she'd seen arguing with Clark shortly before he'd been run down and killed two and a half blocks away. That had been enough for Jake, who had come straight from the bar to make the arrest. By the end of the night Jerry had been charged with Clark's murder—no action yet on the attempt on Alix—and had engaged a lawyer. At first he had stuck to his "I hit a deer" story, but as of this morning, with his lawyer's counsel, he was admitting he had indeed argued with Clark, and that it was Clark he'd hit, and not a deer, but that it had been an accident; he'd had a couple of drinks—the waitress verified this—he'd been rushing to catch up with Clark to talk some more, and must have hit the accelerator instead of the brake pedal when he tried to stop. He hadn't gone to the police because he'd realized how bad it would look for him.

As to what it was that they had argued about and what exactly was going on with the Copleys, that was still undergoing revision by Jerry and his lawyer, but Jake had pulled enough from the various versions to come up with a working scenario: Jerry had not long ago completed valuating two full-size Copley portraits for an earlier Endicott sale, which had involved a lot of looking at other works by the artist. The two Brethwaite miniatures in question had caught his eye right away and he had gone to Clark to suggest that maybe they were *not* Dunkerleys after all. In Jerry's telling of it, his purpose was strictly to inform the Brethwaite that they were far more valuable than they'd realized. Clark had done some research and determined for himself that they were indeed Copleys. He had prodded Jerry into keeping the information to themselves and instead scamming their way into becoming millionaires.

Who had prodded whom was open to question, but Jake had little doubt about the bones of the enterprise. Jerry would keep the estimate low for the auction and they would find a proxy to buy the panel for them. (This was where the shadowy gentleman from *Mitteleuropa* came in; an acquaintance of Jerry's, it had been Jerry who had brought him into it.) Once the panel had been bought, they would get rid of ten of the twelve miniatures and stow the Copleys away for a while. They would scratch the glass covers or dump some varnish on them, or mar them some other way. When enough time had passed they would use another proxy to consign them to a country antiques fair or something like it. Then either Clark himself or Jerry would purchase the blurry things under his own name for next to nothing—and get a legitimate receipt that proved he'd bought it at the fair. Let a little more time go by and the new owner would have the fogged glass covers replaced, whereupon he would be astounded and delighted to find out that they were actually Copleys.

When they auctioned them again—this time for millions—there would be little risk involved. Almost no living people had ever seen them, and without the panel itself there was virtually no chance of their being recognized as having come from the Brethwaite. They were on nobody's watch list because they had never been stolen. And Jerry or Clark could prove that he had come by them honestly, at some dinky, quaint antiques fair—*See, here's the receipt.*

Alix hadn't said ten words through all this, and once Ted had covered the main points, he looked curiously at her. "Are you all right, Alix? You're being awfully quiet."

"Oh, sure, I'm fine. So why did he kill Clark? I understand why he tried to kill me, but why Clark?"

"Well, remember, he hasn't admitted to that, but Jake's conclusion is that he no longer liked the split they'd arranged and he wanted a better share, and Clark wouldn't go for it; that would have been the telephone conversation you overheard. So he killed him."

"I see. Or couldn't it simply be that he realized he didn't *need* Clark anymore? Clark still needed Jerry because Jerry was the one setting the auction price. But why did Jerry need Clark? Jerry was the one who'd engaged the proxy, Ferenc what's-his-name, right? Not Clark. So Clark didn't really have any function anymore, other than to keep half the profit or whatever percentage they'd agreed to. If he was out of the picture, it was all Jerry's."

"That's a good point, Alix. Maybe Jerry offered to buy him out of the whole deal, so to speak, for a percentage of what they'd agreed to before, or maybe some fixed amount, and that's what they were fighting about. Clark told him to go to hell and Jerry killed him. No partner to share with, no partner to worry about."

"Mmm."

"Alix, your mind really is somewhere else."

"I suppose it is."

"Well, I don't blame you. You've been through a lot these last few days, enough to give anybody something to think about."

"I suppose it is," she said again, but that wasn't where her mind was at all. They were nearing the end of Tramway Road now. The tram parking lot was up ahead, and Mt. San Jacinto reared up in front of them. It was the top of the mountain she was thinking about again: the intimate lunch, the laughing, merry snowball fight, the warming up with Irish coffees in front of a crackling fire; the finding of just the right moment and the right words to finally set things aright.

"You know, Ted," she would say, "about that lunch we had in DC—I said some things . . ."

27

You know, Ted, about that lunch we had in DC—I said some things . . ."

"Uh-oh," Ted said, "sounds serious."

So far, everything had gone according to plan, as if they were actors following the directions in a script. They'd had a good lunch at the restaurant, they'd had their snowball fight and gotten good and chilled, and now they were sitting in leather wingback chairs in front of a snapping, crackling log fire. They had warmed up, they were about halfway through their Irish coffees, the glow was spreading through their bodies, and the world was good.

"It *is* serious," Alix said. "But it needs to be said."

Shadows and orange highlights from the fire flickered over his face. "Am I going to like it?"

"I hope so."

Ted put his cup down on the cocktail table beside him and re-arranged himself in the chair to face her more directly. "Fire away."

It was easier than she'd anticipated. The words flowed, systemati-cally and coherently. Encouraged by his serious, focused gaze, she got it all out too: how sorry she was for what she'd said at that lunch and the self-righteous way she'd said it; how bad she felt about her arrogance and presumption in lecturing him on the duplicity and treachery of "befriending and betraying," and how far above such perfidious behav-ior she herself was; and on and on, until she'd gotten everything out.

He sat through all of it, contemplative and very still, but with a frown slowly building, and then, when she was done, a single slow shake of his head.

"Well, say something," she said nervously.

"I'm trying to figure out what to say. The thing is . . ." He stopped, scowling at the floor with an unreadable expression. Annoyance? Confusion? Displeasure?

A sudden gust of queasiness swept through her. *I blew it. I unloaded too much on him. He was coming around, he was forgetting that damn lunch, I know he was, and now I've brought it all back, center stage. Will I never learn to shut my mouth? All I had to do—*

"The thing is," Ted said, and now he lifted his eyes to hers, "I don't remember any of that."

Her jaw dropped. "You don't *remember* it?"

"No."

"I don't believe you. You're trying to make me feel better."

"Alix, I'm telling you, I do not remember. It was a year ago, for Christ's sake. Oh, sure, I remember the lunch, all right, but those things you said you said? Not really, no."

"Well, then why did you avoid me all this time?"

"I didn't avoid you, *you* avoided *me*."

She was flabbergasted. If things got any more bizarre she'd know she was dreaming. "How can you say that? You never talked to me again after that lunch, not once. You made sure to be out of the office anytime you knew I was coming in. You—"

"Sure, because I was trying to do what you wanted."

She jerked her head in frustration. "Ted, why would I want to avoid you?"

"Because you were rightfully ticked off at me for the way I screwed up on that cruise assignment. I was like some stupid kid trying to make an impression on you—*Hey, look what a big shot I am*—and so I put you in with no backup and no training, and I damn near got you killed. I let you in for what had to be the worst experience of your life."

"But I never thought that, not for a minute. That cruise was one of the *best,* most exciting—exhilarating—experiences of my life."

They had been leaning earnestly forward, toward each other, and now Ted sagged back in his chair and puffed out a breath. "I'm a little confused here."

Alix fell back too. "I'm . . . I don't know what I am."

"I'll tell you what I do remember about that lunch, Alix. I remember how cold and distant you were."

"And superior? And condescending?"

"Okay, that too, maybe, a little. But the main thing is, you flat-out turned down an assignment I really thought—I hoped—you'd love, along with the chance for us to work together again. That was more than enough for me. Who remembers what reasons you came up with? I took it to mean you didn't want anything to do with me. That's what I remember."

She gave her head a shake. This was too much, too fast. "Ted . . . a minute ago you said you were trying to make an impression on me. Why?"

Ted put his coffee down again, wiped his hands on a cocktail napkin, straightened the shoulders of his sweater, cleared his throat, and cleared it again. He was taking his time, making a production of it. In the meantime, Alix truly grasped for the first time in her life what it meant to have one's heart in one's throat. *Come on, Ted,* she willed him, *say it, say it!*

"Ted . . . !" she gritted through clenched teeth when she couldn't stand it any longer.

"Because," he said at long last, "I love you, dimwit."

Her teeth unclenched, her heart went back where it belonged, and she burst out laughing. "That's got to be the most romantic thing anyone's ever said to me."

"I'm glad you approve. Now, is there anything you would like to offer back in return?"

"Yes, there is. I love you too, dimwit."

"I'll take it," Ted said with a smile. He reached out to grasp her hand and when they touched she felt a little shock. Was this the first time they'd ever touched, skin to skin? It seemed incredible, but she thought it might be.

"We really have been a couple of dimwits, haven't we?" she said.

"We've wasted a lot of time, if that's what you mean."

"That's what I mean."

"You know," Ted said, and now he had both of her hands in his, "I've got a good idea as to how we might start making it up."

She waited. Had she ever been this happy before?

"I have two weeks' vacation time that I can take in March or April. My brother has a sailboat he keeps down in the Virgin Islands, on Tortola, and he's not using it, so it's mine if I want it. I was thinking about going down there and spending a couple of weeks just drifting around the Caribbean, seeing the sights, getting a tan. Lazy days, warm, starry nights."

"And?"

"And while I've sailed it solo before, right now I'm thinking that it'd be nice to have some company, somebody to share the pleasures."

"And the grunt work."

"Absolutely. I know you know your way around sailboats, and it occurred to me that maybe you'd like to come along, if you can get free. It's not another mega-yacht, I'm afraid, just a thirty-seven-footer.

I thought it would give us a chance to get to know each other a little better, you know?"

"Well, you're right about that," she said archly. "Two weeks on a thirty-seven-foot sailboat would give us *plenty* of chance to get to know each other."

"On the other hand," Ted quickly added, "there's lots of room for privacy, if you're concerned about that. Two separate berth areas, one aft, one forward—"

Alix put a hand on his forearm, and leaned even closer—about as close as they could get in the two big chairs.

"And who said," she whispered with the tiniest of smiles, "that I was concerned about privacy?"

Acknowledgments

Several skilled professionals have generously shared their expertise to help us get Alix London out of trouble (and into it as well) in *The Art Whisperer*. Our particular thanks to:

Mitch Spike, Detective Bureau Lieutenant, Palm Springs Police Department (with our apologies for taking a few liberties with his name in the book)

Barry Bauman, conservator; fellow, the American Institute for Conservation

Patricia Siegel, forensic handwriting expert and certified document examiner, examiner, Patricia Siegel Enterprises, Inc.

Arlin Lindstrom, Service Director, Wilder Auto, Port Angeles, Washington

ABOUT THE AUTHORS

With their backgrounds in art scholarship, forensic anthropology, and psychology, Charlotte and Aaron Elkins were destined to be mystery writers. Between them, they've written thirty mysteries since 1982, garnering such awards as the Agatha Award for the best short story of the year, the Edgar Award for the year's best mystery, and the Nero Wolfe Award for Literary Excellence. The pair revels in creating intensively researched works that are as accessible and absorbing as they are sophisticated and stylish. Charlotte was born in Houston, Texas; Aaron in New York City. They live on Washington's Olympic Peninsula.